CHERISHED LOVE

CHERISHED LOVE

ROSANNE BITTNER
DENISE DOMNING
VIVIAN VAUGHAN

St. Martin's Paperbacks

CHERISHED LOVE

"For the Sake of Love" copyright © 1997 by Rosanne Bittner.
"An Impetuous Season" copyright © 1997 by Denise Domning.
"A Wish to Build a Dream On" copyright © 1997 by Vivian Vaughan.
Excerpt from *Dream a Little Dream* copyright © 1997 by Antoinette Stockenberg.

ISBN: 0-312-96171-5

Printed in the United States of America

St. Martin's Paperbacks edition/May 1997

St. Martin's Paperbacks are published by St. Martin's Press, 175 Fifth Avenue, New York, NY 10010.

10 9 8 7 6 5 4 3 2 1

Contents

FOR THE SAKE OF LOVE

Rosanne Bittner

For the sake of love
I will dare to risk all . . .
For nothing is so important as love,
Not my name,
Nor my station in life,
Nor what others think . . .
Only love matters,
To those who give love . . .
And to those who need love.
There are those who will condemn me
For loving you,
But love you I will.
I will risk all, my darling . . .
For the sake of love.

Chapter One

*O*n this unusually warm but windy day, Sandra Brooks had decided to grade her students' papers outside on the veranda. April did not ordinarily bring this kind of heat to northern New Mexico, but the weather was always unpredictable in this high, wide rangeland, where a pocket of warm air sometimes would hang between the two surrounding mountain ranges for weeks at a time. She only hoped this was not a portent of an even hotter than normal summer. Thank goodness there were only six weeks of school left.

She set rocks on top of the papers to keep them from blowing away, then winced when another gust of wind carried sand with it, stinging her skin and eyes and leaving grit in her mouth.

"I give up!" she muttered. Gathering up the papers to go back inside, she wished she could be as seemingly unaffected by the weather as her son. The nine-year-old did not care if it was a hundred degrees or five, windy or still. Whatever the weather, Billy liked being out in it, hated having to sit inside for school. Without a man to help keep him in line, Sandra often wondered how she was going to keep him under control as he grew older.

It's your own fault your son has no father, she thought. All these years she'd blamed the Apache for her and Billy's situation, but deep inside she blamed his father for being the adventurous, wandering man he was—and herself for being young and impetuous enough to blindly marry Danny Brooks at a young age. Still, she supposed she'd do it again if she had the chance. Danny had been easy to love, handsome, energetic, a man who would have been a great success some day.

She breathed a deep sigh as she walked into the parlor of the comfortable stucco home that belonged to Carl Sloan, owner of the Lazy C Ranch. She boarded here for free, in return for her teaching services. She glanced into a mirror as she passed it, wondering how long it would take for the hot New Mexico sun to wrinkle the still-smooth skin of her face. She set down the papers and looked closer in the mirror, touching her face with her fingertips. She supposed it didn't much matter whether she was still pretty, since there had been no man in her life for six years now.

Oh, how she'd loved Danny, enough to run off and marry him in spite of her parents' warnings she would one day hate moving place to place because of his job as a railroad construction engineer. They had been so sure Danny was not the settling type, but she and Danny had not been married long enough for her to find out.

Apache! The damned Apache had robbed her of the love of her life, robbed Billy of a father. It still sickened her to think of the torturous way Danny had died. The years had not softened the horror of it, but loyalty to Danny's memory was beginning to become less important. She'd been long widowed, and at only twenty-seven years old, she was beginning to want a man in her life again. Billy needed a father, but if she was going to find one for him, she figured it had better be soon, while she still retained some of her youth.

She walked to a window and watched Billy toss a ball into the air. He was so much like his father, with the same adventurous spirit, and in looks. His skin tanned easily and did not burn like her own fair skin. Billy had Danny's dark hair and eyes. She saw nothing of herself in the boy, who hardly looked as though he belonged to his green-eyed mother who sported a few freckles on her nose and arms, and who had to keep her strawberry blond hair covered with a slat bonnet to keep the sun from drying it out and from burning her face.

"You stay in front of the house where I can see you, Billy," she warned.

"I will," he answered.

She smiled, but that smile quickly faded when one of the ranch hands rode in, stopping to greet Billy. Her heartbeat quickened. It was John Casey, better known as Blade to most, a half-breed Apache! She had never spoken to the man, never seen him up close, for she always avoided him. She did not care to go anywhere near a man with Apache blood, not after what the Apache had done to Danny. A man like that had to be sinister, dangerous. She could not imagine what had possessed Carl Sloan to hire him, although Carl swore Blade was dependable, and the best horsetrainer he'd ever had.

There had been occasions when Sandra could not help having to walk past the corral where Blade worked breaking horses. A secret part of her had to admit he seemed to have quite a striking build. She was curious about his parentage and background. Just how "Indian" was he? Carl said he'd lived among the Apache for several years. He was saying something to Billy now, and her trusting son stood there talking to the man as though they were old friends.

"Billy! Don't be talking to the help," she ordered through the window. "I am sure Mr. Casey has better things to do! You come inside and do your homework!"

Blade reined his horse a few feet back from Billy, glancing at the window. Sandra felt a little pang of guilt for the remark, suspecting the man knew her real intentions—she did not want her son talking to a half-breed. Carl Sloan had said the other men had not welcomed Blade too readily, that he was rather an outcast among them. He was quiet and kept to himself. He caused no trouble, but neither was he a man any of the others wanted to cross. Sandra noticed that today he wore fringed, deerskin leggings and moccasins, rather than the denim pants and leather boots he usually wore, the common garb of the other ranch hands. Other than the leather vest he wore his arms and chest were bare, because of the heat, she supposed. Maybe it was the savage in him, unconcerned about exposing his body in front of others. Part of her was offended, and part of her felt a disturbing attraction at the sight of his muscular build.

She drew in her breath at the realization, angry with herself, and with Billy for still talking to the man. "Billy!" she shouted. "I told you to leave Mr. Casey alone."

Billy stepped back and waved to Blade, who nodded to the boy, then glanced at the window again, frowning. He turned his horse and rode toward the bunkhouse and horse barns.

Sandra turned from the window, upset with the way the man had of stirring her emotions in a hundred directions. Carl's wife, Frances, didn't want the half-breed on the premises any more than she did. Only a few weeks ago in town, he'd shown the nickname of Blade fit him when, according to Carl, a man had badgered and insulted him, then challenged him to a knife fight. Blade apparently had no choice but to defend himself, and he had won the fight with only minor cuts to himself; but the whole town had been in a buzz about how it had taken the doctor several hours to sew up all the wounds the other man had suffered. As soon as he was healed, he had left for parts unknown, apparently not wanting to ever see John Casey again. What irritated Sandra most about the incident was how fascinated Billy had been by the story, a look in his eyes that told her her son thought Blade as some kind of hero.

What a preposterous notion! For six months she and Frances had prevailed upon Carl to fire Casey, but he refused, determined Blade was of great benefit to a rancher with thousands of cattle to keep track of and rustlers to watch for. *He could probably track a bird by smelling the air,* Carl had argued. *He can hunt, find stray cattle nobody else can find, and he can speak the Apache tongue. He's talked the Apache out of stealing my cattle and horses a time or two, and there's an honesty and loyalty about him that I like. He's quiet, keeps his distance from the other men, doesn't drink or run with the whores in town, and he's the best bronc buster on the ranch, or anywhere else, for that matter.*

Sandra had trouble believing the man could be virtuous in any way, and it worried her that Billy had apparently taken an interest in the half-breed. The boy went to the corral every Wednesday after school to watch Blade break in new horses. He claimed the man had a special way with them, that he could "talk" to the horses. Sandra thought it was all ridiculous, and she wished she could find a way to discourage her son from being anywhere near the man. She had reminded him it was Apache Indians who had killed his own father, but he only said Blade would never do that. He wasn't "bad" like the other Indians. He was very brave, and he had once fought a grizzly and had even scouted for the railroad for a time.

Sandra wondered at all the stories the men had been telling her son about Blade, wondered, too, if Blade had told Billy the stories himself. They were probably not true, and she determined not to believe anything that made the half-breed appear heroic. She decided she must do something soon about keeping Billy away from all the help *especially* John Casey!

She picked up the school papers, then realized Billy still had not come inside as she had told him to do. She turned back to the window to see he was gone. With a frown, she set the papers aside again and walked outside onto the porch. It angered her that Billy had disobeyed her. It was not like him, and she attributed his misbehavior to the bad influence of the ranch hands.

She looked all around, saw him nowhere.

"Billy Brooks, you little devil!"

Other than a frequent rush of wind, everything was quiet. Normally there was considerable noise and activity on the sprawling ranch, with many daily chores to do and many men to do them. But today was Sunday. A church service had been held at the little school where she taught, a little over a mile south of the ranch. She and Billy had attended with the Sloan family, Carl and Frances and their twelve-year-old daughter, Roxanne. As always, upon returning, she had helped Frances with Sunday dinner and helped clean up afterward. Frances and Roxanne had gone upstairs to nap then, while she graded her school papers.

Every Sunday was the same—church, dinner, napping, reading, grading, Billy playing in the yard before coming in to study later in the afternoon. The hired help on the ranch who had family spent the day with them, and those without family spent the afternoon recklessly, usually drinking, although Carl Sloan did not allow his men to get too rowdy or they risked being fired. She never went out to see what actually went on, but according to Carl the men needed a day to "let loose," and they usually spent it breaking wild horses, sometimes racing horses and betting on those races, often playing cards. Occasionally there was a fist fight, when a simple wrist-wrestling challenge turned into something more.

None of them was fit for the job of setting an example for the boy, except maybe Carl Sloan himself. But he was a wealthy, successful man who was so busy running his huge spread that he had little enough time for his own daughter, let alone a boy who was not even his.

Had Billy gone to the bunkhouse? She debated going there to look for him and get him out of there. She did not care to have to face those men, and although she had no use for them, she did not want to insult them by dragging Billy away as though they were vermin. Most were good in their own rough way, and all had been respectful toward her . . . all except Joe Clayton, a new man Carl had hired. She didn't like the man one whit, didn't like the way he looked at her.

A grandfather clock in the hallway chimed three o'clock. Billy Brooks should be in the house doing his homework! She stared at the bunkhouse in the distance, taking a deep breath for courage. Carl Sloan had gone to town for some kind of meeting, so she could not ask him to go. She would have to get Billy herself. What annoyed her most was that he could be with John Casey, which would mean having to confront the man at close range, and she would rather avoid that . . . for more reasons than she cared to admit.

Chapter Two

$\mathcal{S}$andra did not relish walking into a den of drunken cowhands, but she would do what had to be done to keep Billy away from them.

"Hot damn! Where'd you get a hand like that!" a man shouted. The doors and windows to the bunkhouse were wide open because of the heat. "I ain't never been beat with four deuces!"

Gambling! Swearing! And such poor English! Billy was most likely hearing and seeing every bit of it. Her son was becoming much too infatuated with the life these men led, and that sometimes gave her a feeling of helplessness. It seemed she was losing control of Billy, and of her own life. She had no choice but to live here for the time being, as Carl Sloan lived closest to the school and was the only one in the area with a house big enough for guests. With a child to support on her own, she especially appreciated the free room and board.

In wild country like this, Sandra knew a woman should not live alone. There was too much danger from outlaws, Indians and just plain lonely men. It was understood that a female school teacher must have a reputation beyond reproach and must live in the safety and shelter of a sponsor's home if she had no husband.

For the first few years after Danny died, she had lived in the nearby town of Sloan Springs, a little settlement that had grown from a supply depot Carl Sloan built for the delivery of ranch supplies brought in on the Atchison, Topeka & Santa Fe Railroad. The city of Santa Fe, twenty-five miles south of Sloan Springs, was the closest larger town. Sloan Springs was a rugged, still-growing town, but she'd stayed simply to be near Danny's grave. She had worked at a boarding house there, helping with cooking and cleaning, in an effort to support herself and Billy; but when Gretta Beucher, who ran the boarding house, noticed her teaching Billy to read and write, the woman came up with the idea that she could teach other children. The townspeople had agreed, and Carl had built a schoolhouse just for that purpose, close enough to the ranch for his daughter and the children of the ranch hands to also attend.

Once Sandra officially became a teacher, it had been decided the boarding house in town was not the proper place for her to live. Carl offered his home, deciding it would be nice for his lonely wife to have another woman about. Sandra didn't mind, since Sloan Springs was filled with saloons and painted harlots, and other sources of bad influence for Billy. In spite of the rough ranch hands, this place was still better than town.

She had considered going to a bigger town, or home to Illinois, but here she had friends now, people who cared. In Illinois she would have to face her parents, who would gladly say "I told you so." She didn't want to hear it. Her mother had begged her in letters to "leave that godforsaken land where Danny Brooks dragged you off to and come back home!" She knew her parents were still angry with her for running off with Danny, and she refused to do one thing to add to their confidence they'd been right in their judgment of him. She'd loved him and had been willing to follow him to the ends of the earth.

She stopped walking, still hesitant to approach the bunkhouse. She thought how "the end of the earth" was a rather fitting description of this land after all—rugged mountains, wide-open valleys—places where a person wondered how any plant life survived, a mixture of magnificent beauty and

utter desolation. It was wild and untamed, but here Danny
had died, and here she would stay. Her husband's career with
the Atchison, Topeka & Santa Fe had been cut short by
Apache warriors who resented the building of the railroad
through prime hunting grounds. They had attacked a party
of surveyors with whom Danny had been working . . . back
in '72. . . . Danny had died a brutal death, found hanging by
the ankles from a telegraph pole. She had not even been
allowed to view his body. The thought of it still gave her
shivers.

The damned railroad was finished now. She could hardly
believe it was 1878 already. Billy had been only three when
his father was killed. He hardly remembered the man.

She tried to put such thoughts from her mind as she continued her walk to the bunkhouse. The laughter and swearing
from inside grew louder. She'd had more than one encounter
with drinking men on the streets of Sloan Springs, and those
in the bunkhouse, no doubt, were no different when full of
whiskey. She was well aware that many of them would ride
off to town by nightfall and visit the whores in town. She
suspected Carl Sloan himself had been just like them at one
time, since he seemed to understand their needs and never
berated or fired a man who got back late on Monday morn-
ings looking as though the devil himself had dragged him
through hell.

*Those men respect me more and work harder for me be-
cause once a week I let them raise cain and get what they
need in town,* Carl had told Frances once. Frances had been
arguing that he should not let them drink. *If I set rules like
that,* he'd argued back, *I'd lose half of them tomorrow.
They're all good men, and I need them.*

Sandra wondered if John Casey also visited the whores,
although Carl swore he never did. *The way he was raised,
he's probably had his fill of women like that.* The man made
no other comment about it, and Sandra wondered what he
meant by the remark. The way he was raised? What on earth
kind of life had the man led, being accustomed to whores,

living with Apache Indians part of his life! And her son could be talking to him right now!

She held her chin high as she reached the bunkhouse, where a man sat in a tipped-back wooden chair, holding a bottle of whiskey in his hand.

"Well! Hello there, Teacher Brooks!" His bloodshot eyes moved over her as though she stood there naked. "Come right on inside. Me and the others will make you right at home!"

I just bet you would! Sandra fumed inwardly. It was Joe Clayton, the last man she wanted to face right now. He was never clean shaven, and his clothes were always stained and dirty. It was difficult to tell his age since his face was lined heavily from too much New Mexican sun, but he had a healthy build, and she thought he could be a decent-looking man if he'd clean up. Still, it was the way he looked at her that made her dislike him. She generally tried to see the good in people, but there was something about Joe that told her there was no good to be found. She simply did not trust him and was sure that although Carl was usually a good judge of men, he'd been wrong to hire this one.

"I am looking for my son. Can you tell me if he's inside the bunkhouse?"

Joe shrugged. "I ain't seen him. Check the stables. He's took a likin' to horses. We've been teachin' him to ride. A boy has to learn them things in these parts, you know."

"Yes, I know," she replied, rolling her eyes. "Thank you, Mr. Clayton."

He grinned, his eyes stripping her again. "Any time, Teacher Brooks. You be careful now. I ain't seen the breed around. Maybe the boy's with him. You know what they say about Injuns and white women. Maybe you ought not to let yourself get caught alone in the stables with that devil. You want I should go with you?"

Sandra suspected she was no safer alone with Joe Clayton than she would be with John Casey. "No. I'll be fine. I'll let out a good scream if I need help."

The man nodded. "You do that."

Sandra turned away, shading her eyes as she walked to the stables, wishing she'd put on her bonnet first. Already she could feel the sun burning her nose and arms. She wore a short-sleeved, light cotton dress of yellow gingham, with only one slip under it, but still she felt too warm, and her skin began to prickle and sweat. She did not doubt it was from nervousness more than the warm day. Still, she could feel her hair beginning to wilt and fall in strands from the bun that earlier had been pinned neatly on top of her head, and she was growing more irritated with Billy for making her traipse around searching for him in this heat.

She entered the stables, feeling some relief from the sun in the shade of the building, momentarily curling her nose at the smell of horses and hay. She took a moment to let her eyes adjust to the shade, and as she waited a few seconds, she heard voices . . . a man and a boy.

"Here's what you look for in a good horse," the man was saying. "See the straight back on this one? The broad chest? A horse has no connecting joints in front at the shoulders, Billy, like our own shoulder and collar bones. The legs are connected by mere muscle and skin, so you want a well-muscled horse like this one for breeding. And look how he holds his head. He's a proud one, this stallion. He'll make a good stud horse, give life to strong foals."

Sandra's eyes widened at the words. Stud horse? What on earth was this man teaching her son? She made her way toward the voices, saw a man step out of the stall. She stopped short, a tumble of emotions plaguing her, for in spite of her anger, she could not help being rather stunned by what she saw. There stood John Casey, looking more Indian than she had ever seen him. She had expected him to still be wearing his deerskin leggings, but now he was next to naked! He'd removed the leggings and vest and stood there wearing nothing more than an apron-like garment around his hips and privates, a pair of low moccasins, and a silver concho at his throat, tied there with a rawhide string. His long, black hair was gathered to one side of his neck with another piece of beaded rawhide, and that was the extent of his dress.

Sandra could not quite find her voice. She had heard rumors that sometimes on hot days this man showed his "savage, uncivilized" side by wearing next to nothing, seemed to think there was nothing wrong with that. She felt her cheeks going hot, and was mortified that in spite of the man's near-sinful exposure of his body, she was secretly infatuated. That part of her deep inside that had not been allowed to appreciate a man for six years was surprisingly stirred by the beautiful specimen of man who stood before her. His tall, broad-shouldered frame seemed bigger inside the shed than when he was outdoors. No woman could deny he was handsome, in spite of his looking so Indian, and in spite of a white scar just under his left eye and another one on his chin—scars that betrayed a man who had led a brutal life—a man no woman should look at twice, not even once if she could help it.

She swallowed as his black eyes quickly moved over her appreciatively, and his face broke into a quick grin, showing white, even teeth. "You're looking for your son?"

Sandra took a deep breath. Oh, how she hated herself for momentarily thinking what a magnificent looking man he was! There was an animal-like air about him, reminding her of a dark panther that might be docile but could also be vicious. She realized she did not truly hate him so much as she feared him.

My God, he's part Apache! she reminded herself. *He has the same blood as those who murdered poor Danny, and look at him! He's nearly naked!* Joe's warning that she not let herself be caught alone in the stables with this savage suddenly hit home, and she finally found her voice. "I will thank you not to speak to my son about . . . about stud horses and such," she answered. "When I feel he is ready for such talk, I will explain things to him myself. And you know, Mr. Casey, that he is not allowed around the ranch hands."

Blade frowned. *What a beautiful woman,* he thought, impressed not just by her lovely looks, but by the fact that she had called him Mr. Casey. No one ever called him that, let alone put a little ring of respect into it. Sandra Brooks had certainly not gone unnoticed by him. There were few white women he liked or respected. God knew his own brutal whore of a mother didn't deserve any respect. As soon as he was old enough he had gotten out of the brothel where he'd been raised and had gone to find the Apache, to learn the ways of his father's people, although he'd never known his real father and never would. Living among the Apache had given him some inner peace, a true identity. It had instilled in him some pride, something he'd never felt before then.

"Your son is old enough to begin learning about life, Mrs. Brooks. There are some things only a man can teach him. He asks many questions, and I am glad to answer them. I know what it is like not having a father."

Sandra was slightly taken by the words, realizing she really knew nothing about this man's background. Part of her sympathized a little for the fact that he must be a rather lost man, torn between two worlds, probably ridiculed and unwanted by both. Still, she again chastised herself for having any interest, most certainly for having any sympathy for the man.

"My son has no father because Apache Indians tortured and murdered the man," she answered coolly, hoping she'd shock and embarrass him.

"I know. The boy told me." He remained calm.

"Not all Indians are bad, Mom," Billy spoke up.

Sandra only then realized her son had walked up to stand beside Blade. She saw the defensiveness in Billy's eyes. He had apparently talked to this man several times before, had probably been seeing him secretly, afraid to tell her. Billy knew how she felt about Indians, and she had expected him to feel the same way, yet she had taught him to be a Christian, that all people deserved to be loved the same. She realized that with a child's innocence he had taken that Christian teaching literally.

"Blade says lots of the Apache are good people. They're just scared 'cause people are taking away their hunting grounds and killing all the animals. When they kill people, it's just to try to scare them back, chase them away, make them leave them alone. Blade says soldiers and other white men have killed lots of Indians, even the women and little kids. It makes them cry and makes them scared, so they fight back. Blade says—"

"I don't want to hear anything more about what Blade says!" Sandra interrupted firmly. "You have been very disobedient, Billy Brooks! You know you are not supposed to be out here with *any* of these men, Indian or white. Now get to the house!"

Billy frowned, and Sandra could feel Blade's dark eyes on her. She didn't have to look at him to know he in turn was looking right through her, his gaze burning into her soul. Did he sense the shameful woman deep inside who was drawn to his brawny good looks, drawn to the animal grace about him, drawn to his sure loneliness? She must not allow it!

To her chagrin, Billy grabbed hold of Blade's hand. "I'll go, but first you have to promise to teach Blade to read and write better. He says he doesn't know how very good. He's been teaching me things about horses and riding, and I want to do something for him. He said he'd like more schooling, 'cause his ma never let him have any. I promised him you'd teach him, but he said you probably wouldn't want to. He told me not to ask, but I told him my mother is a good lady who likes to help people."

Sandra was furious at the way the boy had put her on the spot. Yet how she loved him for being so caring! He had always been like that, loved animals, tried to save wingless butterflies, never said good night without a kiss and a hug. She studied the honesty and trust in his eyes, then moved her gaze to meet Blade's dark gaze, his eyes unreadable.

"Is this true? You need schooling?"

Blade looked away, embarrassed. "I guess so. I only had a little learning when I was young, from a—" He hesitated, meeting her eyes again. "I'll explain when the boy is not present. I know I look Indian, Mrs. Brooks, and I've lived with the Apache, understand their ways and the reasons behind the things they do. But half of me is white, and I know that to survive in the white man's world and make something of myself, I need more schooling. I want to own my own ranch some day. I'm thirty-three years old and have no possessions to speak of, no family. It doesn't seem right for a man to live his whole life that way. I figure maybe some learning might help me."

Sandra could not help respecting his determination to better himself. For that brief moment she saw him as just an ordinary man wanting the same things other men wanted. "I will have to get the approval of the school board, and Mr. Sloan."

He nodded. "Fine. Carl Sloan likes me well enough. He won't object."

She could not help dropping her eyes to drink in once more the sight of his magnificent body, then felt embarrassed for it. "You must promise to dress decently during lessons. You are sinfully . . . exposed . . . Mr. Casey."

He flashed the disturbing smile again. "Yes, ma'am." *I'll just bet you'd like to strip half naked yourself in this weather,* he thought. *And I'd sure as hell like to watch.* He had quietly watched her at times when she had no idea he was looking. She had grace and charm, a goodness to her soul that shone through in spite of the act she put on of hating anyone with Indian blood. She *had* to be good, to have raised a kid as nice as Billy. And he suspected there was a wild passion under all those skirts and behind that very proper behavior. He knew her husband had been dead for six years now . . . and women like Sandra Brooks didn't go to a man easily. He could tell from the way Billy talked about their lives that she'd not had a man since then. Too bad she was so untouchable for a man like himself. A half-breed brought up in a whore house with little education was not fit for a woman like Sandra Brooks.

"You come with me right now, Billy," she was saying to her son. She reached out for him, her eyes still on Blade. The boy finally took her hand. Sandra turned and walked brusquely away. "I will let you know about the teaching, Mr. Casey," she called out to him without turning around.

Blade watched the sway of her slender hips. He wished he could believe she'd agree to teach him, but he suspected she'd find an excuse not to do it. He turned back to brushing down the stallion he'd been tending.

Outside Billy decided to plead his case further. "I like him, Mom," he said excitedly. "He's taught me lots of things. He never tells me to get away and leave him alone like the other men do. I feel kind of sorry for him. He doesn't have very many friends. The other men stay away from him because he's Indian, but they won't get into a real fight with him because they're afraid of him. He's strong, and they say he can be mean. I don't think he's mean, because he's always real nice to me, but you heard that story about what he did to that man in town he got into a knife fight with."

Sandra stopped walking. She turned to look down and face her son. "Billy, you have to be careful around men like that. Remember that he is half Indian, the same Indians who killed your own father."

"But that wasn't Blade's fault! He wasn't there. He hasn't lived with the Indians for ten years, since he was twenty-three, he says. He had a real mean mother, and he ran away from her when he was fourteen and went to live with the Indians. They were real good to him. They were the only family he ever had, except he never did know who his real pa was."

Sandra rolled her eyes. "He told you that?"

"Yes, ma'am. His ma was a bad woman who slept with lots of men. She was real mean to him because she didn't really want him."

"Dear Lord," Sandra muttered. "He should never have told you such things!"

"It's okay, Mom. I'm big enough to understand. There's good people and bad people. Some folks think all Indians are bad, that Blade is bad just because he's so dark and wears his hair long, and because his ma was bad and he doesn't know who is father was, but that's not his fault. He can't help that. And he's not bad, Mom! He's really not. You'll see when you start giving him lessons. He's real smart, and he'll be respectable. You'll see.''

''Well! I see you survived the Indian without gettin' your clothes ripped.''

The crude words came from behind Sandra. She turned to see Joe Clayton. ''That was an unnecessary remark, Mr. Clayton!'' She took Billy's hand to march him to the house, but Clayton grabbed hold of her arm.

''Hey, lady, why are you always so uppity to me?''

Sandra jerked her arm away. ''I have not had enough association with you, Mr. Clayton, to be opinionated one way or another, but the crude remark you just made in front of my son causes me to fast *form* an opinion! I will thank you to never touch me again!''

The man pursed his lips and cocked his head in a mockery. ''Ain't we the special one now? I just wonder if the pretty widowed schoolteacher is feelin' a little frustrated, maybe?'' He leaned closer, whiskey on his breath. ''Need a man, Mrs. Brooks? Maybe you liked layin' eyes on that big buck in the horse shed.''

Sandra raised her hand to slap him, but he caught her wrist. Billy then kicked the man hard in the shin, and Joe let out a yelp, releasing his hold on Sandra.

''You little brat!'' he growled. ''I oughta—''

''Clayton!''

All three of them turned to see Blade standing not far away. ''Leave the lady alone.''

Joe took a couple of steps closer to Blade. ''You ain't got no right speakin' for a white woman, one way or the other.'' He looked Blade over. ''And you ain't got no business showin' yourself half naked in front of her neither, unless maybe she ain't such a lady after all.''

Blade slowly walked closer, and Sandra noticed Joe swallow nervously, but he stood his ground. She supposed he wanted to look brave in front of her, but when she looked at Blade again, she had no doubt any average man would be afraid of the fire in Blade's dark eyes at this moment. Suddenly Blade grabbed the front of the man's shirt and jerked him forward, reaching down and yanking the whiskey bottle from his hand. He tossed it against a rock, breaking it.

"You can insult me all you want, white trash! I am *used* to insults. But you will never again insult Mrs. Brooks! Do I have to tell you what will happen to you if you do, even if you make remarks to the men when she is not present?"

Joe swallowed again, his breathing more labored. "I reckon' not, you murderin' savage!"

"Good!" Blade shoved the man hard, making him fall on his rump. "Go join the others in the bunkhouse!"

Billy giggled as Joe got to his feet. He gave the boy a dark look, then glared at Blade. "Some day, Indian—"

"I am ready whenever you are!"

Blade stood unflinching, and Sandra could not help another quick look at his physique. Out in the sunshine, his dark skin glistened. His thighs and hips were well muscled, his back straight, his arms—*dear Lord*! she thought. *I am admiring a man who is half Apache*! Had she lost her mind? The fact that she truly *wasn't* thinking like a lady would be humorous right now if not so devastatingly real and shockingly wrong.

Joe backed away, obviously not desiring any further confrontation with Blade. He turned and walked toward the bunkhouse, and Blade looked at Sandra and Billy. "You all right?"

"We're fine," Sandra answered curtly, taking Billy's hand again.

"You sure showed him, Blade," Billy spoke up.

Blade kept his eyes on Sandra, seeing her disapproval of the way men behave. He also thought he saw something else there . . . a fascination for how he was dressed, perhaps? A hint of admiration? He wasn't used to women like Sandra Brooks, wasn't sure what to make of her. He'd defended her as a proper lady, but he hardly knew what a proper lady was. He couldn't quite describe it. It was just something a man sensed about a woman.

"I . . . thank you," Sandra told him, not sure what else to say.

"See what I mean, Mom?" Billy told her. "Blade protected you. He's a good man."

Sandra rolled her eyes again and turned, marching her son to the house. When she reached the veranda she stopped and turned, looking out at the stables. A half-naked Blade emerged, riding a large Appaloosa stallion bare-back. He charged off on the animal at a hard gallop, man and horse looking as one. She realized that a secret attraction to the man was already growing deep inside, and it frightened her. The last man who should stir her emotions again was one with Apache blood, but she could not help being impressed by his defense of her. A woman would never have to be afraid with a man like that around.

"I will judge for myself just what kind of man John Casey really is," she told Billy. "In the meantime, I don't want you hanging around *any* of those men. Do you understand?"

The boy sighed, his lips puckered into a pout. "Yes."

Sandra looked down at him, touching his hair. "You're a good boy, Billy, and I'm proud of your soft heart. But you have been neglecting your lessons lately. I promise to try my best to be allowed to teach Mr. Casey, but you must promise in return that you will study harder yourself. If you do, I'll let you help Mr. Casey with his lessons."

The boy's eyes lit up with hope and happiness. "Really?"

"Yes, really."

"Okay!" He ran inside. "I'm going to finish my homework for tomorrow!"

Sandra turned back to watch Blade ride the Appaloosa, but man and horse had already disappeared beyond a distant hill.

Chapter Three

*S*andra hesitated at the doorway of Carl Sloan's study. John Casey stood beside Carl's desk, this time wearing the more familiar denim pants, and a blue calico shirt, which looked clean. The shirt was open at the neck, revealing the silver conch necklace against the dark skin of his chest. He wore more silver on one of his wide, powerful-looking wrists, a bracelet that showed up well because he'd rolled up his shirt-sleeves against the heat. His knee-high leather boots were worn and dusty, and he wore a weapons belt that held the infamous knife, as well as a six-gun in a holster at his side.

There was that same pull again at her insides. Damn him! She caught an odd flicker in his dark eyes when he looked at her, something that looked like pleasure, something that moved her in ways she would rather not feel moved. He was clean shaven, and his hair looked fresh-washed, slicked back from his finely chisled face and tied at the base of his neck. He nodded slightly to her but said nothing.

She turned her gaze to Carl. "Frances said you wanted me to come and see you after dinner," she said, "but apparently I have interrupted something—"

"Not at all. I wanted Blade here as well," Carl answered. "Come in, Sandra."

Carl was not tall, but he was stocky and robust, a man in his late forties whose hair was thinning and turning gray. In spite of his being rather blustery and sometimes downright ornery, Sandra respected him for his honesty and hard work. Out here a man had to be that way to survive, especially when he was in charge of a bunch of wild drifters like those who helped work the Lazy C.

He rubbed at his leathery neck and a face that was weathered by spending too many years in the sun building his little empire. He had gained most of his wealth in recent years, since the cattle industry began to boom after the Civil War. With the advent of the railroad, making it easy to ship cattle to the slaughter houses of Omaha and Chicago, there seemed no end in sight to the wealth a cattleman could gain, as there seemed to be no end to the demand for beef back east.

Carl looked at Blade. "I will expect you to call this lady Mrs. Brooks at all times, Blade. I only call her by her first name in private. She's been living in this house for nearly three years now. Since she has become such good friends with my wife and is so well liked by my daughter, we've all decided that there is nothing wrong with us being on a first-name basis." He looked at Sandra. "You can call me Carl in front of Blade here, Sandra. He understands. Come in and sit down."

Sandra tried to keep her gaze averted from Blade. She moved inside to sit in a deep green leather chair as Carl had directed. She liked Carl and Frances Sloan, who had treated her with friendship and respect. Although at times Carl seemed to enjoy flaunting his growing wealth, he was basically a kind and generous man.

"I think we can kill two birds with one stone, so to speak," the man was telling Sandra. "Sit down, Blade."

Blade took a chair a few feet away from Sandra, his big frame making the whole room seem smaller. She had told Carl that Blade wanted some schooling, and she presumed that must be the reason for this meeting.

"Blade, I heard some bad news in town today," Carl said. "It seems there is a band of outlaws in these parts who have been doing some ugly things. Seems they're made up of some renegade Apache Indians, as well as a few white men who are utterly without morals or feelings. The Baggett

ranch was attacked last night, and Mrs. Baggett was—'' He
hesitated, glancing at Sandra, who reddened at the realization
of what he was trying to say. ''Manhandled,'' he finished.
''In the worst way. Then they took off with the Baggetts'
fourteen-year-old daughter. They said something about sell-
ing her to Comancheros down in Texas. From there I have
no doubt captives are taken on to Mexico to sell as slaves.
A man doesn't have to think too hard to figure out what
young women are used for.''

Sandra shivered.

''Sorry, Sandra, but I want Blade to be fully aware of the
dangers we're facing, since I'm going to ask him to risk his
own neck to help me.'' He looked back at Blade. ''A posse
has gone after the bunch who took Susan Baggett. God only
knows what the poor girl will suffer. The sheriff in town
says he got a wire saying the same thing happened at a ranch
a few miles southeast of here, which means they might not
be done working this area. I don't aim to leave my daughter
vulnerable while those bastards are on the loose.'' He
glanced at Sandra. ''Pardon my choice of words, Sandra.''

''It's all right.''

''You asking me to try to track them?'' Blade asked.

''No. But I want you to guard my daughter, and Mrs.
Brooks. I wouldn't put anything past these animals. I'm the
wealthiest man in these parts and it won't take them long to
figure that out. Maybe they think I'd pay a lot of money for
my daughter, and I would.'' He looked at Sandra. ''And you,
dear woman, are very beautiful and would make quite a prize
for men like that. They would consider you quite valuable.''

Sandra felt embarrassed at the meaning of the remark, flattered at the compliment, and irritated at the sudden realization that she was wondering if men like John Casey
considered white women beautiful. She drew in her breath
at the ridiculous thought, still refusing to look straight at the
man. ''Surely they wouldn't come here, Carl. You have a lot
of men guarding this place.''

''That's right, but not guarding the school. In that school
house you're alone and wide open for trouble. We're trying

to civilize this country, but we haven't quite managed that yet. It's still a dangerous land full of bandits and Indians, and I think for a while you and your son and my daughter should have protection going to and from school as well as during the hours you are there.'' He looked at Blade. ''Is it true what Sandra told me, that you're wanting some schooling?''

Blade shifted, appearing a little embarrassed. ''Yes, sir.''

''Well, I think it's very good that you want to learn more. It's education that's one day going to civilize this land.'' Carl ran a hand over his balding head and looked at Sandra. ''What I am getting at is you and my daughter need protection, Sandra, so I'm assigning Blade to ride along with you to the school, stay there with you, sit in on the lessons and get some schooling while at the same time he'll be protecting you. He'll ride back with you so you have protection both ways. He'll use Saturdays for breaking horses. I need him for other ranch work, but this is more important.''

''I'm just one man, Mr. Sloan,'' Blade put in. ''You said there is a whole gang of men in on these attacks.''

Carl laughed lightly. ''One of you is worth five of any other man. I saw you the day you cut up Ben Hinton, and I've seen you in a fistfight and watched you at shooting contests. You have the stamina and keen instincts of an Apache because you *are* half Apache, and although I don't have a great deal of love for them, I respect their skill and their survival abilities.'' He leaned forward, resting his elbows on his desk as he directed his attention to Blade. ''Since it's only a little over a mile to the school, you're close enough that you could give three warning shots in case of trouble, and I can have more men there in no time. It's time for spring roundup and branding, and I just can't spare any more men for the moment, so I picked the best man for the job of protecting Mrs. Brooks and my daughter.''

Blade shifted again, seeming restless. ''Thank you, sir.''

Carl stretched and clasped his hands behind his neck. ''You've been a loyal employee, Blade. Others might say I'm wrong to trust you, but I don't think I am. I have a feeling you're the kind who would put someone else's life before his own. I'll pay you a little extra, and you'll get an education out of it besides. Are you willing?''

Blade glanced sidelong at Sandra, and she felt a little unnerved at the teasing sparkle in his eyes, as though he were getting a little fun out of the situation he'd put her in. She could tell he was feeling rather victorious, and it irked her to realize she really had no choice in the matter.

"I'm willing." He turned his gaze back to Carl. "If Mrs. Brooks is. She might not care to be accompanied by a half-breed. I'm not ignorant of how most folks feel about me, Mr. Sloan." He looked at Sandra again. "Especially proper ladies."

Carl eyed Sandra with raised eyebrows. "Well?"

Sandra sighed in resignation. "If you approve, Carl, then it's fine with me. Billy seems to think highly of Mr. Casey. I am a teacher, so I will teach. I do appreciate your concern for my safety."

"Fine then." Carl rose, taking his own wide-brimmed hat from a rack behind his desk. "It's settled," he said, a man who was usually blunt and in a hurry. "Tomorrow morning Blade will ride alongside your buggy when you take Billy and Roxanne to school." He put on his hat. "I've got to go out to the barn and check on that new foal. And I think Sadie is about to drop her foal before the night is over, Blade. I'd like you to come out in a few minutes and check her out with me. Nobody knows horses like you do."

"Yes, sir."

Carl walked out, and Sandra rose, refusing to look Blade in the eye until he called her name.

"Mrs. Brooks."

She turned to face him. "Yes?"

"You should not be afraid of me."

"I have no choice but to trust you, Mr. Casey." Again she wondered at the feelings that rushed through her body. "I am willing to teach you because it's what Billy wants, and my son is all I have. He means the world to me."

"I know. I am very fond of him myself. Being with him

gives me a chance to relive my own boyhood in the way I would have liked to live it."

She frowned. "I've been wanting to talk to you about that."

The look of a hurt little boy came into his eyes, strange, for such a big, tough-looking man. "What do you mean?"

"You apparently had a rough childhood, Mr. Casey. I am sorry about that; but I do not appreciate you telling things to my son he isn't ready to learn about, like . . . your stories about never knowing your father, about your mother being some kind of bad woman. It leaves a boy curious, wanting to understand better."

His jaw flexed with apparent repressed emotion, and his dark eyes showed hurt, and not a little anger. "You mean you don't want to have to explain what a *bastard* is? He already knows, Mrs. Brooks, and it's good that he knows. A child needs to learn about the bad in this world just as much as the good. It helps him understand who to trust and who not to trust, and it helps him see that not everybody that *seems* bad really is, and not everybody that seems good is all they're cut out to be. Bastard is a cruel brand to put on a man . . . makes him spend half his life fighting to prove his worth." He put on his hat. "I'll be ready to ride with you come morning."

He walked past her, and she touched his arm, surprising herself at the gesture. She just as quickly pulled her hand away when he stopped and looked down at her. She stood there, feeling stunned and embarrassed. She wanted to apologize. She had not meant for him to take her remark the way he had, had not even given thought to branding him a bastard. Apparently he had heard that word too many times in his life, and suddenly she felt a wave of pity for the man.

"I didn't mean to insult you," she said. "And I . . . I thank you for apparently not telling Carl about the incident in the shed, or the confrontation with Joe Clayton."

"Billy told me you didn't want Carl to know."

Sandra again felt irritated with her son, who had apparently talked to Blade again, against her orders. "I wasn't sure what Carl would think. A woman in my position has to be careful of her reputation. He might have been upset that I'd gone alone to the bunkhouse. Since no harm was done, I decided not to mention it.''

"No harm except for a big purple egg on Joe's shin bone," Blade replied.

She met his eyes and saw him smiling, and she had no doubt Joe would have suffered something much worse if he'd harmed her in any way. It gave her a feeling of security, something she had not enjoyed in a long time.

"Thank you again, Mr. Casey."

He tipped his hat. "Any time, Mrs. Brooks."

He turned and left, and Sandra closed her eyes and rubbed at her head, which was beginning to ache. She felt like an ignorant fool for some of her remarks to Blade, and now she wondered how she was going to feel comfortable being around him every single day. The next few weeks were going to be a real test of emotions. If she had any sense, she'd leave this ranch and her teaching position right now and go home, but Sloan Springs was home now, and she did have a responsibility to good people like Carl and Frances. Now she'd gone and promised to teach John Casey to read, and she was not a woman who broke her promises.

Chapter Four

$\mathcal{F}$or the first week that Blade accompanied them, Billy talked excitedly to the man on their trips to and from school, asking unending questions about the Apache, about horses, and how Blade seemed to know what a horse was thinking.

"Billy, you are becoming a pest with your questions," Sandra objected on an especially talkative morning. "I am sure Mr. Casey is tired of answering them."

"I don't mind, Mrs. Brooks," Blade answered. "The boy needs—"

"I know. I know. He needs to know these things." *And I suppose I do, too,* she thought. She had learned a lot herself about the Apache through her son's questions, and although she would never forgive what they had done to Danny, she had to admit she was beginning to understand the reasoning behind some of their desperate exploits as well as gaining an understanding about Apache culture and custom. Still, she could not agree that such barbaric behavior was acceptable under any circumstances. And there remained the fact that the Apache had brutally murdered Billy's father.

Apache or not, she was learning to see John Casey with more tolerance, seeing him more every day as just a human being struggling to better himself. Some things about him remained a dark mystery—details about his mother and his own boyhood. He avoided all questions from Billy about those things, and Billy had been ordered not to ask the man about how he got his Apache blood.

Sandra could not help wondering if the man's mother had been raped, and the thought naturally made her wonder about her own safety, even though Blade had done nothing to suggest he was anything but respectful toward her. Sometimes there was a kind of teasing glitter in his dark eyes that frustrated her, a look that told her he knew exactly what she was thinking. She chastised herself for often judging him as surely savage at heart just because of his blood.

One week grew into two, then three. Every day, once classes started, Blade sat silently in the classroom, listening to her lessons, ever watchful. Sandra explained to the children he was only there to protect them, suspecting Blade would be embarrassed if they knew he was there to learn with them. The children seemed to like the man and were fascinated by him, and Sandra could not deny the secure feeling it gave her having him around. She had never seen John Casey use his weapons, but anyone could see he was a man who knew how to handle himself. When he rode beside her buggy on his big Appaloosa, he often reminded her of an animal, protective, wary, a cunning look in his dark eyes. He watched every shadow, every hill and rock above them. He rode first on one side, then ahead of them, then the other side, then behind them, sometimes seeming to literally sniff the air. Just looking at his build and the sure way he sat his horse, seeing the array of weapons he wore, the small scars on his face, all spoke of a man most men would be wise not to tangle with.

Inside the school house Blade sat on a bench against the wall, and in spite of his attention to lessons, he would often rise and watch out a window, or walk outside for a while, ever alert. Sandra admired him for not being too proud to admit he needed more education, but she seemed unable to stop that admiration from growing into something more, a deep attraction to his dark handsomeness, a sympathy for the little boy in him that had apparently never been loved, a great respect for his being able to rise above a lifetime of being labeled a worthless bastard.

She tried to ignore the tingle she felt when he was watching her, told herself she shouldn't wonder if he thought she was pretty, shouldn't feel drawn to a man who was totally forbidden, not just socially, but personally, in her own heart. She should be angry for the way his eyes raked over her sometimes. If any other man would have looked at her that way, she would be furious, yet somehow she didn't mind when it was John Casey . . . Blade . . . half tame, half savage . . . all man. It was as though he was seeing more than the outer woman, as though he could read her thoughts, and she didn't want him doing that, for her thoughts had gradually begun to include John Casey much too often.

No! She must stop this! He was half Indian, the very same tribe that had murdered her beloved first husband. Maybe if she got rid of this guilt over her own attitude, she would quit feeling sorry for him. She would clear the air, that's what! She decided it had to be done, and at the end of one schoolday she dismissed the children and told Billy and Roxanne to go outside and play on the new swing. When Blade started to follow them out, she called to him to wait. "We need to talk."

Blade turned, unnerving her with his all-knowing look. He walked back to the bench and sat down, leaning against the wall, his knees spread in a relaxed fashion, his long legs sprawling outward in a casual pose. Today he wore no hat, and his black hair was brushed clean and straight over his shoulders, a bandana tied around his forehead.

"Talk away," he told her.

Sandra carried a reading book over to him. "This is a high grade level reader. Read to me from it."

He met her eyes with a frown. "You said you wanted to talk."

"I do. First I want to see how much progress you have made. I've never given you a lesson one-on-one, nor have I asked you to read aloud with the other children. I didn't want to embarrass you by asking. We're alone now, so read to me.''

He knitted his eyebrows in thought as he opened the book, obviously a little nervous and embarrassed. He studied a page, then took a deep breath and began rather hesitantly, but finally he read two pages without a flaw before Sandra took hold of the book and sat down next to him.

"That was perfect. I'm very proud of you, Mr. Casey."

"A couple of women friends of my mother taught me a little bit when I was small." He met her gaze with a show of defiance. "Did you think a half-breed bastard couldn't learn very easy?"

She refused to look away. "I deserved that. I had a feeling you were still angry about my remarks that day in the horse shed, but believe it or not, I don't look at you the way you think I do. No one's intelligence can be blamed on their race or birthing, Mr. Casey. I admit to judging you that way in the beginning. I resented you greatly when Carl Sloan hired you, and again when he appointed you the one to guard Roxanne and me. I can't help holding a great fear and dislike for anyone with Apache blood, after what they did to my husband. But my son is right. That was certainly none of your doing. As far as my remark about your mother, I was only trying to tell you that it's difficult to explain such a thing to a boy Billy's age. It had nothing to do with me seeing you as a bastard. I abhor that word. How can any child be blamed for how he or she was . . .'' Her face reddened, and she glanced down. "Conceived," she finished, realizing the mental picture the word created.

Blade sighed, leaning forward and resting his elbows on his knees. "All right, Mrs. Brooks, you want the truth, so I'll tell you," he said flatly. "I was *conceived*, as you put it, in Albuquerque, by a filthy white whore and a drunken Apache Indian. The whore lured the Indian to her bed just to find out what it would be like to lay with an Indian. She didn't figure on him getting her pregnant."

Sandra felt her cheeks growing even more crimson. John

Casey had a way of putting things very bluntly, but she wanted to know all of it, so she let him talk.

"My mother was as wicked as a woman can get," he continued. "She didn't want me. She made that damn clear as I was growing up. The only reason she didn't get rid of me was because she'd seen some of her slutty friends die from abortions. She fed me goat's milk because she wasn't about to let a 'dirty Indian bastard' feed at her breast." He snickered in bitter disgust. "It was okay to go to bed with a full-blood Indian she didn't even know, but she couldn't nurse her own child."

He rose, and Sandra could feel his anger fill the room as he walked to look out the window to watch Billy and Roxanne play. "If it wasn't for some of the other whores in the brothel feeling a little sorry for me, I'd have starved to death. They're the ones who fed me. My mother tried to give me away, but nobody wanted a half-breed. I got slapped around a lot, more than slapped some times. I grew up hearing how worthless I was, how I'd never amount to anything, how I was too stupid to ever make anything of myself and how I'd never fit in the white man's world. I ran off at fourteen to find the Apache—figured maybe I'd fit better in their world. In most ways I do. They took me in, taught me their ways. I even had a spiritual experience while I was with them, and that's when they gave me my Indian name, Singing Hawk."

Sandra thought what a beautiful name that was.

"For the first time I felt like I belonged someplace," he went on, "but then there was a big uprising, lots of misunderstandings that led to the Apache massacring a lot of white settlers. The Indians were hunted down. They scattered in every direction, mostly deep into the mountains, some farther west. A lot of them were rounded up and arrested, some hanged. The three men who had helped me the most were among the ones hanged. I could see the future right then and there. White settlement, buffalo hunters, the railroad, discovery of gold, all those things will bring an end to the Indian's way of life as he once knew it. Being half white, I figured I'd try to make it in the white world. It was the only way I could have some kind of normal life, if that's possible.''

He turned and faced her. ''I've been in a lot of fights, a lot of trouble, but others always start it over the fact that I'm a breed. The only thing that keeps me from going crazy and killing about a dozen men I'd like to sink my knife into is the inner peace I learned to find through living with the Apache. There is a lot you can learn from them, Mrs. Brooks, a beautiful way of looking at life, a spiritual experience of being one with the earth, the animals; the peace of knowing who you are, how strong you are, comes from the inside. I am who I am, and I've accepted it. Others can think what they want. I'll just go on doing what I need to do to show them I'm just as smart, just as capable and can be just as successful as any of them. I'm true to myself, which makes me true to my word. I'm loyal to people who deserve it, like Carl Sloan, but most who give me trouble usually wish they would have left me alone. Most know to stay out of my way.''

Their eyes held, each thinking thoughts they were afraid to express. ''Yes, I'm sure they do,'' Sandra replied. She looked away. This was not working as she'd planned. She thought a good talk would help her deal with unwanted feelings, rid her of all guilt, but both emotions had only been enhanced.

''As I said, I never meant my remark to be taken the way it was,'' she added. ''I apologize for offending you, Mr. Casey, and I'm so sorry about . . . the way you were raised.'' She felt sick inside at the thought of an innocent little boy, no different from Billy, being brought up with such brutality, and with not one ounce of love. She met his dark eyes again. ''Do you even . . . do you understand anything about love, Mr. Casey?'' Had she really said that? ''Not . . . not the kind between a man and a woman. I only meant . . . the way you were raised . . .''

''I know what you meant. Sure, I understand it. I learned it from the Apache, one young Apache woman in particular, but she was killed by soldiers. I was twenty-five. She was sixteen.''

He quickly turned away. Sandra felt strangely privileged, suspecting this man was not in the habit of telling the details about his past. What he had just told her about the Indian girl struck her as something very private that perhaps he had never told anyone.

"I'm sorry, Mr. Casey," Sandra sighed. "I do seem to be saying that a lot today."

Blade ran a hand through his hair. "Well, now, you don't exactly have to be sorry about things you had nothing to do with, do you?" He cleared his throat and finally faced her again. "As far as the boy, I just happen to like him a lot. He's open and honest, curious—a good kid. He's getting to the age where he's full of questions, and I just figured maybe some of them were things that would be hard for a mother to answer. They are things he needs to know, whether you like it or not; but I guess I stepped out too far taking it on myself to tell him something about my mother. So, you have *my* apology. From now on I'll not get into any details with him about—" His dark eyes moved over her again. "Men and women, things like that. He, uh, he's already seen horses . . . you know . . . how mares get pregnant. And he's watched foals be born."

Sandra stood up and moved behind her desk, feeling suddenly hotter than could be blamed on the weather. She felt herself breaking out in a sweat, and she fanned herself with an arithmetic paper. There was a moment of silence, and finally she met his eyes again, noticing a hint of a grin on his face.

"It's all a natural thing, Mrs. Brooks. There's nothing wrong with the boy seeing and understanding."

She fanned herself again. "I suppose not."

Blade forced back an urge to laugh at her reaction. *It's been a long time for you, hasn't it, lady?* God, he loved that about her, all that "properness," the way she blushed so easily. "You've done a fine job with him, ma'am. As far as both of us being sorry about past things we had nothing to do with, I'm sorry about what happened to your husband. There are all kinds of reasons people do what they do, and sometimes innocent ones have to suffer, like I suffered as a little boy, like your husband suffered at the hands of Apaches. Billy is damn lucky to have a mother like you. I have to ask, why haven't you ever gone back east? You must be from someplace back there, have family there."

Sandra sat down. "Illinois. My parents and a sister. I've visited a couple of times, and they came out here once to see me." She sighed. "I know life would be more comfortable with them, and I've debated many times about going back, but . . . the first few years I couldn't bring myself to leave Danny's grave so far behind me . . . and mostly I can't bear the haughty looks my parents give me. They didn't want me to marry Danny, said his job would drag me all over the country, which it did. I don't know what it is that keeps me here. I just don't feel like I belong back there any more, and I know a teacher is badly needed here. When I got the offer from Carl Sloan and others to teach their children, I decided that if I can be a part of helping civilize Sloan Springs and bring education to the children here, I'll have a little more purpose to my life."

He folded his arms, and Sandra could not help noticing the powerful muscles that bulged beneath his shirtsleeves when he did so.

"You're a brave and honorable woman," he told her. "I admired you before I ever got to know you better, and I admire you even more now. I knew by the way Billy talked about you that you were quite a lady."

Again she felt the strange flush moving through her. "Thank you, Mr. Casey."

He grinned. "Just call me Blade."

What a handsome smile he had! Why was she beginning to like this man? More than that, why was she beginning to desire him? Why was she wondering what it would be like to be touched by him . . . held . . . kissed. . . . She looked away, deciding she had simply been too long without a man. "I prefer to call you Mr. Casey, and not because I'm worried how it would look to others if I called you Blade." She met his eyes again. "I prefer Mr. Casey because you *deserve* to

be called Mr. Casey. Using your surname has a ring of respect to it, makes you equal with any other man. Blade is a
nickname given you by people who have seen you use that
knife you wear, but it speaks of someone wild and vicious,
which only makes people look at you that way. Perhaps you
are wild and vicious when the need arises, but you don't
really want that. I think some day everyone will call you Mr.
Casey.''

His smile faded, and he dropped his arms. ''Do you really
believe that?''

''Yes, I do. Finishing your schooling is just one step in
the right direction. Earning Carl Sloan's respect is also a
help. Billy sees the good in you, Mr. Casey, and that means
a lot to me.'' Suddenly she could not take her gaze from his
own. ''You are a man of many sides. I have a feeling you
have shown me a side most people never see. Most keep you
on the defensive, so you remain proud and silent, and you
let them draw their own conclusions about you, judge you
with their simple, prejudiced minds. I for one admire you for
your ability to rise above a childhood that would have turned
most men to drink and probably crime. Perhaps it is the Indian side, but there is a deep, inborn pride in you that would
not allow your mother and those who ridicule you to pull
you down to their level. That takes a lot of strength and
intelligence.''

She could see he was touched. He nodded, his lips set
tight for a moment before he finally spoke. ''Thanks.'' He
turned away. ''We'd better head to the ranch house.''

Sandra picked up some papers and put them into a car-
petbag she carried. She walked near him to take her slat
bonnet from a peg on the wall, then tied it on. She turned,
realizing only then he was standing directly behind her. She
raised her face to look up at him, having to arch her head
back a little farther than normal because of the wide brim of
her bonnet. ''I'm ready,'' she told him.

For more than you think, Blade thought. *I think I'm in
love with you, Mrs. Brooks.* ''You're quite a woman,'' he
told her, not quite knowing how in hell to try to hint at his

true feelings. Would it do any good? Why would a woman like this one entertain any thoughts about letting a half-breed bastard touch her, even if she did respect him the way she said? The cold facts remained . . . he was part Indian and in her world a man with little honor. She was untouchable, like a china doll, or a precious gem. Not only was she totally proper, but she was educated and independent, a female school teacher, expected to behave in the highest manner, with perfect morals and good judgment. Still . . . what was that in her eyes? Desire?

"And you're quite a man, Mr. Casey."

He could not resist touching her arm. He thought how small it was, how he could never touch Sandra Brooks with anything but gentleness.

Sandra looked down at his big, dark hand on her arm. A wave of desperate need and desire swept through her with such force that she drew in her breath. No! This could never, never be! Yet she found herself putting her own small hand over his for just a moment, thinking how good it felt to be touched by someone so strong. It made her think briefly how nice it would be to be held by a man again, to feel strong arms around her, to let someone else take over, help her with Billy, care about her, protect her. . . .

This was ridiculous! She pulled her arm away and hurried to the door. "I think the danger of outlaws is over, Mr. Casey. There have been no more problems. Perhaps it isn't necessary for you to accompany me any longer. I'll talk to Carl about it. I'm sure he needs you for other things." She opened the door. "I can give you books to continue your studies, and you can submit a paper to me each week showing your penmanship and spelling and I will grade it for you."

She walked out and called for Billy and Roxanne to get into the buggy. Blade stood there staring at the door. "Sure," he said quietly. He walked out and closed the door, mounted his big Appaloosa gelding and rode off ahead of her. Sandra watched him. Had she really thought for a moment that she could love such a man?

Chapter Five

$\mathcal{I}$t was done. It had been decided John Casey was no longer needed for guarding Sandra and Roxanne. There had been no more incidents of raids by renegade Indians and outlaws; but just in case, Carl had decided to give Sandra a rifle. She was to fire three warning shots if she felt she and the children were in danger. After another week of teaching, having to be in John Casey's company daily, having to fight deepening feelings for the man, Sandra was finally free of him.

Poor Susan Baggett had been found by the posse. She'd been badly abused mentally and had been beaten, but not sexually abused. They had been saving her virginity so she would bring a higher price in Mexico, according to her tearful story. The posse had tracked the outlaws, and when they nearly caught up with them the girl had been turned loose just to stop the posse from trailing the outlaws any farther and perhaps discovering where they hid out.

The townspeople and Carl Sloan were satisfied that the same outlaws would not try something so foolish as to come back to this area again. They would most likely direct their raids farther south, perhaps in northern Texas. They had got away with something and should be damn glad they were not caught and hanged. The Baggetts had their daughter back, and that was all that mattered. The school was only one mile away, and Sandra's insistence that Blade was no longer needed had finalized the decision. Besides, there were only two weeks of school left. Children were needed to help on ranches and farms for the summer, so Roxanne would herself be safe on the ranch soon.

Now Sandra waited in an open area behind the ranch house. Blade was to show her how to shoot the rifle. She wished Carl himself or someone else would help her, anyone but Blade. But at least after this she would not have to see so much of him. It was best that way. Spring roundup was finished, and besides calves needing branding, and a whole new herd of wild horses had been penned. Blade was needed now to tame and break those horses. That was his expertise.

Carl had decided that rather than have someone go back and forth to school with her, he would have two men less needed than Blade keep watch from vantage points on the hill over which she drove daily to get to school. The only trouble was, one of those men was Joe Clayton, the one man she disliked most on this ranch. Carl insisted the man was dependable as long as he was sober, and Sandra was glad he at least only watched from a distance and she didn't have to talk to him.

She couldn't help arguing with herself over whether she'd been right to convince Carl that Blade was no longer needed. She'd promised to give him more lessons over the summer, but she knew she couldn't even do that. Being close to him was too dangerous . . . dangerous for her heart. When she was away from him, she ached for him. She could not allow these feelings to continue. Still, the days without him riding beside her, sitting in the classroom, seemed boring and empty now. She missed his company, but she would have to learn to live with those feelings.

"Have you done any practicing at all?"

She turned at the words to see Blade walking from beside the house, wearing snug-fitting denim pants, the sleeves of his blue shirt rolled up past his elbows. Instantly the rush of unwanted desire returned, and she quickly looked away. "No. I really see no need for this. I don't need to know how to aim or anything. All I need to do is shoot this thing into the air."

"Maybe. Then again, you might be inside a barricaded schoolhouse shooting at outlaws . . . or Indians." His voice was closer now, right behind her. "Heaven forbid the savages should get hold of you."

Sandra caught the intended humor and felt like hitting him. "Yes, heaven forbid," she answered. She noticed how dark his skin was when he reached around her and took the rifle Carl had given her, a Winchester. He explained the mechanism of the gun, showed her how to load it, and she could not help noticing the way the muscles of his hands and forearms worked as he used the gun. Today his hair was tied to one side of his head, and he wore no hat or headband. He raised the rifle and shot it off a couple of times, retracted the lever to spit out shells and load more in. "Your turn," he told her, pointing to a tin pan already full of holes that hung on a fence post in the distance. "We'll know by the sound if you hit it. Here."

Sandra took the rifle and raised it to her shoulder.

"A little higher," he said. "Tuck the butt in good and tight against your shoulder. It's gonna kick. I'll give you some support until you get used to it."

He reached around her from behind, helping her position her hands, her elbow. Sandra could hardly think straight. Her mind was only on how good it would feel to be embraced by strong arms again, the arms of a man who would die for his woman. That was the kind of man John Casey was, she was sure. He helped her hold the gun for the first couple of shots, but she missed both. She tried the next one on her own, her eyes widening with delight when she heard the bullet ping against the pan. "I hit it!"

She looked up at Blade, and he was grinning. "You sure did. Keep practicing and you'll learn how to aim and shoot quicker."

If men could be beautiful, that's what I'd say you are, she thought. More and more she knew she had to get away from this place all together.

"Show me how fast you can shoot," she told him, handing him the rifle.

He seemed a little embarrassed then, but his male pride won out. He took the gun and quickly reloaded it. In what seemed only a second, he aimed and fired at the pan, hitting it, retracted the lever and fired three more shots in split-second movements, hitting the pan every time. Sandra could not help wondering if he had ever shot at whites while riding as an Apache.

He handed the rifle back to her. "You reload it yourself this time."

She obeyed, took three more shots of her own and hit the pan with one of them. "This does seem rather silly, with only not quite two weeks of school left," she commented.

"Seems rather silly that I should have to quit watching over you with that short a time left, too," he answered. "Don't think I don't know why you insisted I stop. I understand."

"What?" Sandra met his eyes, and he took the rifle from her, rapidly discharging the last shell, his dark eyes boring into hers.

"Ladies like you don't allow themselves to be attracted to men like me. It goes both ways, Mrs. Brooks. I know forbidden fruit when I see it. I'll find some other way to keep learning. Maybe the next schoolteacher will be a man."

Sandra's face reddened with a mixture of guilt and shame, desire and anger. "It seems you've misread—"

"I haven't misread anything. One thing I know is women, Mrs. Brooks. God knows I ought to understand that certain look they get in their eyes sometimes. Actually, I'm honored. A little part of me hoped maybe you were strong and fiesty enough not to care what other people think, like when you married your first husband against your parents' wishes. I guess I was wrong."

She stepped farther away, keeping her back to him. "You're wrong about all of it," she answered.

"Am I?"

She rubbed nervously at her arms, wanting to cry, to shout at him, hit him. "My situation, not just as a teacher, but . . .

considering how my husband died . . . surely you understand.''

"Oh, I understand, all right. I told you that." Suddenly he was right behind her again. He handed out the rifle, reaching around her to do it. "Here. You can finish practicing by yourself. I've enjoyed knowing you, Mrs. Brooks. You going back east after school is out?''

She swallowed back a lump in her throat. "I suppose. I might just try to find a teaching job in a bigger city, maybe Denver.''

He sighed. "I'll miss you, Sandra.''

He had never called her by her first name before, and the gentle way he'd said it. . . . "Believe it or not, I'll miss you, too, Mr. Casey.''

Blade grinned at her insistense on calling him Mr. Casey. God, he loved her! He leaned closer, and she did not move when he kissed her lightly on the cheek. "Good-bye, Sandra.''

She turned, tears obvious in her eyes. "Good-bye, John. I hope . . . I hope you don't take this as personally as I fear you do.''

He put a big hand to the side of her face. "Oh, I take it very personally.''

Their gaze held in painful understanding, and Sandra could not make herself turn away when he bent close and met her lips with his own in a delicious kiss that made her want to throw her arms around his neck, but she resisted. Part of her wanted to scream at him to please hold her in his strong embrace, to lean on a man again; and part of her was horrified she was even allowing him to kiss her.

His dark eyes glittered with what she was sure was love. He said nothing more. He simply turned and walked away, and Sandra watched after him, her insides screaming to be with a man, her better judgment telling her John Casey was not the one who should fulfill that need. She touched her lips. What a lovely, gentle, warm kiss he'd given her, surprisingly sweet for such a rugged man. She reminded herself where he'd learned how to handle women.

She quickly wiped at unwanted tears and walked back to the house, determined she was doing the right thing by leaving this ranch and Sloan Springs. She had to get as far away from here as possible, and as soon as possible.

Three more days passed, and Sandra saw no sign of John Casey. She knew he was making a point of avoiding her, for her own sake, maybe even for Billy's. The boy adored him, and she felt guilty for taking him away from here. Blade probably knew it was best not to see Billy before that day came. To continue their relationship would only make a good-bye even harder, not just for Billy, but for Blade.

She moved through lessons with her normal routine, dismissed the class, gathered her paperwork and closed up the school, realizing it had come to the point where she actually was afraid she wouldn't see Blade again without going to find him. But that would be much too forward.

No. It was best this way. She walked outside, forgetting to bring the rifle with her. It remained standing in a corner of the schoolroom while she climbed into the buggy with Billy and Roxanne. She hated having to leave Frances Sloan, and also Roxanne, who was at that awkward age where she really was not a girl, but not yet a woman either. She needed a woman's counsel and attention, but Frances was a very shy woman and did not always understand the girl's problems and feelings. Roxanne had begun confiding in Sandra at times.

She raised the horse whip, then realized Joe Clayton was waiting on his horse not far away.

"Where is Pete?" she asked, referring to the second man who was supposed to also be watching over her.

"He's farther up on the hill," Joe answered, scratching at a several-day growth of beard with dirty hands.

Sandra wondered why Joe had come here to meet her instead of just watching from the hill the way he and Pete usually did. She whipped the horse into a gentle trot and headed toward the hill beyond which lay the ranch. She reached the base of the hill, where for a short way the road narrowed between a tumble of huge boulders before rising up over the lowest level of the hill.

"Hold up there!" Joe called out.

Sandra frowned, reining the horse to a halt. Something seemed amiss, but she could not put her finger on what it was. "What is it, Mr. Clayton?"

He rode up beside her. When the man pulled out his six-gun and held it on the children, whose eyes widened in terror, Sandra felt as though the blood was draining from her body. "Turn the buggy left," he ordered Sandra.

"What is this?" Sandra demanded. "I'll not do anything but take Roxanne and Billy home to the Lazy C!" She whipped the horse to make it start running, but a moment later a rope came around her horse's neck, and the animal jolted to a stop and whinnied in confusion when the rope was jerked tight. Sandra tried to get it going again, but the horse only tugged fruitlessly at the rope. She turned to see it tied around a stubby tree. She reached for her rifle, only then realizing she had left it behind! She wrapped the reins around the buggy post and kept her small whip in hand, realizing it was her only weapon, not even sure what Joe Clayton had in mind.

"Children, get out and run!" she told Billy and Roxanne. "Run for help!" She was sure she was Clayton's only interest, and she didn't want the children hurt. Roxanne obeyed, but Billy stayed.

"I'm not leaving you, Mom!" he told her with a determined scowl. "I don't like Joe. Him and Blade almost got in a fight once. He says bad things about Blade. He's a bad man."

Joe's horse galloped past the buggy, and Sandra stood up, the whip ready in hand. She watched in growing terror as Joe thundered up to the fleeing Roxanne and reached down, grabbing her up by her long, blond hair and flinging the screaming girl over his horse in front of him.

"Shut up, or I'll knock you senseless!" he ordered.

Then Sandra noticed three more men galloping toward the buggy from behind. Had help come? No! These men had apparently been hiding in a stand of aspen trees to the left of the boulders on the east side of the road. She wanted to hope they were Sloan men, that maybe Pete was with them, but the way they rode . . . the fact that they had apparently been in hiding until now. . . .

"Get out of the buggy, Teacher!" Joe was ordering.

Sandra looked back to see he had a sobbing Roxanne perched in front of him now, one of Joe's strong arms around her in what looked like a painful grip, while he held his six-gun to her cheek.

"What in God's name are you doing!" Sandra demanded. "Where is Pete!"

"Pete's dead, Teacher, and so will your brat of a son be if you both don't get down out of the buggy! We're all takin' a little trip together, and soon as these men here have you well on your way, I'll be headin' back to the ranch to report how Comancheros came along and attacked us, killed Pete and stole you three away! I'll give wrong directions to Sloan, so's he'll send a search party on a wild goose chase, while these men here take you down to a holding camp where their boss will decide where you go next." His eyes raked over her the way they had the day she spoke with him at the bunkhouse. "God knows you'll bring a pretty penny down in Mexico, and Roxanne here will bring a fine ransom from Sloan, only he won't really get the girl in return. She'll bring yet more money down in Mexico! Pretty young virgins are as valuable as gold to some men, so me and the others make out doubly good."

Sandra felt sick at the words, rage burning through every nerve end. "You stinking coward! *Traitor*! You'll never get away with this! You're part of the Comancheros aren't you? You were sent here by them to get a job with Carl Sloan and figure the best opportunity to kidnap poor Roxanne! She's just a child! Let her go!"

A powerful hand grabbed her left arm painfully and jerked hard, yanking her from the buggy. She screamed, felt her feet touch the ground for only a moment before her arm was jerked upward in an agonizing and awkward position. Her yellow cotton dress ripped under the arm. Another hand came around under her right arm, grasping one of her breasts as the man who'd pulled her from the buggy lifted her onto his horse in front of him. He grabbed hold of her hair then, pulling it hard, while with his other hand he yanked a knife from its sheath at his belt and held the big blade to her throat.

"No more screaming, woman!" came the command.

Sandra's breath came in gasps as she looked into the face of an Indian, this one nothing like John Casey. He was unkempt, his black hair dull and unwashed, his face pockmarked, some of his teeth missing. There was a bad smell about him, something worse than just the perspiration that glistened all over his bare, dusty arms and chest. She wished she had worn more than a simple cotton camisole under her summer dress. She'd left off a corset and thicker support because of the heat, but her attire made it easier for her captor to feel her breasts through the thin material of her cotton dress and undergarment.

"You scream again, my friends will slit the boy's throat!" The Indian warned. "And I can cut you just enough that you'll never use your own voice again!"

Sandra blinked back tears, wishing Blade had been with her today. She was sure he would have known what to do about this, would have been able to stop these men, would have known they were waiting here.

"Mom! Mom!" she heard Billy cry out. She heard a slap then.

"Shut up, boy!"

"Why do we even have to bring the boy along?" someone asked. "Why not just kill him right here?"

"No!" Sandra pleaded, tearing her gaze from the black, menacing eyes of the renegade Indian who held her. She took a good look at the other three men. Besides Joe and the Indian who held her, there were two other Indian renegades just as wild and menacing looking as her captor. One of them had Billy on his horse with him, a thin rope around his neck, which he pulled just tight enough that poor Billy could not talk or scream. He was the one who had suggested they kill Billy.

"Please!" she begged. "Please let my son go! He's just a child."

The big blade at her throat pressed tighter, and she felt its sharp edge begin to sting her skin. "I told you to shut up, woman! Perhaps you would like us to strip you naked in front of your son and teach him all about mating!"

She met the Indian's eyes again, wanting to vomit. Instinct told her all she needed to know. She was going to be sold somewhere into prostitution, most likely, and until they got her wherever they were taking her, she was in a bad situation. She was not a virgin. If she were, she would probably not be touched wrongfully. At least Roxanne was probably safe from rape for the time being, but not herself. Still, why did they need Billy?

"The boy stays with us," she heard Joe explaining. "As long as we've got him along, the woman will do whatever we ask just to keep us from hurtin' the brat."

Sandra looked at Joe, wishing this were all a bad dream. "You filthy coward," she groaned. "You aren't worth the horse dung on the bottom of your boots!"

The man only grinned. He rode closer, Roxanne still with him, her head hanging, her shoulders jerking in sobs. "Call me all the names you want. Here's how it is, lady. Roxanne here is gonna bring us a good sum of money. Her pa's rollin' in it. Once he pays us off, the girl gets sold down in Mexico to a real wealthy Spaniard who purely loves light-haired virgins. Billy can be sold, too, as slave labor on the man's ranch, and believe me, he's got ways of breakin' people so's they do what he tells them to do. Now you . . . he might want you for a servant, and maybe to add to his pool of women for a little variety . . . or maybe he'll want to drug you up and set you to work at the whorehouse he owns. White women there bring a lot of money. One of these men here is gonna put a wound on me so's I can show Carl Sloan I was wounded tryin' to defend you and the girl here. Then I'm gonna' send Sloan's men off in the wrong direction while these men take you to their leader."

"You'll never get away with this! A posse caught up with the last raiders!"

Joe shrugged. "We decided raidin' settlers wasn't the best way to go about this. Too much commotion—tracks too easy to follow, posses formed too quick. We decided to do it quietly this time, get you well away before I go report the attack. There's a couple more men waitin' over there in the trees. They'll make tracks in the direction I'll tell Sloan's men you went, so's his men will be followin' a fake trail. Ain't no posse gonna find the captives this time." He took a note from his shirt pocket. "Here's the note I'll be givin' Sloan tellin' him how much it will cost him to get his baby girl back—ten thousand dollars! Ain't a cowboy in this land who could make that much in a lifetime." He put the note back, laughing. "Even my share of it will get me by on whiskey and women for a good long time to come. Once this is over, I'll join up with the rest of this bunch here, take my money and celebrate! Maybe I'll come down to Mexico and use some of that money to have a turn at *you*, you stuck-up bitch!"

He grinned through tobacco-stained teeth and turned his horse, riding to the third man, who reached out and yanked poor Roxanne onto his mount. The girl cringed when the Indian put a rope around her neck the same as had been done to Billy. Joe looked back at Sandra. "The girl ain't no child like you think," he told her. "Where she's goin', she'll be considered woman enough." He rode closer to the Indian who held Sandra.

"I'm ready, Many Crows, but make it look real."

Sandra gasped when in a split second the Indian's knife left her throat and slashed out, cutting into Joe's upper left arm. Joe cried out and grasped the wound, and blood began to ooze between his fingers. "Jesus Christ, Injun', I'll bleed to death!"

"Wrap it tight, white man. It will heal."

Sandra thought Joe actually looked like he might cry. "You idiot!" she chided. "You're actually stupid enough to let yourself be wounded for *money*? I hope that wound gets infected and you lose your arm, or better yet, your *life*!"

Instantly the big blade, still bloody from slashing Joe, was at her throat again. "Perhaps you would like me to demonstrate again how good I am with this blade," the Indian holding her said. "They will pay good money for you in Mexico, even with a scarred face! It is only that part of you from the neck down they care about!"

Sandra swallowed, most afraid for Billy. He was the most expendable of the three of them, worth the least to them. She realized the only way to keep her precious son alive was to act as though she would obey every order as long as they did not harm Billy. "Just don't hurt my son," she pleaded.

The Indian turned his horse. "Give us fifteen minutes," he told Joe. "Then go and report the attack."

"You won't get far!" Billy spoke up, tears on his face. "Blade will come after us! He'll find us and he'll kill *all* of you!"

"Blade? Who is this Blade?" Many Crows asked.

"He's just one man," Joe answered, untying a bandana from around his neck and holding it to his wound, pain evident in his eyes. "He's a half-breed ranch hand who I suspect is sweet on the woman there. He's supposed to be damn good with a knife."

"Let him come then!" Many Crows said, holding up his own blade. "It might be fun!"

"He won't be comin'. I'm gonna throw all suspicion about this on Blade. He'll be sittin' in jail, or maybe, hanged. He had the duty of guardin' the woman and kids here for a while, so I can make it look like he set this whole thing up. Hell, he's half Apache. People will believe he might have had somethin' to do with this, that he wanted the woman taken because he's got a yen for her. He's familiar with the whole setup, knows Sloan's daughter would be worth money."

"You can't blame this on Blade! He's a good man," Sandra spoke up, afraid for Blade. How easily people thought the worst of men like Blade. Joe was right. He very well could be hanged, no questions asked.

"He'll come help us!" Billy declared again. "He'll—"
His words were cut off when the Indian holding him yanked
hard on the rope around his neck again, choking him into
silence. "Let's go!" commanded the others. He turned and
rode off with Billy. The other Indian followed with Roxanne.
Many Crows shoved his knife into its sheath and grasped at
Sandra's breasts before putting a powerful arm around her
ribs.

"Hang on, white woman! Do everything I say, or I will
slice the skin from your son while he is still alive!" He rode
off with her, and Sandra struggled against a feeling of desperate helplessness. *Please, God, protect Roxanne and my
son,* she prayed inwardly. *Give me the strength to bear what
I must bear to keep them safe.* She was sure the children's
safety, especially Billy's, depended on her cooperation. The
way Joe had described how this would be reported, she already took little hope in being found. She wished she had
the same confidence as Billy that Blade would find them; but
the man would first have to be allowed to search for them.
By the time Joe got through throwing suspicion on poor
Blade, he would be lucky to avoid being promptly hanged.

She struggled against tears of terror, against the sick feeling of horror deep in her belly. Visions of how Danny had
been tortured stabbed at her memory. She should never have
convinced Carl Sloan to remove Blade from his guard duty,
all because she was afraid of her feelings for the man. The
savageness of this lawless land had killed Billy's father; now
it might be Billy himself who was killed. How could she
forgive herself if her actions hurt her son?

Chapter Six

Blade stayed just inside the stable doors, listening quietly. He'd never trusted Joe Clayton, didn't believe what the man was telling the others now was the whole truth. He tried to piece together the story, thinking it a little strange that Sandra and Billy could have been taken by a gang of outlaws, with Joe and Pete keeping watch, without one gunshot being fired. At least one of the two men should have had a chance to shoot at someone. Pete's dead body still lay over a horse nearby, an arrow in his back. If Joe's wound had been as devastating, it would be easier to believe neither man could have shot at the *Comancheros*. But there was only a bad cut on Joe's left arm. He still could have used his right hand to shoot at Sandra's abductors.

He leaned against the wall, breathing deeply to stay in control, rage ripping through him like fire at the thought of Sandra with those men! She was in more danger than poor Roxanne. Roxanne was a virgin. They would save her. But Sandra. . . . He felt a wrench in his gut at the thought of other men touching her, especially men like that. *Comancheros*! He knew what they were capable of. And it wouldn't take much fight from Billy for them to kill the boy. He had no doubt Billy would try to defend his mother.

His mind raced with confusion, while outside Joe carried on about the abduction, how lucky he was to get away alive. He had the men, including Carl Sloan, so riled up that they weren't thinking straight. They were too excited to put two and two together and make some kind of sense out of how the abduction had taken place. Carl was beside himself with worry over Roxanne, and Frances stood off at a distance, weeping uncontrollably. The wife of one of the ranch hands was trying to console her.

Whatever Carl Sloan did to get his girl back, Blade suspected that even if the outlaws kept their word to return her unharmed for money, Sandra and Billy's fate would not be so harmless. They might never be seen alive again . . . unless someone went after the outlaws and got them back by force! What worried him was Carl Sloan was talking about doing exactly what the outlaws demanded, paying them off for his daughter's return. Joe was saying the instructions were for Carl to give the ten thousand dollars to Joe to deliver at Wolf Creek, where Roxanne was to be returned. They had warned that if a posse was formed, or more than one man showed up, Roxanne would be killed, according to Joe's explanation.

Blade's hands moved into fists. He was sure Clayton was lying, maybe even in on the whole thing. Couldn't anyone see the reason *Joe* was to take the money? He'd deliver it, all right, and keep right on riding with the outlaws. Even if the sonofabitch was not involved in this, he'd probably ride off with the money and never be seen again. Either way, Joe was the last man who should make the delivery, and he didn't believe Roxanne would even be brought to Wolf Creek. He was pretty damn sure she and Sandra and Billy were already being hauled to Mexico.

He turned and walked quickly to the little shack behind the horse barn where he'd been living alone. He gathered together some food and ammunition, deciding to do a little scouting of his own. He already knew where Joe had said the abduction took place. Maybe no posse would be formed, but that didn't mean one lone man couldn't go after Sandra and the children! He loaded up his saddle bags with the food and a good deal of ammunition, strapped on his six-gun and his big blade, tied the holster strap around his thigh. He donned his hat, grabbed a couple of blankets and his rifle and headed back into the horse stalls to saddle his Appaloosa gelding. It was then he heard the shouting.

"The sonofabitch ought to be hanged!"

"You see?" Joe was saying. "He ain't even brave enough to come out here and join us, help us figure what to do! He was in on it, I tell you! He had to be! He knew the best spot for those outlaws to attack poor Mrs. Brooks and little Roxanne. Hell, he's half Apache himself! He ain't no different from them damned renegades who did this to me and Pete!"

Blade was not about to go out there and argue with any of them. Most of them had their minds made up. Joe Clayton was doing a good job of trying to blame this on him. He quickly finished tightening the cinch, shoved his rifle into its boot, tied on the blankets and threw the saddlebags over the horse's rump. All the while he heard Carl Sloan arguing that he couldn't believe Blade had anything to do with the abduction. "He had a hundred chances to go off with them, all that time he rode guard to and from the schoolhouse!" the man argued. "Blade's a good man, one of the best and most dependable I've ever hired!"

"You did wrong trustin' that half-breed bastard," Joe argued. "Any man who's half Indian, brought up in a whorehouse like rumor has it . . . just think on it, Mr. Sloan! A man like that pants after white women like a dog sniffin' after a bitch in heat! And bein' raised like he was, he knows all about prostitution, what white women is worth to Indians and Mexicans. It all makes sense. Why would the man work here for a few dollars a month when he can make hundreds stealin' and sellin' women? I tell you, you can't trust the man. If I was you, I'd string him up right now. Why ain't he here helpin' us? I'll tell you why. He's afraid to show his face, 'cause he knows the truth! He's the one who helped them outlaws get away with this! He's probably a part of them, and he's fixin' to go join them right quick!"

"I don't know, Joe," Sloan answered. "I can't think right now. I have to figure out where and how soon I can get that money! I don't have that kind of cash. I'll have to go to Santa Fe and wire my bank in Omaha. What I have in Santa

Fe won't cover it. They'll have to dip into other people's funds for the rest, and they'll need a guarantee from my bank in Omaha that it will be replaced from my account there. This is going to take a couple of days. Do you think they'll leave my daughter unharmed that long?''

"Hard to say. I'm just the messenger, Mr. Sloan. Only reason they didn't do me more harm is because they needed me to bring you that note," Joe answered. "I expect as long as you don't form no posse and go lookin' for them, they'll not touch the poor girl. They must know it could take you a couple of days to get the money. You'd best be on your way, sir.''

"Dear God, I hope Roxanne won't be brutalized by those bastards!" Carl groaned.

Blade mounted up. More commotion rose outside, men riled to fury over the abduction of pretty, sweet Roxanne Sloan and the very proper, respected Mrs. Brooks and her son, whom everybody liked. Through a window without glass Blade could see Carl Sloan heading toward his house, the man's sobbing wife on his arm. Already Joe was again getting the rest of the men heated up against Blade, swearing they ought to find him and beat the truth out of him, hang him from the pulley post at the top of the barn. The men were easily convinced. After all, some of the abductors were Apache Indians, and John Casey was half Apache. He knew the lay of the land, knew Carl Sloan would pay big money for his daughter, was familiar with the girl's comings and goings and had friends among the Apache, or at least they believed he did.

It was obvious none of them were in the mood to listen to reason, and Sandra could this very moment be being forced to submit to some stinking outlaw. And Billy's life was definitely in danger. He cared very much for that boy, and he damn well did know the kind of money men would pay for a pretty young virgin like Roxanne. She was a sweet girl. She didn't deserve this kind of terror. They had to be found quickly, before the money arrived, and he was the best man to do it. He turned his horse and headed out the back side of the barn.

"Hey! Hey, it's him! It's the breed!" Joe yelled. "He's runnin' off! See? See what I told you? He's goin' to join them! He knows he's been found out, and he's tryin' to get away!"

The shouting and cursing began to fade as Blade rode hard. He heard a zinging sound, another, another, a couple of strange little rushes of air shot past him. Bullets! They were shooting at him! He crouched low and rode his steed at a furious pace until he was sure he was out of range.

Wolf Creek. That was where the money was to be taken, according to Joe. Blade suspected that was a fake location, but he decided to head there, just to throw Carl's men off track if they tried to follow, which they surely would do, in spite of Sloan's asking that a posse not be formed. They would be forming one for John Casey, not to chase down the outlaws. But they would follow him to Wolf Creek and find nothing, because none of them would expect him to circle right back to the schoolhouse road, which was exactly what he would do. He needed to go there, study the tracks. Joe had said they'd headed east, which made no sense. Was the man only trying to fool them? Wolf Creek was to the east. He'd cut back to the site of the abduction and head west or south if he saw any tracks going in that direction. That was the more likely route.

He knew that running only sealed his guilt in the eyes of the others, but he'd take the chance to save Sandra Brooks. A man did crazy things sometimes for the sake of love, and he damn well loved that schoolteacher. He'd track her and Billy all the way to Mexico if he had to!

"He'll find us, Mom. I know he will." Billy sniffed, the dirt on his face smearing when he wiped at his tears.

Sandra's heart ached at how brave the boy was trying to be, and she realized it was his faith in Blade that was keeping him brave. The boy absolutely idolized the man and had complete confidence in him. She hated to dash his hopes, but she was afraid that by now Blade had already been hanged or was being beaten in an effort to force some kind of admission of guilt from him. She knew how ready people would be to believe he'd been a part of this. If she didn't already know him as she did, she'd probably believe it herself. She realized now how prejudiced she had been against men like Blade before she'd really come to know him better. The hell of it was, she loved the man. That realization only added sorrow to her terror and the horror of being a captive in this filthy outlaw camp.

This was her fault, for fighting her feelings for Blade, for refusing to admit even to herself that she loved him. It had happened so unexpectedly, slowly, quietly, gently. Now it might be too late to do anything about it.

She wrinkled her nose at the smell inside the shack where she and Roxanne and Billy had been chained to iron posts secured into the damp cement floor on which all three of them were forced to sit or lie. One wrist was chained, the other hand free to use for eating or tending to personal needs, embarrassing for all of them. The shack was lit only by slits of sunlight that managed to get through cracks between the outer boards. Each of them had a chamber pot close enough for use, but they were never emptied and they had no lids. They also each had a bottle of water and a loaf of bread, their only food, and one blanket each, hardly enough to warm them at night when they had to lie on the cool cement, no pillow, nothing to buffer them against the hard floor. They had seen rats running around the outer walls, and Sandra worried the horrid rodents would eat up their bread . . . or perhaps they would begin feasting on the prisoners.

As far as she could determine, this was the second day since she and the children had been kidnapped. She had no idea where they were, and she could not imagine that even if Blade was free, he would know how to find them. She forced herself to be strong, knowing she must not break down in front of the children and add to their terror, no matter what was done with her. For now Roxanne was safe, and as long as she herself made no fuss, Billy was also safe.

I'm the one they'll come for, she thought. She had already heard the eight men outside arguing over who got to have a turn at her first. The only thing that had saved her so far was the leader, called Manuel. He insisted they not abuse her right away. He didn't want her "all used up" before they even got her to Mexico. "When the time comes, I will be first," he had announced. The thought made her skin crawl. She could only pray the man would not choose to "abuse" her right in front of the children. Such a horror would scar both of them emotionally for life and put such fear in young Roxanne as to drive her mad. The girl already just sat staring, speaking to no one, constantly shivering. None of them had slept more than a few minutes all night, constantly afraid of what was going to happen next, unable to find any comfort against the hard, cold floor.

"Blade can track anything," Billy told his mother. "He told me. He's even showed me things about tracking."

Sandra closed her eyes against an urge to shout at him to stop talking about Blade coming. He was not coming! He was probably dead or in jail, and even if he could come for them, no one, not even Blade, could possibly find them in this hidden, desolate canyon. They had ridden over rocks to get here, places where surely no tracks could be detected. Their fate was sealed. She just wished there were a way to get the children back to safety, but it was obvious these men would take the ransom money and never return Roxanne. They would take Roxanne on to Mexico and get even more money for her there.

"Billy, we went through places where no one could possibly track us, over rocks and—"

"He'll find us!" the boy interrupted, his lips puckered with determination.

Sandra chastised herself for the remark. She reminded herself not to destroy the boy's hope. "I'm sorry, Billy." She fought her own tears. "I just . . . I'm so frightened, and you're so brave."

The boy's chest jerked in a sob. "I wish . . . I was bigger," he told her. "I'd help you if I was big like Blade. I bet he could lick all eight of those men out there."

Sandra closed her eyes and forced herself not to tell him how ridiculous the thought was. The men outside were all well armed, ruthless and experienced . . . but then so was John Casey.

"Blade showed me things . . . like how you can tell if a rock is recently tumbled," Billy was saying. "That means somebody rode through there and stirred up the littler stones. He can even see tracks over flat rocks. You look real close and you can see the sand and dust on top are stirred up. Horses are heavy. They break off little twigs while they're walking, and heck, all horses leave their droppings along the way. Blade's got a nose like a wolf. He can sniff the air and smell things we can't. He can smell horses and campfire smoke from far away, things like that. He learned all that from the Apache. You'll see. He'll find us."

Sandra smiled through tears, thinking how her son's hope and confidence, and his talk of Blade's skills, was infectious. He was even beginning to give her a little hope. At least his trust and confidence and their conversation gave her a kind of strength to keep going, and helped pass the time and keep her mind off of what might lie ahead for her.

"Besides, Blade loves you," the boy added.

The remark startled her. "What?"

"He loves you. He told me, only he said not to tell. Only reason I'm telling you now is 'cause maybe it will make you feel better. If he loves you, he'll try even harder to find you and help you."

Suddenly all the horror outside the shed was for the moment forgotten. "He *told* you flat out that he loved me?"

"Yes, ma'am." Billy grinned. "I was talking about how pretty you are, and he says, yup, she's a damn pretty woman. I don't mean to swear, Mama, but those were his words. I asked him if he liked you, and he said yes. I asked if he liked you a *lot*, and he said yes, he did. Then I asked if he *loved* you, and he thought a minute, then looked at me, and he said yes, he supposed he did love you, but that I shouldn't

tell you that. He said ladies like you are too nice and educated and all for somebody like him. He said that didn't
make him any less respectable than any other man. It was
just a fact of life, he said. Sometimes two people can like
each other a lot, but they're too different to really be together. I said it shouldn't matter, if you love each other. Do
you love Blade, Mom?''

Sandra thought a moment, realizing the boy deserved for
her to be as honest with him as Blade had been. She wondered at her son's ability to understand such things, and she
realized he was much more mature than she had given him
credit for. Yes, perhaps he *did* need a man to teach him
manly things now. ''I think maybe I do, Billy.''

''Then you should be together.''

She sighed. ''It isn't that easy. Mr. Casey was right, about
how different we are. And other people would be very upset
if I was with someone like Mr. Casey. I could lose my teaching job.''

The boy shrugged. ''So? You could go some place else
and teach.''

Such simple words. He made it sound so easy. ''I suppose
I could.'' Voices rose outside. Another argument was taking
place. She prayed it wasn't over her. The shouts brought her
back to the reality of her situation. ''It might not even matter
now. First we have to find a way to escape these men. We'll
probably be all right until that money gets delivered. Then
they'll take us farther away, where we'll be harder to find.''

''Blade will find us before they can do that,'' the boy told
her.

She reached over and touched his face, leaned closer to
kiss his hair. ''I'll pray that you're right, Billy. If Mr. Casey
is to find us, it's God himself who will have to do the helping.''

Chapter Seven

*B*lade slung his rifle over his shoulder, a leather bag of ammunition over the other shoulder. He left his horse tied behind a hill, suspecting he was close now. The animal might be too easily spotted. He had to go the rest of the way in on foot.

He prayed his hunch and his tracking instincts had been right. He had not followed the tracks that headed east from where Sandra and the children had been taken. He'd seen plenty of tracks headed west, then south, figured there to be at least three horses at first, then more had joined the first men beyond a stand of aspen trees.

He'd followed the tracks to Rock Canyon, certainly suitably named. Although there was a creek and a little green in the canyon bed about two miles ahead, there was no other life here, nothing but rock and clay. Apache war parties had used this place more than once to hide from soldiers. It made sense that renegade Apaches would know about it.

He tracked carefully for the next mile, using every sense to its fullest, smelling the air, listening keenly for the distant sound of a voice, hoping his hunch that the outlaws were camped at the creek on the other side of this canyon wall was right. If so, he had to be very careful. It was likely a lookout had been posted. He stayed in shadows as much as possible, using the cover of boulders and ledges, watching every step. It was dead quiet here. One wrong step on a dry plant that might snap, one small tumbled rock, and he would be found out.

One thing he knew for sure, he'd have to shoot fast and sure. If he was caught, he couldn't even run to his horse to escape. He also had to keep the outlaws busy shooting at him so they would not kill their captives during his attack.

His only saving grace might be the element of surprise. These men had not counted on someone following them who knew this country as well as he knew every line on his own face. They had not figured on Apache tracking Apache, or that someone would follow who knew the best hiding places, places few white men knew about.

This had to be the place! It was close enough for Joe to catch up with the money, far enough and well hidden enough to dare to stay there with their prey until the money arrived, and to still have time enough to get a good head start south before anyone could trace them here. The creek would have plenty of water this time of year, with spring melt-off in the surrounding mountains. A man could stand on a high wall of the north side of the canyon and see someone coming for at least two miles.

He waited for the cover of full darkness before going the last mile, wanting to be sure no one spotted him. Not many men could make this last trek after dark, through the maze of dry, scratchy plants and rocks that lay along the way, but he knew this place, had been here with Apache warriors himself several times when he lived among them. Still, even for him, coming through here at night was difficult. His shirt was ripped in several places, and his arms, chest and back were covered with stinging cuts, but he ignored them. His own condition was nothing compared to what might have happened to Sandra.

Again his insides raged at the very thought of it, such a beautiful, gentle, proper woman, untouched since her husband's death. He'd come to think of her as belonging to him, even though that could never be. He felt as though the outlaws had stolen away his own woman. He cherished her above anything he'd ever owned, above anyone he'd ever known. She was like a perfect jewel, a woman of pure honor. And Billy! He loved that kid. If those men had harmed him, there would be hell to pay! Fact was, there would be hell to pay either way.

He just hoped he'd made it here before Joe did with the money. It would take Carl Sloan at least one full day to get to Santa Fe. He'd probably have to wait a while to get things straight with the bank, another day to get back home, which he had probably managed today, but most likely not in time for Joe to leave before dark. He had to make his move tonight, or Joe Clayton would be here tomorrow, tomorrow night at the latest, one extra man to go up against.

He was relieved that he'd seen no sign of a rider headed this way. Joe was supposed to take the money to Wolf Creek, and he most likely would do that at first, just in case someone was following. There might even be men there to shoot anyone who tagged along. That was where everyone thought the outlaws waited, not here at Rock Canyon.

He crept up the north wall of the canyon, his fingers bleeding from grasping and climbing over rocks. He finally reached the top, then moved stealthily along the ridge on noiseless moccasins. He had exchanged his hard boots for the moccasins before making his way here. Boots made too much noise against crunching gravel and rocks.

Finally he spotted the lookout. He crouched low, watching as a second man approached. They spoke to each other in Spanish, and Blade understood enough to know the second man was a relief man. That was good. He'd wait until the first man went below. Once a new man was sent up, the men camped in the canyon below would think nothing of not hearing from him the rest of the night. That's when he would make his move and quietly eliminate the lookout. In the meantime, he would move to a spot where he could see below, count the men, measure his odds . . . figure which one should die first! He'd dearly love to kill them all the Apache way, torture them, take several days to let them die, but there would be no time for that. He must be quick, sure, and he must shoot to kill!

* * *

The beginning of another miserable night brought the one
thing Sandra had been dreading. She could hear another argument. Manuel was declaring he'd "try" the white woman
for himself and see how much she was worth. She was ter-
ribly weakened from eating nothing but bread and water, and
she felt filthy and tired, but all senses came alert when the
door to the shack creaked open.

"It is time, *señora*," came a gruff voice.

"You stay away from my mother!" Billy yelled at Manuel, who stepped into the shack. Roxanne began whimper-
ing, and she curled as far against the back wall as she could.

"You will keep silent, little *gringo*, or you will be dead!"
Manuel warned.

"Please leave my son alone," Sandra asked quietly, feign-
ing cooperation.

Manuel stepped closer. "I will leave him alone, as long
as you come with me with no trouble." He bent down to
unlock the tight cuff about her wrist, where her skin was
chafed raw.

"Please unchain my son and poor Roxanne for a while,"
she begged. "Their wrists are bleeding."

"Children are too much trouble. They might try to run
off. It would be difficult to find them in the dark." He freed
her wrist, then yanked her close. "Or would you rather they
came outside and watched what I will do with you?"

Sandra could smell whiskey on his breath.

"I will inspect you, strip you and decide what your body
is worth. Then I will try you on for size, if you know what
I mean." He laughed. "Then I think perhaps it will be time
to get rid of the boy. He is just one more mouth to feed. I
do not think he is worth taking all the way to Mexico."

"No!" Sandra said, shrinking back from the smell of his
breath and body. "You promised to leave my son alone if I
cooperated!"

The man shrugged. "I am known to break promises," he
said, his teeth showing white by the light of the campfire
outside.

"You leave my son alone, or you'll get no cooperation from me!" Sandra snarled.

"Oh, but I like a woman with fight in her," Manuel answered.

"Then you will get one!" Sandra screamed. Summoning what strength she had, she picked up her chamber pot and flung it at him, spilling the debris all over the front of the man. He screamed in horror, stepping back, cursing loudly. He backed out of the shack, looking down at himself.

"Bitch! You bitch!" he yelled. "Go and get her!" he ordered someone. "Bring her out here! I will beat her until she dies!"

Men laughed, and through the open door Sandra could see them stepping away. Quickly Sandra picked up the key Manuel had dropped and began unlocking Billy and Roxanne's cuffs, forcing herself to hurry.

"I ain't goin' in that mess!" one of the men shouted between guffaws.

Manuel began ripping off his clothes, still screaming obsenities, throwing his clothes into the fire. Suddenly a shot rang out. Another. Another. By then Sandra was near the door with the children. They watched a half-naked Manuel fall, blood on his back. Two more men cried out and fell, one with an ugly hole in his cheek, the other gripping his chest.

"What is happening?" someone yelled. "Where is Lou?"

"It's him, Mom!" Billy yelled. "It's Blade! I told you he'd come!"

Sandra did not know what to think. Whoever it was, perhaps a posse, someone had found them. She could only pray it wasn't just another band of outlaws out to steal what this bunch had already taken.

"We have to get out of here!" she warned. "They might try to kill us for spite!" They could hear more gunshots. Someone else cried out in pain.

"Damn it, I can't see him!" another cursed. "How many are there?"

"Don't know—eeeahhh!" came another cry.

"Get the girl! That will stop them! Hold a gun to her head!" someone cried.

Sandra ran to pick up another chamber pot. One of the men rushed inside the shed, and she threw the contents of the pot directly at his face. The man screamed and stumbled out, gagging and choking and cursing. Another gunshot. Sandra grabbed Billy and Roxanne and ran to the back of the shed, kicking and pushing at one of the flimsy wall boards until it broke loose. She hurried Roxanne and Billy through the opening, and they ran into darkness, away from the light of the fire, waiting, not even sure for what . . . or for whom.

"I know it's him!" Billy whispered. "See? I told you he could track us!"

They heard a piercing war cry. Surely it was Indians attacking the camp! Their fate with Indians could be even worse than what Manuel had in mind for them, Sandra thought. She spotted a few bodies. One outlaw ran for his horse, and a man in a torn shirt, his long, black hair flying, charged into the outlaw, landing a big blade into his back.

The Indian whirled, and it looked as though his arm was bleeding. It was then Sandra realized Billy was right. "Blade!" she whispered in disbelief.

"I knew it!" Billy jumped up, but Sandra grabbed hold of him.

"Wait! Don't distract him!"

There was one man left, and he approached Blade, waving a knife. Sandra recognized Many Crows, the wild renegade who had first brought her here on his horse. He arched over, arms poised to strike, circling Blade, who in turn made ready for battle. Sandra realized he had somehow lost his rifle, but he still wore a six-gun. Why didn't he use it? He had probably already used up his six shots. The knife must be all he had left with which to defend himself.

The two men circled, lunged, tumbled to the ground, wrestling in the gravel.

"He's wounded!" Sandra lamented. "He can't win this!"

"He will, Mom," Billy declared. "He's fighting for you!"

Sandra could not help feeling a deep pride and a vast love

at the remark. Both men rolled, each one struggling to keep the other's knife hand away. They got back to their feet, and Many Crows took several swipes. Sandra gasped when one of them cut across Blade's chest, but Blade seemed unaffected, a man bent on doing what must be done, ignoring his own wounds. He waited for just the right moment, then in a flash he lunged immediately after Many Crows took another slash with his knife. Blade landed his own knife into the man's middle, and Many Crows grunted and stood still for a moment. Blade yanked out his knife as the renegade backed away, staring at Blade, until finally he went to his knees and keeled over.

Blade whirled, taking a look at the rest of the men. A couple of them groaned. They were still alive, but he was not going to help them. He was going to get Sandra and the children out of this place, if they were indeed still safe. He'd only guessed they were in the shed. He headed for the little building, calling their names. He stopped when he saw one man he'd shot lying on his back with the contents of a chamber pot all over his face, the pot lying nearby. He grinned at the thought of what must have happened. *My woman is clever and brave,* he thought.

"Here!" Sandra cried. "We're over here!" She and the children stepped out of the darkness hesitantly, but then Billy ran up to Blade and hugged him.

"You came! I told Mom you would! I told her you loved her, Blade, and that's why you'd come and find her! She told me she loves you, too."

The boy seemed oblivious to Blade's wounds, but Sandra could see they were serious. She stepped closer, Blade's dark eyes on her. She could not remove her gaze from his.

"This is true?" he asked.

Sandra shivered from both shock and relief. "We'll talk later, Mr. Casey. You're hurt. Let me find some supplies and dress your wounds as best I can."

His eyes moved over her as though he were looking at a ghost. "They did not touch you?"

She blinked back tears. "You got here before—" It hit

her then how he had risked his life for her and the children. "I don't know what to say." She stepped closer, touched his bloody arm. "How can I ever thank you enough? You could have been killed!"

"It would have been worth it to free you." He turned away, afraid to believe what Billy had just told him. He kicked a body out of the way and sat down on a log. "Do what you can," he told her. "At first light we will go back. You are right. This is not a good time to talk about . . . other things." Perhaps she didn't want to talk about them because it wasn't true. Maybe Billy was just wishful thinking. The boy should not have told her of his feelings. He glanced at the children. "You are unhurt?"

Roxanne just sniffled and sat down near the fire.

"We're okay," Billy answered. "Roxanne is just real scared, but I was never scared," the boy bragged. "I knew you'd come, Blade."

"Did you now?" Blade grinned through his pain. "You make too much of me, boy."

"Billy, look in the tent over there. See if you can find some whiskey to put on Mr. Casey's wounds, something to wrap them with."

"Yes, ma'am!"

Blade looked at Sandra. "I am sorry you had to see me use my knife on that man, but my gun was empty, and one of the others had kicked my rifle away."

Sandra felt suddenly weak. She sat down near him, putting her head in her hands. "It's all right, Mr. Casey."

"Mr. Casey?" he asked softly. "You still feel you should call me Mr. Casey?"

She raised tear-filled eyes to face him. "Yes. After tonight you deserve more respect than ever."

They did not speak of love. This was not the time. But Sandra saw it there, in his eyes, and Blade saw it in her own. It did not seem possible. Loss of blood was making him weaker. He prayed he could hang on long enough to get this woman and the children to safety. After that they could talk about this love neither of them wanted to admit to.

"How can I thank you."

"I do not need thanks. It is enough to know I got here before you were harmed." He glanced down and saw the raw skin on her wrist. Carefully he reached out and grasped her forearm, raising the wrist to his lips. "I am sorry for this," he told her, kissing her wrist gently.

Fiery passion ripped through Sandra's body, in spite of the terror she had just suffered, in spite of her sorry condition. "John." She didn't know what else to say, but he seemed to understand the way she had finally used his first name. He reached out and pulled her into his arms. How she needed to be held, to feel his strength! She collapsed against him, not caring that the children looked on.

Chapter Eight

*B*illy grinned as Blade handed a bouquet of flowers to his mother, and Sandra could see by Blade's face that he felt a little awkward. "There's a place east of here where these grow. They're kind of pretty," he told her.

Sandra smiled when she took the bouquet of tiny blue, white and pink forget-me-nots. "Thank you." She handed them to Billy. "Will you ask Frances or Roxanne to put these in a vase for me?"

Billy took the flowers and glanced up at Blade. "You and Mom have fun," he told him, total excitement shining in his dark eyes. He ran off, and Blade looked back at Sandra, thinking how utterly beautiful she was today, with color on her cheeks, her reddish-blond hair done up in pretty curls. She wore a soft green dress, and a straw bonnet was tied under her chin with green ribbon, all of which accented her beautiful green eyes. Did he dare think she had got herself all fixed up like this just for him?

"You look real nice."

Sandra smiled, wondering if he could tell by her eyes how impressed she was with how he also looked . . . so utterly handsome! He wore a dark suit, every bit the respectable man, certainly a totally desirable man standing there so strong and tall, a neat string tie at the collar of his white shirt. The shirt made his skin seem even darker. His long, black hair was tied neatly at the base of his neck, and his eyes sparkled with what she knew was love. It made her heart pound harder to think they would be totally alone for the first time since they had known each other. "You look wonderful yourself," she answered. "How are you feeling?"

He flexed his left arm. "I'm healing. You ready?"

She picked up a picnic basket. "Yes."

He took the basket from her and led her to the waiting buggy. Today teacher Sandra Brooks would go on a picnic alone with Mr. John Casey, who had garnered a good deal of respect from the Sloan family, the men at the ranch, and even the townspeople . . . who had promptly dragged Joe Clayton off to the gallows after a quick, rowdy trial. Blade had not only brought back Roxanne, Mrs. Brooks and her son alive and untouched, but in spite of his wounds he had also gone after Clayton, who had already left with the money. In spite of some people's suspicions that the half-breed would surely ride off with all that money, he had returned again with both Joe Clayton and the ten thousand dollars. Now people were beginning to talk about making John Casey their new sheriff. Sloan Springs needed more law and order.

Carl Sloan couldn't thank Blade enough. He had given him one hundred fifty acres of good, grassy land from the better section of his ranch, as well as a five thousand dollar reward. He'd had no objections when Blade asked if he could court Sandra Brooks, and Sandra herself certainly had none. She no longer cared what the town might think of such a relationship.

Blade drove the buggy to the section of land Carl had given him. It was pretty, with plenty of high grass for horses or cattle. He drove to a grove of cottonwood trees, where he helped Sandra down, and they laid out a blanket. They ate and talked about Blade's plans for the future. He would capture and break wild horses and sell them in Santa Fe and to ranchers. He had plenty of money now, could maybe buy up even more land adjacent to what Carl had given him. He was having a cabin built, "a real nice one, plenty of room for a wife and kids. It's going to have a big stone fireplace, a hand

pump for water, real wood floors, windows with curtains . . ."

Sandra met his eyes, and she knew they had both talked
around the real subject on their minds long enough.

"You've done a lot of planning, Mr. Casey."

He nodded. "I'm hoping . . ." He looked away, rubbing
at his eyes. "You know I love you, Sandra."

It was the first time he'd actually said it himself.

"And you know I love *you* . . . John."

The air hung silent for several seconds. He still would
not look at her. "That is hard for me to believe, a man like
me—"

"You're no different from any other man, except perhaps
a little smarter, much braver, more skilled, certainly more
handsome. More than that, my son looks up to you. He thinks
you're wonderful, a true hero . . . and so do I."

He finally looked at her. "I love that kid. You know that,
don't you?"

Her eyes suddenly teared. "Yes."

He bent his legs and rested his elbows on his knees. "Sandra, I had planned on doing this right. I mean, courting you
a good long time, making sure this wouldn't mess up your
teaching job, making sure the townspeople wouldn't lose
their respect for you—"

"You've proven yourself to me many times over, John
Casey, *and* to others. No one is going to think less of me
for seeing you, and right now I couldn't care less if they
did."

He watched her lips move, wanted to taste them. "What
I'm saying is, I don't really want to make a long courtship
out of this," he told her. "I already know how I feel. I just
need to know for sure how *you* feel. I love you. I'd honor
you, treasure you like the most precious gem. A woman like
you . . . she's something a man like me would normally never
dream he could have. I don't drink, Sandra. I've seen enough
of drinking and womanizing and gambling and all that when
I was growing up. And I've seen what whiskey does to the
Apache. I'll never let that happen. You don't have to worry

about me getting drunk and mean. I'd treat you like a piece of delicate china. I'd—''

''Are you asking me to marry you?''

Their eyes held, and Sandra smiled at the realization that he was actually blushing a little. ''Yes, ma'am, I'm asking.'' He reached out and touched her face gently. ''I want you like I've never wanted any other woman. I want you to belong to me. When I heard those men had taken you and Billy, I thought I'd go crazy. I didn't go after you just because it was the right thing to do. I did it because I couldn't stand the thought of any of them touching my woman. That's how I'd come to think of you, and that's what I'd like you to be. I'd take good care of you, protect you, provide for—''

''Yes,'' she interrupted.

''What?''

''Yes, I'll marry you, but I will always call you John, never Blade. I cannot think of a more honorable man to have for a husband, a better man to be a father to Billy. And I . . .'' Did she dare say it? Was it too brazen? ''I also . . . want you.'' She looked down, feeling the flush come to her face. ''I want you to hold me. I want to feel a man's strength again, to feel a man . . .'' She swallowed. ''All these years, I've hardly thought about what's been missing in my life, my needs and desires as a woman. You awakened all of that. I never would have dreamed I'd fall in love with any man, after what happened to Danny, let alone a man with Apache blood in his veins; but you've shown me a man can't be judged that way, and I'm sorry for being guilty of that.'' She met his eyes again. ''I only know that I love you, and I would be honored to be John Casey's woman, as you put it; honored to call you my . . .'' She could see the fires of desire in his dark eyes. ''My man.''

He came closer, his full lips meeting her mouth, parting her own lips. In that one moment, just their second kiss, they both knew what they had been craving from each other for weeks now. Exquisite desire filled Sandra's every bone and muscle, every nerve end, every sense, touch, taste, smell, even sound . . . the sound of his soft groan as he unfolded his legs and stretched out beside her, laying her back on the blanket . . . and sight . . . the sight of John Casey moving to hover over her while their kiss lingered, burning deep, growing more desperate, more demanding.

Oh, it had been so long since she felt this way! She couldn't remember ever desiring Danny with this much passion and intense need. She felt a big, strong hand at her ribs, and she daringly grasped his wrist and moved his hand to where she knew he would like to put it, wanting to feel a lover touching her breasts again.

"God, Sandra," he groaned, their kiss growing wilder, deeper.

The awkwardness was broken. Both knew what they needed. Both were mature adults who cared little at the moment about properness. This was something they had wanted for too long, and Sandra had no misgivings, no worry that this man would think any less of her. "Make love to me, John," she whispered. "I need you so. I don't want to wait."

It happened like in her dreams, and she wondered if perhaps she was actually only dreaming again. Light clouds floated across an intensely blue sky, and a soft breeze caressed them. Kisses moved to intimate caresses. Somehow she found herself lying naked beneath John Casey. His hair was undone now, falling about her shoulders, and he, too, was unclothed. There was the scar on his broad chest, put there when he fought Many Crows to save her; the scar on his arm from a gunshot wound suffered for the same reason. Then his big, strong hands were gently massaging, caressing, exploring, hands that could so easily break her, but were now so gentle.

She could hardly get her breath. She gasped as he guided himself into her. She gloried in being a woman again, taking this powerful, brave man inside her in sweet ecstasy. John Casey was as good at making love as he was at breaking horses, or wielding a knife or using a rifle. No, he was even *better* at this.

* * *

The little schoolhouse was full to overflowing, not with children, but with townspeople and ranch hands, all come to see the marriage of Sandra Brooks to John Casey. Roxanne carried flowers for Sandra, and Billy carried the wedding rings. Frances played a wedding song on a piano donated to the school by one of the local saloons.

Sandra had stayed in the coat room until it was time. She emerged and walked down the short aisle, and she could tell by the look in John's dark eyes he thought she looked beautiful. She had never primped and fussed over herself the way she had today, flowers in her hair, color on her cheeks and lips. She wore a dress made of ivory lace. Sara Stafford, the town seamstress, had insisted on making the dress for her, and she had done a wonderful job on the dress with its ivory taffeta underskirt and bodice, overlaid with handmade lace ordered all the way from New York City. Waiting for the special lace had been agonizing, but it had arrived in time. The wait for this day, too, had been agonizing, but John Casey wanted to be able to take his new wife home to a decent house, insisted on finishing their cabin before they wed. They had both agreed, after that first afternoon of passionate lovemaking, that they would wait until marriage for more.

It had not been an easy decision. That first time had been out of desperate need, long-buried desire, and the sweet taste of love had left them both hungry for more. Still, it seemed only right that they wait for this moment. It had been nearly three months, the longest summer Sandra could remember; but it had been a good summer for Billy and John. Man and boy had become even closer, Billy helping John work on the cabin every day. They had not let her even come inside until two weeks ago, when they both proudly showed it off to her, a wonderful stone fireplace, just as John had promised, three bedrooms, wood floors, a water pump and sink. She had only to decorate as she liked.

They would be happy there, a family . . . the family John Casey had never had and never thought he could have. She would give him more children. He would be able to be the father he himself never had, and he would be a better father for it. She had written her parents, but they had not replied. She knew they would not understand this. She could only pray some day they would realize the kind of man John was. It did not matter that he carried Indian blood. Some would look down on her for this, but she felt nothing but pride. For the sake of love, she would not let their looks and remarks make her waver. For the sake of love, she would risk whatever she had to risk . . . for this handsome, brave man who had risked his very life in order to save her from a fate worse than death.

How wonderful he looked! Before the incident involving Roxanne Sloan, people would have run her out of town for marrying this man, but he had proved his worth. Most had agreed they would still allow Mrs. John Casey to teach their children, in spite of her husband being a half-breed. How foolish to judge people in such shallow ways. How many people like John were wasted because of that, never given a chance to make something of themselves? She had a feeling that even Danny would understand this, that he blessed this marriage from somewhere above.

Vows were spoken. Rings were exchanged. John Casey kissed his bride, a delicious, warm, sweet kiss that hinted of things to come. She wondered how she was going to get through the next few hours of celebrating before they went alone to their new home to spend their first night there together. Billy would stay tonight with the Sloans. He'd had a lot of talks with John. He understood.

Tables were spread out in a grove of trees behind the schoolhouse to shade people and food from the hot August sun. They ate, opened gifts, visited. It was wonderful to see how people were treating John, with the respect he deserved. He was ''Mr. Casey,'' now, just as Sandra had said he should be called.

She ached for him. How long this day had become! Finally he was at her side, his strong arm about her waist. He was walking her toward a big Appaloosa gelding that had only a blanket where normally a saddle would be. People were throwing rice at them, a few making suggestive remarks that made her blush. To her surprise, John lifted her onto the horse. "I will take my bride to our dwelling the Indian way," he told her, "on horseback, not in a buggy." He turned to Billy, who stood watching with a big grin on his face. He leaned down and gave the boy a hug. "We will come for you tomorrow, Billy. Be a good boy for the Sloans."

"Yes, sir." Billy clung to him for a moment. "I love you, Blade."

Never had the man been more touched. "And I love you, Billy."

"Can I . . . call you Pa now?"

Pain pierced Blade's heart . . . all the years he'd wished he had a father, wished he could love and be loved. "That's what I am now, isn't it?"

Billy nodded. "I gotta' always keep a picture of my real pa, though, always remember him."

"Of course you do." John reached out and tousled his hair. "It is right to honor your real father." He turned to see tears in Sandra's eyes. "This is no time for sadness and tears." He leapt onto the horse behind her with grace and skill, put his arms around her to take up the reins. "Let's go home, Mrs. Casey," he told her.

Fire ripped through every part of her. "I am ready, Mr. Casey. I can hardly stand the wait."

He grinned, a smile that melted her every time she saw it. More rice was thrown at them as they rode off toward the ranch, and on the way Blade used one hand to pull the leather tie from his hair so that the hair fell out loose. He stopped the horse for a moment, took off his suitcoat, the tie, the white, ruffled shirt. "There are some white man's clothes that I hate," he told her. "For the rest of the night I will be Singing Hawk, an Apache brave who will mate with his new bride."

Sandra watched in surprise as he removed his shoes and socks, throwing everything to the ground. He was transformed from white man to Indian, and it astounded her how easily he could do so. He sat there naked from the waist up, no shoes, his hair blowing in the wind . . . as handsome a specimen of man as any woman could set eyes on. "I am honored to be your bride, Singing Hawk."

He met her mouth in a heated, provocative kiss, his hand gently fondling her breasts, breasts that lay under the ivory lace dress, aching to be touched, tasted. How sweet it was to give this man pleasure, for she took so much pleasure in return. The kiss lingered, both of them groaning with need.

"We'd best get going," he said, nearly breathless. He kicked the horse into a gallop, keeping one strong arm tightly around her as horse, man and woman disappeared over the hill toward home, the first real home John Casey had ever known. Both of them had risked all . . . for the sake of love.

From Rosanne Bittner . . .

$\mathscr{I}$ hope you have enjoyed the story of Sandra and Blade. I have written many novels about the American West and American Indians, all set in the 1800's. If you would like more information about me and my writing, along with a list of titles and publishers, just send a #10 (letter-size), self-addressed, stamped envelope to me at 6013 North Coloma Road, Coloma, Michigan 49038. I will mail you a newsletter and bookmark. Or you can visit my home page at http://www.parrett.net/~bittner. Thank you!

AN IMPETUOUS
SEASON

Denise Domning

To Elizabeth Stramel, who at ninety-six is everything I hope to be at the same age. Your memories of Victoria made Kansas real to me.

Chapter One

Seated on the chancel step, Verity Standiford, the black ewe of the Rycote Standifords, stared at the ruined nosegay in her hands. A single rose petal remained. She plucked it, then let the soft bit of flower fall from her fingers. As it settled atop its brothers in her satin-clad lap, all hope of ever having a family of her own shattered.

Verity sighed as bitter disappointment ached in her. What a fool she'd been to dream she could escape her fate. Not even Ralph, who was no man at all, wanted used goods. She was doomed to the same barren, purposeless existence as that dried-up old battle-ax who claimed to be Great Aunt Faith. When word of this, her second abandonment at the altar, spread, as it surely would, the quiet scorn and hissing whispers she already endured would become open laughter.

"Coward," she scolded herself. She wouldn't let anyone see how this hurt her. To do so would only prove they'd beaten her and no matter how true it was, she'd never let them see that. It was in defiance that Verity sent the bundle of stems flying across the chapel. It bounced off a high-backed wooden pew, then skittered across dank, stone flooring.

From the chapel's arched doorway came the sound of footsteps. Verity looked up. August's bright sunlight outlined her father's stocky form making Wilson Standiford's formal at-

tire gleam, all dark blue silk and starched whiteness. A cool
breeze teased what little was left of her father's light brown
hair.

"Child, it's time to leave." Papa's voice was as mild and
indolent as he.

It was pointless to remind him she was hardly a child,
having reached her nine and twentieth year. Instead, Verity
came to her feet in a shower of petals and yanked off the
circlet of orange blossoms topping her upswept hair. Dropping the girlish headdress with its fine, white veiling, she
strode for the portal.

"So Papa, what's next?" she asked, her voice as bold as
ever. She threaded her arm through her sire's. "Were I you,
I think I might sue Ralph to retrieve the sums you expended
in buying him for me."

Her father's broad and fleshy features tensed as he eyed
his taller daughter, his mouth a narrow line beneath a mustache that would have done credit to a walrus. His eyes, the
same clear gray of her own, narrowed, his look growing just
a tad anxious. "Buy him for you, indeed. I did no such
thing." Behind his stuffy words lurked a touch of shame.

"And, here I was thinking you'd paid Ralph's debts to
tease him into marrying me." Verity raised a chiding brow.
They both knew very well Papa had arranged this abortive
wedding as an apology of sorts, now that he'd had time to
regret the vengeance he'd wreaked on her all those years ago.

Papa glanced away from her look, color creeping up his
neck and Verity relented with a sigh. "Ah well, I, too,
thought the arrangement a fair one. In exchange for marital
respectability, I would have spared Ralph the complaints
some naive virgin might have made against the men he took
to his bed."

Wilson yelped, his eyes widening in shock, then shot a
frantic glance over his shoulder to see if anyone was within
hearing distance. "Have a care with your tongue, Verity,"
he hissed in panic. "Gadzooks, you shouldn't even know
such things, much less say them aloud."

Again, bitterness touched Verity's heart and echoed in her

short laugh. "You're wrong, Papa. Only I, 'that brazen Standiford woman' can say these things." If her second desertion had freed her from society's bonds, it was a cold sort of freedom she'd gained, offering her nothing but endless years of emptiness.

Anger flared beneath Wilson's usually bland expression. "So, you'll use bold rudeness to punish me for what Ralph has done, will you?"

"And, what sort of gratitude would that be after all you've done?" Verity pressed a kiss on her father's balding pate, ignoring the fact that it was Papa who'd destroyed her all those years ago. "No, it won't be me bringing scandal down upon the Standiford name. I'll gladly leave that chore to Johnnie, who's ever so much better at it than I."

Her father grimaced. His youngest son's most recent excesses resulted in Johnnie being exiled in April past to the United States. The youngest Standiford departed England with Sir George Grant, a wealthy Scottish industrialist, for some place called the Kansas Frontier. Sir George vowed the roughness of American cattle ranching would make a man out of an otherwise well-established rakehell, at the same time it increased the family's fortune.

"We are quite a family, eh, Papa?" Verity offered.

"That we are," Wilson agreed with a hopeless sigh as he led his daughter out into the hot, heaviness of Lammas day. She and her father strode apace down the flagstone path as they made their way toward the gate in the lime hedge. Their carriage waited beyond that exit, yet bedecked in the garlands and ribbons of a wedding conveyance.

Cowardice returned so suddenly, Verity's feet froze to the ground. Wilson stumbled to a halt beside her. "Verity," he cried in stark surprise.

Verity stared at the great loops of roses and greenery on the carriage's sides. Their ride home would be nothing more than a ludicrous advertisement of her desperate grab for home and husband. Why couldn't she have realized the utter hopelessness of her state before today?

"Have Benton tear off the flowers, Papa," she said quietly.

Wilson rolled his eyes in exasperation; he wanted his study and his port. "Can it not wait until we're home, child?"

Dear God, she'd never survive it if anyone witnessed her return to the Standiford estate in that thing, but there was no way to achieve it unless she begged. Verity swallowed that craven desire as she tried to convince herself there was no one to see her. Everyone who was anyone was still in London finishing out the season. Fear fell into an uneasy grave, buried beneath a merry laugh.

"How right you are, Father. I must hurry home, rushing to my mother's side where I will attempt to soothe her nervous distress. After all, it is her continuing failure to rid herself of me that lies at its root." Although Verity shot her father a wicked, laughing glance, within her woke a niggling sense of unfairness. Since her fall from grace all those years ago, Heloise Standiford had barely endured her daughter's presence. Meanwhile, Johnnie's debts, gambling and drunkenness were tolerated as the appropriate sowing of masculine wild oats.

"You are a cruel, cruel child," Papa whispered in approval, making no attempt to defend his wife for whom he'd long ago ceased to care.

He led his daughter from the churchyard to the carriage door and handed her up into the conveyance. Verity shook out her skirts before seating herself on the upholstered bench. When Papa took his place across from her, he again leaned close.

"Truth be told, I wouldn't trade either you or Johnnie for another of our Fred. Stodgy old man at five and twenty, he is. You two make life interesting."

"I love you, too, Papa," Verity said, offering her father a brilliant smile to hide her pain.

Leather snapped and wooden wheels squeaked as the carriage jerked into motion. Verity watched the deserted stone church with its ivied walls and hydrangeas pass from sight.

Her tattered girlhood dreams would forever remain locked within its moldy embrace. Again, her cold and childless future loomed.

The ride progressed in silence, the tree-lined lane blessedly empty. Rather than torture herself by watching for other travelers, Verity forced her gaze to the passing scenery. Thatched roofed cottages were clustered in fives and sixes, neat stone barns sat amid lush fields, while sheep filled the open meadows. In one sunny glade there stood an old byre, half sunk into the earth and so covered in moss, grasses and clinging flowers its walls looked more like grass than stone.

It was as she studied the ancient structure that she realized the futility of trying to hide what had happened this day. Whether her retreat was witnessed or not, it wouldn't take long for news of this latest debacle to spread. Even as loyal as her few guests were to Papa, they couldn't help but talk about this.

Panic rose. She wasn't ready to face this, at least not yet. She had to escape until the bulk of the gossip died down.

Verity lay a hand on her father's sturdy knee. "Papa, I have a sudden yen to travel, see new sights."

Her father's eyes narrowed until they almost disappeared into folds of fat, a calculating gleam in his gaze. "Do you? How far? Perhaps, say, the United States? Your mother does so pine for her sweet Johnnie and Aunt Faith absolutely refuses to travel among American heathens and ignorants."

With a swift breath, Verity recognized what her father was offering. She could run, but only on his terms and he wanted freedom from his wife. Was she truly so desperate, she'd consider traveling with her mother?

The carriage came around a curve, then slowed. Two horses walked toward them. It was Mr. Wakefield and his new wife, the former Miss Blackworth. Wakefield tipped his hat to Wilson, ignoring Verity, while the tittering idiot riding at his left averted her eyes. A modest woman didn't look upon the fallen Miss Standiford. Mrs. Wakefield didn't wait until they were out of earshot to cry out, "Whatever is *she* doing in such a getup?"

"America." The word almost leapt from Verity's mouth. "The Frontier. Savages. What a heady thought. Yes, I think I'll go."

Mr. Standiford grinned and reached into his coat. Withdrawing a thin flask, he helped himself to a goodly swallow of brandy. "That's my Verity girl. Always the helpful sort."

"Oh, do hold your tongue, Papa," she snapped.

When her father offered her the flask, Verity snatched it from his hand and let fiery liquor wash the taste of cowardice from her mouth.

Chapter Two

*T*he piebald's coat gleamed with sweat in the late afternoon sun. As the massive plow horse slowed to a walk, he lowered his head toward the dense carpet of buffalo grass. Seated on the horse's broad, bare back, Seth Adamson glanced ahead at the justice's far more spirited pony. Mr. Jenkins was more than a hundred yards ahead of him. Seth jabbed his booted heels into his neighbor's workhorse. "Come on, you pig-headed fool, keep pace." With a snort of disappointment, the big horse lifted furred hooves into a canter.

The child seated before Seth took a wild bounce. Gemima Adamson's dark braids flew and her pink sunbonnet slid back to nestle at her nape. With a frightened cry, she clutched her rag doll even closer to her chest. Seth's four-year-old niece had never ridden a horse; Gemima liked neither the height nor movement of this tall creature.

Seth drew his only remaining blood relative back into the cradle of his body. "We're almost there, Gemma," he told her in a paltry attempt at both reassurance and apology, using his niece's pet name for herself.

The sweeter of his two charges shot him a wet look over her shoulder, the bright blue of her eyes naming her an Adamson. In Gemma's gaze lingered traces of the shy resentment she'd aimed at him since her parents' death last February. Seth smiled to hide his disappointment. Stepping into the role of father hadn't been easy for him, an unmarried man. Hell, he hadn't even known his brother had a child until a year ago.

With a sigh, Seth turned his attention back onto the road, if that's what one could call the dual ruts cutting across the gentle roll of Western Kansas's landscape. A lingering meadowlark trilled as a gentle breeze rustled through drying grasses and thistles. Without a house or tree to tease his eye, Seth's thoughts drifted to his elder brother, Matt.

The War between the States and Matt's mishandling of their father's estate after the War's end had separated them, permanently, or Seth had believed. Instead, for some reason beyond any understanding, Seth's thirty-fourth birthday brought with it the need to restore familial bonds. It had taken some searching, but he'd finally located Matt in Fort Hays, Kansas. His brother had found himself a wealthy merchant's widow to marry and seemed to be living a prosperous life. After welcoming his prodigal brother with open arms, Matt proposed Seth take up residence with them to continue his interrupted education in the law. A lawyer, Matt insisted, was just what Hays needed.

Seth's mouth twisted at that thought. He'd been an idiot to trust Matt for a second time and even more of a fool to reawaken the desire for the life he'd once assumed was a right. Four months later, Matt and his wife were dead, killed in a wagon accident.

In Matt's inimitable style, his generosity had been well mortgaged. By the time the debts were paid, all that remained were a few pieces of furniture, a filthy, landless soddy and the girls. This time Seth's sigh was bitter.

The girls, sweet Gemima and lovely, nasty, conniving Sarah Jane. Living with a fifteen-year-old who hated him and continually pointed out he wasn't even her blood kin, but only her stepuncle was like going to hell. Ah but if that was true, than today was a glimpse of heaven.

Guilt stabbed through him. It was wrong to find relief in Sarah's downfall. Still, if Standiford admitted he'd fathered Sarah Jane's child, it'd be Standiford who kept the little vixen—at least until the Brit's parents freed him of the marriage. Seth found himself hoping the divorce took a year or more. That way, by the time Sarah Jane returned, babe in arms and far more humble, he'd own his law license and income enough to support them all, beyond even Sarah's somewhat plebeian standards.

Once again, Gunter's stubborn plowhorse slowed to a walk. Seth glanced toward Mr. Jenkins. The sun gleamed off the justice's brown broadcloth suit as he drew his pony to one side. Ahead of them, bumping and jolting along this track, was a mule-drawn wagon. Folks on this trail could only mean another brace of damn fool Englishmen come to play at pioneering. A new ranch sprang up almost every day around Victoria.

Seth's thick brows lowered and his eyes narrowed in scorn at the sight of parasols. These fools happened to be of the female persuasion; two women were seated on trunks in the wagon's bed. These women looked as out of place in Kansas as he would, were he to return to Harvard wearing his present worn, red shirt, sturdy trousers and thick brogans.

The older of the two was dressed in a maroon traveling outfit thick with swags and jet beads. A ridiculous, brimless hat perched atop her grizzled frizz, studded with enough long feathers to make a pheasant jealous. Overdressed for the prairie's afternoon heat, she sought relief with her parasol and a vigorously plied fan. The dark vee of sweat on her gown's back evidenced her failure.

The second passenger was substantially younger than her companion. Outfitted in green and cream plaid, her fan lay neglected in her lap, while her parasol was cocked uselessly over one slender shoulder. Instead, it was a sensibly brimmed straw hat that shaded her from the sun.

"Ladies," Justice Jenkins offered, his voice as stringy as he, and doffed his bowler. With his bushy mustache and his oiled hair slicked against his narrow skull, Jenkins looked like an oversized otter. Once his hat was again fixed firmly upon his head, Hays's marrying man rode past the wagon.

As he and Gemma drew alongside the slow moving con-

veyance, Seth glanced at the younger woman and his disapproval softened. Her skin was pale and clear, her eyes a
lovely gray. Honey-brown hair nestled softly against her
nape in braided loops. If her features were a tad long, her
nose was straight and her chin gently rounded. Fool she
might be, but she was a damned fine-looking one.

In the next moment, the corners of her mouth lifted and
her gaze filled with a sort of amused reproach. Aw, hell.
He'd been staring, the height of rudeness. Years of saddle
tramping and associating only with women he'd paid for had
turned him into the yokel he looked.

Well, there was no sense trying to amend his faux pas.
Instead, Seth swept the battered reminder of his stint as a
cowhand off his head in a mocking tribute to the fine lifestyle
of his upbringing. "Ma'am."

At his parody of elegance, she freed a sultry laugh and her
face came to life. Prettier and prettier. Seth compounded his
earlier sin by winking at her, then ran a quick hand through
the heavy, curling strands of his black hair before clapping
his chapeau into place.

"Of all the impertinence!" The words dripped icicles. The
older woman had turned on her trunk to fix him with a chill,
blue stare over the arched bridge of her nose. Her mouth was
pursed and her pointed chin jutted outward in disgust. "Verity, look away this moment. You're only encouraging the
witless oaf."

Seth quirked a brow at the biddy's arrogance. This particular witless oaf had a bloodline as pure as hers, studded with
notables, not the least of which had been his father, the sen-
ator.

"I don't think she's very nice, Uncle," Gemma said, peer-
ing over his arm at the harridan.

"Oh, don't mind her, child," this Verity replied. "Mother
finds herself dismayed by the lack of organization she sees
around her. She thinks you Americans a very careless sort
of people."

Seth drew a swift breath. Not only was her voice as sultry
as her laugh, there was an odd intimacy to her manner that

sent a shiver through him. Desire followed, strong and not the least bit subtle.

'Mother' had already turned her back to him, her spine stiff against her daughter's veiled insults. "That is quite enough, Verity."

"If you say so, Mama," Verity replied, then offered Seth and Gemma a cheery wave and another lovely smile.

Seth again kicked his ungainly steed into a trot. It was a few minutes before he caught up with Justice Jenkins on his sprightlier mount. Only a few more moments passed before the justice waved them toward a faint new trail marking the dense grass. In the distance to their left there was a cluster of buildings.

"If I was counting rightly, this here's the Standiford place, Adamson," the justice called to him as he turned his horse toward the buildings.

When they'd passed the stone foundation of what would someday be a spacious home, Seth let Gunter's horse slow into its favorite plod. Behind the stonework stood a much smaller, but complete, frame house, with a ceilinged porch clinging to its south and west sides. This dwelling was so new it didn't yet wear paint and so narrow it couldn't consist of more than a bedroom on the second story with a sitting room and dining room below. One blistering Kansas summer had already warped a number of its wooden shingles, revealing the tar paper underlining.

Where Seth's early years had taught him to sneer at so tiny a home as only fit for servants, experience had long since changed him. Now, he looked longingly at it, craving wooden walls and floors. This place was a mansion compared to his present address.

Two expensive horses appeared in a corral behind the dwellings. The bright bay was a hunter, or so the binding of its mane and bobbed tail proclaimed. The other was a gray whose compact lines revealed a goodly dollop of Arab blood. The steeds whickered a friendly greeting to more of their kind. There were no pigs, no milk cows, no chickens.

Like many of Victoria's ranches, this spread was occupied

by a wealthy and unmarried man of substance. As a whole,
these young swells came to make a fortune off cattle and
sheep ranching, not the wheat and sorghum farming of their
less monied neighbors. This was not to say the Brits intended
to work with their hands, no, not at all. They hired others to
do their chores and build their homes, while they hunted or
drank in Tommy Drum's saloon at Hays. The good Lord
knew Seth had made more than a few dollars working for
them, as had Sarah Jane in her position as cook and house-
keeper for one of the families, the MacDonalds.

Once again, guilt rose in Seth. He shouldn't have allowed
Sarah's earnings to blind him into placing her among so
many young men. Moreover, when Sarah vowed to catch
herself a wealthy husband, he should have understood how
it was she meant to achieve her goal. True, Standiford
shouldn't have made free with Sarah, but Seth had no doubt
the greedy little spitfire had done as much seducing as had
been seduced.

Jenkins drew his pony to a halt before the porch and dis-
mounted. Once he'd helped Seth lower Gemma to the
ground, the justice retrieved two shotguns from his saddle
holsters. Afoot, Seth took his own weapon from Jenkins,
setting it into the crook of one arm. With Gemma's hand in
his, he led the way up the porch stairs to the door. It took a
moment to manufacture the right amount of outrage. He
lifted a fist and knocked loudly.

Above them, hidden by the overhanging porch roof, a window squeaked open. "Who is it?" The voice was young and
masculine, the accent proper British English.

"Seth Adamson, Mr. Standiford. I'm Sarah Jane's uncle.
It seems we need to talk," Seth replied.

"Oh my God." Even the man's voice blanched, then he
freed a nervous, girlish giggle. The sound tangled with a
quiet, female shriek.

Gemma gave a happy jump, her face alive with excitement. Her precious doll, dangling from one tiny, grubby fist,
leapt with her. "Sarah Jane," she called, "come down! I
want to see you!" What with Sarah employed since June,

Gemma's contact with her half sister had been limited to Sundays.

This command only woke another female yelp from above. There was no mistaking Sarah Jane. Seth had heard a harsher version of the same sound far too many times over the term of his guardianship. He lowered his voice to the deeper tones of a threat. "Standiford, you'll do right by my niece."

"Best do as he says, young fella," Jenkins added in his nasal tones. "We'll make things as painless as possible. Relatively speakin', that is."

The window slammed shut. Seth glanced at the justice, whose head barely reached his shoulder. "Best you go around back." It was a quiet remark.

" 'Magine you're right," Jenkins replied.

As the justice disappeared around the corner of the house, Gemma looked up at her uncle, all excitement gone. She worried her lip with tiny, white teeth, her blue eyes solemn. "Why won't Sarah come down?"

Seth looked at his niece. "I think she's afraid of me, darlin'."

"Oh." Gemma frowned as she thought this through. "Can Sarah come home to stay with us now?"

Seth sighed, then squatted until they were face-to-face. He tugged Gemma's green sprigged dress straight around her body, then pulled her bonnet back over her black braids and delicate ears. Why hadn't he left her in Hays with Matt's friends, the Evans? When would he ever learn to think like a parent? He shouldn't have exposed her to her sister's downfall. Lifting a hand, he ran a work-hardened palm over the soft curve of her cheek. "No, Gemma, Sarah will have to stay here."

Tears filled Gemma's eyes and her lower lip trembled. "I want Sarah Jane." She pulled her ragdoll close into her embrace, seeking comfort from the lifeless toy.

Seth drew the child against him. "Darlin', she can't come. She's gone and grown up on you. Sarah and the man who lives in this house must get married. That's why Mr. MacDonald came to speak with us this morning, to tell me what

Sarah had done. Now,'' he said, setting her away from him so he could look at her, "you'll have to keep a secret for me.''

"A secret?" Excitement battled distress in Gemma's gaze. Secrets were a favorite game of hers, one she and little Mina Evans played when they were together. "I like secrets.''

"I know you do,'' he said with a smile. "Listen closely. In the next few minutes I may sound very angry. The secret is I'm only pretending. Promise you won't tell?" Seth could only pray the few, fragile bonds he'd woven between them this past summer would hold beyond the coming event.

"I promise,'' she said. It was less vow than the response she knew as part of her game. Then, Gemma's gaze flickered to the gun. "Are you going to shoot Sarah Jane?''

Seth loosed a quick laugh as he came to his feet. "That I will not.'' No matter how often he'd wished he could.

As his niece wrapped an arm around one of his legs and leaned her head against his hip, Seth tried the door handle. It was latched tight. He glanced down at her.

"Remember your promise,'' he said. Then, raising his voice to a threatening level, he shouted, "Standiford, open up or, by God, I'll blow a hole in your door and let myself in.''

"Lookee what I caught me.'' Jenkins sailed back around the corner, Sarah Jane's arm tight in his hand.

Sarah's blond hair hung loose around her shoulders. She wore a new dress, a pretty yellow shirtwaist. That it was misbuttoned down the front spoke to her haste in dressing. Her face was still flushed with the telltale signs of lovemaking, but her green eyes were wide with fear.

"Sarah!'' Gemma cried joyously, leaping for her half sister.

"Gemma! Come to me, sweetheart.''

As Sarah leaned down to embrace her sister, Jenkins moved his grasp to the back of her dress, allowing her to lift the child. Sarah shifted her half-sister in her arms, seeking to use her as a shield against her stepuncle. Seth wasn't so easily deterred. He came to stand in front of her, then crooked a finger beneath her chin. She had no choice but to meet his gaze.

"Mrs. MacDonald suspects you are in the family way. Is this true?"

The blunt question brought a rosy blush to her cheeks. Sarah nodded, the movement of her head almost shy. He released her chin.

"You little fool," he told her in soft scorn. "Well, I'll see you married today to give your child a name, but don't set your sights on keeping him. His sort has grander plans than a ragged orphan like you."

"If I'm poor, it's because you sold everything and took the money for yourself," Sarah retorted, her eyes widening in anger. "I'm every bit Johnnie's equal."

Seth shook his head. No doubt, when judged against the stark poverty of the locals here, she had seen herself as well-to-do, but she was hardly a fit wife for the young Brit. Releasing a harsh breath, he turned his back on the girl and looked at Jenkins. "Can he flee through the back door?"

"Jammed it shut, I did. All you gotta do is pry this one open."

"Well then, let's see how much goading he'll endure." Seth again lifted his fist and banged on the door. "Open the door, you piece of cheap English trash." The angry shout reverberated off the porch and into the sky above them.

"I beg your pardon!"

The sultry tones of the woman Seth found so alluring only a quarter of an hour ago brought him around in a hurry, Jenkins and Sarah turning with him. The young woman was balancing precariously on her feet in the wagon's rocking bed.

"We Standifords aren't cheap trash," she called in that smooth as silk voice of hers. "Quite the contrary. We are extremely expensive trash. Ask my father. He keeps paying and paying."

"Verity!" Verity's mother cried, appalled.

Beside Seth, the justice freed a snorting chuckle at the jest, while Seth fought his grin. A woman with a sense of humor. Now, that was a pearl of price.

"Sit down before you kill yourself, ma'am," Seth called to her.

As she more toppled than sat onto her trunk, the elder Standiford woman turned on the wagon's driver. "Faster, you," she cried. "Can't you see my son is in danger?" Using her folded fan as a quirt, she rapped the man repeatedly on the head to encourage haste.

There was nothing but stoic blandness on the driver's broad German face as he endured his beating without once urging his mules to a faster pace. However, when he drew the wagon to a halt near the porch stairs, he made no move toward aiding the women from its bed.

John Standiford's mother glared at Seth as she came to her feet. "What sort of country is this? Imagine! Armed riffraff assaulting a decent man's home. The audacity of it!" The words escaped her in great gusts of outrage.

"Now, Mama," Verity Standiford said, "these men wouldn't be the first to have a perfectly legitimate complaint to air with Johnnie."

The sister of the man about to become Seth's in-law rose. Finding her footing more secure this time, she extended a hand toward Seth. "Do help me down, won't you?"

Seth looked at Sarah Jane. His stepniece glanced from the newcomers' fine attire to her own garment, only now noting the gaping front. With a quiet cry, she set Gemma down and began straightening and buttoning her dress. Although she seemed fully occupied, Seth looked to Jenkins. "Don't let her go, now," he warned, then leaned his shotgun against a porch support and went to the wagon's end.

Verity Standiford's waist was pleasantly narrow beneath his hands. As he lifted her from the bed, the scent of roses came with her. He set her feet on the earth. She was tall for a woman, her brow level with his cheekbone. Desire again spurred Seth; he liked a woman of good size.

She tilted her head to peer up at him from beneath her hat's brim. Her gray eyes sparkled in wholly unwarranted merriment, while her face softened into something damned near beauty. When she leaned toward him, most of Seth melted. If his skin hadn't already been burnt brown by the sun, he'd have feared a revealing blush.

"Be a dear, won't you, and help Mrs. Standiford down," she whispered, then turned to climb the stairs.

Seth did her bidding without a second thought. "Mrs. Standiford," he said, extending his hands toward the heavy-set woman.

The biddy eyed his calloused palms and work-stained shirt with disgust, her mouth growing even more pinched and sour. Drawing two handkerchiefs from her reticule, she offered them to him. "I'll not have you ruin my clothing. Worth, himself, designed this for me."

There was no sense arguing. Seth cloaked his hands in fine linen, then heaved the woman from the wagon. The moment her feet touched the earth, Mrs. Standiford tore free, letting the lace-edged squares drop to the ground as if befouled by his touch. The woman swept up the porch stairs without offering a word of thanks, then turned on Jenkins and the girls. "Be gone with you. Shoo!"

"I don't think as we can be doin' that, ma'am," Hays's justice replied, unperturbed by her rudeness.

"Not just yet, anyway." Seth stepped onto the porch without using the stairs and, again, caught up his weapon. He edged through the crowd porch until he stood beside Standiford's sister.

"Right, then," Miss Verity Standiford said to him, her slender, gloved hand poised at the door. "Let me show you the trick to this door opening thing. Are you watching?"

"That I am," he replied with a quiet smile, wondering if it was possible to want a woman more than he was presently wanting this one.

She tapped lightly. "Johnnie, darling, are you in there?" she called out. There was no response.

"Ma'am," he started, but she tilted her head to look up at him. Seth caught back the rest of his complaint, content to stand and wait as long as she watched him that way.

Chapter Three

*V*erity couldn't help herself. Her gaze caught on his face and wouldn't move. If this man wasn't particularly handsome, at least not in the classical sense, he was as much man as she could ever have wanted.

Tall and very broad-shouldered, his black, curling hair tumbled out from beneath the band of the most hideous hat she'd ever seen to cling in loose spirals to the strong column of his neck and spill over the collar of his shirt. She studied his features, finding it truly refreshing to see a man who didn't clutter his face with beard or mustache. His nose had been broken at least once, for the bridge was flattened and the line of it was now a little crooked. But, his eyes were his most striking feature. Set beneath thick, black brows, they were a startling shade of blue.

The corners of his mouth lifted at her stare. Verity started, realizing he recognized her interest. To hide her embarrassment, she turned her attention back to the door. "One more time," she said, as much to that wooden panel as to him.

She rapped again. "Johnnie darling, this is getting very tedious. Do open up. Come now, Mama's here, just in time to save you."

This time, the door flew open and Johnnie stepped out, finger combing his fine brown hair. His attire was in terrible disarray, what with his shirt only partially buttoned and its tail hanging out over his trousers. His upper lip now sported a wispy mustache, but it was too thin to aid Johnnie in looking all of his two and twenty years. As her brother came face to face with a man half a head taller and at least three stones heavier than he, Johnnie squeaked and eased nearer to Verity.

"Verity, dear sister!" he cried out, his voice cracking. "By Jove, I expected to see Aunt Faith, not you."

Verity's heart hiccoughed at this unwitting reminder of her impending doom. Once again, she fought off fear with a laugh. "One spinster for another, my sweet. Now, do tell me why you weren't opening the door for Mr. . . . ," she paused, then glanced up at the big man next to her, hoping to encourage an introduction.

"Adamson, Miss," he replied, the timber of his voice sending a pleasant chill down her spine. "Seth Adamson. You'll need to move aside now."

"But of course," Verity replied, starting to one side. "Business before pleasure, eh, Johnnie?"

"Verity," Mama called, her voice sharp with command as she tried to elbow past Mr. Adamson without touching him. When the big man refused to move, Heloise shouted over his shoulder, "You'll stay just where you are. I'll not have these rude yokels assaulting our family."

"Oh dear. I suspect this means I must stay put," Verity said, using helplessness as a pretense to ogle Mr. Adamson a little longer.

He was a riddle, this one. Although dressed in what were rags by any standard, his speech patterns revealed more than a little education. So too, was his accent different from any of those she'd heard thus far in her journey. His pronunciation was soft, the words almost running into each other. It made listening to him quite enjoyable.

"I'm afraid I can't allow that," he replied, politely ignoring her bold stare. "You'll need to stand aside, Miss Standiford."

Verity shrugged in compliance and moved to one side. "There's no help for it, Mama," she said.

Mr. Adamson stepped forward and lowered his shotgun until it touched Johnnie's chest. "Is Mr. Standiford the father of your child, Sarah Jane?'' he asked of the disheveled blond at his side.

It was a moment before Verity took in the full meaning of his words. Behind her, Heloise gasped. Verity turned a startled gaze on her younger brother. ''Oh, laddie, what have you done?'' she breathed.

Johnnie flushed, the color bright on his pale skin. ''Egad,'' he said in a tiny voice, then lifted his gaze to his paramour. ''Why didn't you tell me?''

The mother of Johnnie's child was a beautiful little thing, all golden skin and hair, just the sort Verity expected Johnnie to favor. This Sarah Jane paled and, in her sudden nervousness, she set down the child she carried. ''I meant to tell you, but—'' Her voice trailed off into silence.

The scrawny man in the tasteless brown suit smiled, or at least creases appeared on his cheeks. There was no seeing his mouth beneath that mustache. ''Well now, it don't really matter whether she said or not. What's done is done and it takes only a few words to set it right. Adamson, put yer niece next to Standiford. Hold steady there, boy,'' he said as Johnnie paled. ''Right nice of your kin to show up for the event.''

Wicked delight woke in Verity as she recognized what went forward here. She glanced at her mother, but Heloise was still frozen in shock, her hand pressed to the overflow of bosom above her corset. Up until this day her precious son had been a profligate and a drunk, but he'd sired no bastards. Where Heloise saw a redeeming virtue, Verity put the omission up to incompetence on Johnnie's part.

The scrawny man fumbled in his jacket pocket and pulled forth a battered book. ''This here's my favorite part. Dearly beloved, we are gathered here—''

''Stop!'' Heloise's shout was a clarion call, trumpeted to the heavens above. ''You cannot seriously think I would allow my son to marry this little Jezebel! What proof have you that it is Mr. Standiford who fathered her child? She's already got one brat. Dear God, but who's to say how many men's beds she's warmed.''

''Gemma's my sister,'' Sarah Jane blurted out, then her

face crumpled and shamed rolled over her expression. Only now did she recognize her fall from a virtuous woman into whore.

The girl's reaction was no more than a reflection of Verity's own sin. Hadn't she also seen only love's purity when she ran to the Continent with Richard, the man she'd so foolishly deemed her "Shelley"? Drawn by a shared humiliation, Verity retreated to stand behind the girl, resting her hands on the sweet thing's shoulders.

"That was cruel Mama, even for you. Come now, Johnnie," Verity prodded. " 'Fess up. You were the first."

Her brother peered up from his studious observation of his stocking-clad toes. With a nervous giggle, he nodded, then returned his attention to the fascination of his nether digits. "What now, Johnnie?" Verity insisted. "Haven't you anything to say in her defense?"

Johnnie's spine stiffened, at least momentarily. "Mama, truly it's not so bad a marriage if I'm to stay in the United States. Sarah's been a dear and she makes a demmed fine meal. I tell you, you'll be glad of her before a week is out."

"Hold your tongues, both of you," Mrs. Standiford snapped, then turned on the Americans. "I'll not allow this travesty to continue."

Mr. Adamson graced Verity with a swift, considering look, then turned on Heloise. "Ma'am, since the boy admits his wrong in this, there's not much you can do to stop us."

"Humph," Heloise bit out, not yet defeated. "If Mr. Standiford did father her child—mind you, I'm not saying he did—you can be assured we'll settle a sum upon the girl and see her bastard supported." Sarah Jane moaned at the word 'bastard' and Heloise shot her a narrow-eyed look. "The Standifords have always been generous to a fault when shouldering their responsibilities."

"Cain't buy back what yer son took from her," the scrawny man said, his voice gone harsh and cold. "He'll do right by the girl and wed her."

"Of all the impertinence," Heloise retorted. "I demand to speak to the authorities."

The little man's gaze hardened. "Justice Jenkins, at yer service, ma'am. I'm the best ya can get today, the sheriff being outta town and Judge McGaffigan ailing."

Mr. Adamson lay his free hand on the justice's shoulder. "Mr. Jenkins, here, is justice of the peace in these parts. He does our marrying and such as there's presently a dearth of clergymen in this locale."

Heloise brought the force of her personality to bear on Mr. Jenkins. "If this is true, how can you persist in such a miscarriage?"

The bantam of a man fixed his adversary with a steely stare. "The way I see it 'twas your son who did the miscarrying when he went and laid with Seth's niece, her being an innocent girl an' all."

"You'll not misuse me this way!" Heloise turned on the Americans, her arms outstretched as if she meant to shove them off the porch. "Go now, all of you. We'll have no more to do with your sort. Be gone with you!"

The shotgun's blast made everyone jump and the little dark-haired girl began to wail. Mr. Adamson once again lowered the smoking barrel of his weapon until it touched Johnnie's chest, then held his hand out to the crying child. "Gemma, come and stand by me."

"I want Sarah Jane," the wee girl sobbed, pushing past Verity to reach her sister. The bride scooped up her sister, pressing Gemma's dark head onto her own trembling shoulder.

"How dare you try to frighten me." Heloise's voice retained but a pallid reflection of its previous bluster. "You will immediately cease to point that vile thing at my son."

Mr. Adamson pushed his hat back on his head and set a chill blue gaze on his future in-law. "Ma'am, I've been patient up until now, knowing you to be ignorant of our ways. If you plan to stay in the United States for any length of time, best you take heed of this advice. In this country, it's always more sensible to ask the man holding the gun what it is he wants, then be accommodatin' to his needs. Take this warning to heart, understanding my next shot will make your grandchild an orphan before its birth.'' Although his voice never raised out of its casual cadence, there was no doubting he meant to do as he threatened.

This time when Heloise gasped, her hands came to clutch at her chest. Johnnie shot Verity a hopeless, helpless look as he recognized their mother's last ditch defense. Verity only shook her head.

A great moan tore from Heloise. ''My heart! Oh dear Lord, someone help me!'' She staggered toward Johnnie. ''My dearest boy,'' she managed in a quivering voice, ''help me inside. I must sit down.''

Mr. Adamson inserted the rifle barrel between mother and son. ''Enough histrionics. You'll stop or I'll put a hole in one of his legs.''

''Mama, stop,'' Johnnie squeaked.

Mama managed a miraculous recovery and turned on the tall man. ''Don't think you'll get away with this. My husband is a wealthy and well-connected man. He'll see this mockery undone and your niece will be left without a shilling, do you hear!''

''Dime, Mother,'' Verity corrected. ''They don't have shillings in the United States.''

''Do I care?'' her mother raged. ''This is a foul and uncivilized place and none of us will stay here past the morrow.'' She turned on her heel and stormed into the house. The door slammed so hard the upper window rattled. Johnnie giggled, while his bride released a sudden, sad sob.

Gemma looked up at Verity from Sarah's shoulder, her thumb in her mouth. Beneath smooth, dark brows, the child's eyes were the same blue color of her uncle's. Verity stroked the girl's velvety cheek, the desire for her own children aching in her.

Her caress came to a rest atop a tangle of yarn. She looked closer. Caught between the child and Sarah Jane's shoulder was a rag doll. Dark brown loops of yarn served as hair, while tiny, round blue buttons were its eyes. For clothing, it wore a shift of a green sprigged fabric, the same material that made up Gemma's simple, long-sleeved dress.

"Set yer sister down, dearie," Mr. Jenkins told Sarah.

Sarah did as he bid, but when Gemma once again stood on the porch, the child circled around Sarah to look up at Verity. Verity extended a hopeful hand. Gemma frowned slightly and stared at her fingers, then took the offered hand. Her tiny palm was damp. At the feeling of fragile fingers in her own, an ocean of regrets washed over Verity. At least Sarah Jane would take a child with her from her mistake.

"Dearly beloved," Mr. Jenkins intoned.

"Forget it, Jenkins," Mr. Adamson said, his words touched with pain. "Have them say their vows."

It took only a moment for Johnnie to stutter through his promise to his wife, while Sarah's words were wet with tears. When Mr. Jenkins urged the groom to kiss the bride, Johnnie managed a swift peck on his new wife's cheek. Then, much to Verity's surprise, her brother drew himself to his tallest. She smiled as she recognized an amateur actor's portrayal of the jovial host.

"What ho, but you all must come in for a nip to celebrate the moment. I got myself a turkey whilst hunting yesterday and Sarah's made the most marvelous dinner. As it happens, there's one last bottle of wine. We'll toast to the babe's health."

"I think not," Mr. Adamson replied as the new Mrs. Standiford covered her face with her hands.

"Well, if you must go," Johnnie said, his relief gusting from him. "Sarah, say your farewells swiftly. You need to come in and lay the table. I'm starved, I am." With that, he fled into the house.

Sarah's whole body shook with the force of her tears. Verity glanced up at Mr. Adamson and found his gaze filled with masculine helplessness; he had no idea how to address his distraught niece. At last, he simply reached for the younger girl's free hand. "Come, Gemma. It's time for us to be going home."

Gemma unstoppered her mouth long enough to cry out, "I want to stay here."

Verity thought her heart would break as the little lass's

fingers tightened around her hand. For just this instant, she let herself dream Gemma wanted to stay for her, not Sarah Jane. Although she chided herself for a fool, she made no attempt to release Gemma's hand.

"I think she doesn't wish to leave her sister," Verity told the child's uncle, as she indulged herself in the even sillier dream he might allow Gemma to stay here with Sarah for a time. This was a ridiculous hope. Only an idiot would entrust a child as precious and beautiful as this one to a household ruled by someone like Mama. Mr. Adamson was no idiot.

"Sarah Jane must live with her husband now, Gemma," Mr. Adamson said as he set down his gun and reached for the child. Still clutching Verity's hand, Gemma kicked weakly as he lifted her. The rag doll dropped to the porch floor.

As the tall man settled the struggling child on his hip, Verity was drawn closer still. Suddenly, Gemma was cradled between the two of them. Verity almost sighed. This had the feel of heaven to it.

"We must get home for our meal," Mr. Adamson continued, "then rush you to bed as we've a long walk tomorrow. Don't you remember? You're to go into Hays and stay the week with Mina."

Gemma's expression filled with excitement, then dimmed against her sister's continuing tears. Her final resolution was achieved by shoving her thumb back into her mouth and draping herself over Mr. Adamson's broad shoulder, limp in confusion. Verity retrieved her hand as Mr. Adamson offered her a farewell nod and turned toward the stairs.

Sarah Jane leapt for her uncle, grabbing him by the free arm. "Don't leave me here, Uncle Seth," she cried. At this moment, she sounded no older than Gemma. "I want to come home with you."

"Shoulda thought about that afore you laid with him," Jenkins chided in harsh rebuke.

"No more, Jenkins," Mr. Adamson snapped, enclosing Sarah in a protective arm. "She's hurting enough right now. Nothing's served by making it worse for her."

Verity's heart melted in that moment. Here was a man who looked beyond the shame his niece brought his family to offer comfort. It was a luxury, indeed, something not even her previously doting father had given her when he found her in Paris with Richard.

"Pardon," Jenkins said with a swift nod. "No harm intended. Sun's setting and I got me a ten-mile ride if I'm to make Hays afore dark. We'll settle up later."

He turned toward Verity, pressing one set of fingertips to his bowler's brim as he took his own weapon from its position against the porch wall. "Miss. Caint say it's been boring making yer acquaintance." He skittered down the stairs and to his waiting horse.

Sarah buried her head into her uncle's shoulder. "Don't leave me," she sobbed into his shirt.

Mr. Adamson moved a big hand over her slender back in a soothing caress. "Honey, if there were a way to change this for you, I'd do it." He looked at Verity from over the top of the girl's head. "You could help me out here."

Verity smiled as her admiration for him grew. He even looked to recruit comforters from the enemy. "My dear man, you have mistaken me. I'm much too selfish to help anyone." She threw out the words as a gentle test of his sincerity.

"Is that so?" His blue eyes flared to life as the corners of his mouth lifted. "Then, perhaps you'd like to explain why you were protecting Sarah from your mother's attack?"

"One act of kindness and the whole world wants favors," Verity grumbled, pleased that he approved of her actions. She set her hands on Sarah's shoulders once more and turned her new sister-in-law into her embrace. "Come now, sweetling, settle yourself. I won't let you face that old dragon alone."

Sarah Jane lifted her head, her face still beautiful despite her tears. "Promise you won't leave me?"

Verity laughed, her amusement tinged with bitterness. In her life, it wasn't she who did the leaving. "I vow," she replied, placing a hand against her heart in a mock oath.

"Brace yourself, dearest sister. This was one of Mama's better days."

Sarah almost smiled, while Mr. Adamson chuckled, the sound deep and warm. "Sarah," he said, "kiss Gemma farewell, so she needn't go worried for you."

The new Mrs. Standiford took two trembling steps to press a kiss against Gemma's cheek. "I'll be well, sweetheart." Her voice was faint and when she retreated, she fairly fell into Verity's embrace. Gemma sighed around her thumb.

"Goodbye, Gemma," Verity offered, still wishing for ever so much more than she would ever own.

"Say goodbye to Miss Standiford, darlin'."

At her uncle's command, the little girl moved the smaller fingers of the hand against her mouth in a meager wave, then she frowned. "Kiss," Gemma muttered around her thumb.

Verity's breath caught in her chest as the hoping moved into a painful dimension. "From me?" she asked.

The girl gave a brief nod and pleasure rushed through Verity. Without a second thought, she leaned over to press her lips to the girl's forehead. It was possible Gemma's skin tasted of sweat and dirt, but in her happiness she wouldn't have noticed. The child sighed, her hand opening to brush Verity's cheek in a sweet caress. "I like you," she murmured.

"Well then," Mr. Adamson said, stepping to the side to grab up his shotgun.

As he started down the steps, Verity stared after him in desolation. He was leaving and taking Gemma with him. What if she never saw them again?

"Wait," she cried out. He turned back toward her, his brows raised in question.

Words jumbled in her throat. She wanted to know who he was, how it was he lived with his nieces and why an educated man would be in this awful place. Mostly, she didn't want him to go.

"What—where do you live? Will we have to fetch Sarah Jane's belongings?" It was a silly attempt to hide her interest in him.

"There are a few things, yes, but it'll have to wait until next Sunday as I'm away until then. Will you be calling with Sarah?"

Verity's heart pounded and her blood sang at his invitation. "Perhaps I shall. It would be interesting to see how an American lives," she said, trying for a neutral tone. Instead, the words were nothing more than a soft sigh.

The smile on his face was glorious. "Until Sunday, then."

He wanted her to call. Embarrassment followed swiftly on the heels of Verity's infatuation with this man. Before he could see her blushing, she pushed Sarah Jane into Johnnie's house. When she turned to close the door, Mr. Adamson was still standing below the porch stairs, watching her. Verity caught her breath in strong and hopeless pleasure, then firmly shut the door.

Chapter Four

$\mathcal{B}$ack aching, Seth leaned over the open trunk to find his newest shirt, better pair of trousers and clean drawers. Stripping sorghum for a week left him almost grateful to be home. Although the job earned him a generous seventy-five cents a day, the chore was tedious. Moreover, the farm was six miles distant; meaning he'd slept on the ground for the past week rather than coming home to his own bed.

Clothing in one arm and the cloth for washing and the sacking he used as a towel in the other, Seth kicked down the trunk's lid. As he walked toward the table, he glanced into the iron kettle on the stove's top. Tiny bubbles were just beginning to form in the water. The big wooden tub, already half filled with icy well water, sat just inside the soddy's door. It occupied this spot mostly because the doorway was the only open area in this long, narrow room.

Once again, Seth gave thanks to the Evans family. Their offer to keep Gemma another day gave him the opportunity for a leisurely soak. Living with girls in a one-room house made privacy difficult.

As he dropped his clothing onto the table, his shirt spilled over onto his books. Seth set it back atop the heap, then knocked imaginary dust from the top book's cover with a swipe of his hand. The harvest season was in full swing, which left him little time for reading.

It was odd how quickly a man could change. Last week,

achieving his law license meant no more to him than a viable way to support his nieces. Today, the desire to add the title of attorney-at-law to his name burned in him.

The corners of Seth's mouth lifted slightly. And, how much of his sudden urgency to reclaim respectability and regain some of the status he'd once believed his right centered on Miss Verity Standiford? His smile dimmed. Too much.

Even though she called herself a spinster, only a fool would fix his heart on a woman like Miss Standiford. The possibility she might allow him to court her was nil. Her sort never lowered themselves to look kindly on someone in his straits. The only chance he had of marrying her was if he did as Sarah had with her brother, and seduced her into wedlock.

With that thought came a thrill of sensation. His last seven nights had been filled with exceedingly inappropriate dreams about Miss Standiford. Seth forced lust deep into him and locked it there. If a sensible man wanted a woman at his side, he looked to those readily at hand.

He grimaced. It was better to blind himself. Immediately after Matt's death, two farmers' widows had openly approached him with proposals for marriage. In trade for his strong back and warm presence in their beds, they offered to add his nieces to their already substantial broods. Had he accepted, he'd have locked himself into a hand-to-mouth existence for the rest of his life. This was the exact lifestyle he meant to escape when he'd sought out Matt in Hays.

Once more, his memory offered him the image of Miss Standiford, her gray eyes gleaming softly in amusement. Her lips had the sweetest, taunting turn to them. As pretty as she was, he couldn't reason out why she wasn't already married.

He stopped himself. Damn, but he had to put her out of his thoughts. Nothing good could come of wishing she truly meant to visit with Sarah Jane. Which, of course, explained why he'd spent the morning cleaning the soddy instead of studying.

Cleaning the soddy, now there was an oxymoron if he

ever heard one. How did one clean a dwelling whose walls and ceiling were nothing more than thick slabs of Kansas sod, grassy side pointed out? Seth glanced around him, wondering what Miss Standiford would think of this unique solution to building houses in a land without trees.

True, the interior walls didn't look as if they were made of dirt bricks, covered as they were with a layer of white-wash. Overhead, there was only muslin to be seen. The fabric not only obscured the straw and sorghum leaves, which lay between the sod roof and the crossbeams to absorb some of the seeping rain, but kept snake intrusion to a minimum.

Reaching up, he tucked a loose edge into a crosspiece, then sighed. Miss Standiford would think no differently than he might have before the War. This was a hovel, even if the furnishings were unusually fine.

The pieces Seth saved from Matt's creditors were all that was left of his own inheritance, having originally come from their family estate in Southern Missouri. His grandmother's Irish linen tablecloth covered a roughhewn table and a glass fronted cabinet displayed the only remaining pieces of his mother's china and crystal, both cabinet and dishes having somehow escaped the War's ravages. At the other end of the single room, modest, calico curtains created two bedrooms, each with its own walnut-framed, feather bed.

Seth's lips turned in disgust. To think any of this might find favor in Miss Standiford's eyes was to make himself thrice a fool. What could she possibly see but a rude yokel taking on airs? It would be better for him if she never came to call. All in all, it would be far better if he kept as far from the British colony as he could.

The water was at a full boil. He took the heavy container to the tub. Steam rose as he added hot to cold. Setting the pot onto the packed earth floor, he stripped off his clothing and stepped into his bath.

The water was hot enough to sting his skin. Grabbing up a small bowl of freshly made soft soap and his cloth from the tub's base, he washed hair and body as quickly as he could. Then, rinsing the cloth, he laid the warm, wet square

over his face, meaning to soak until the water was cold.
Hiding behind the cloth's moist dimness, he tried to escape
the disappointment that filled him at the thought of never
again seeing Miss Verity Standiford.

The late morning sun shone in the intense and vaultless blue
of the sky, the air filled with the crystal clarity and crispness
only autumn could bring. Verity stared out over the green
and gold sweep of grassland. The emptiness of this place set
a quirk of fear in her heart, then pricked her into nervous
conversation with her brother's temperamental riding horse.

"Emeer, how does anyone tolerate this loneliness?" she
asked the high-strung beast. "Where are the trees, the roads,
the villages? A body could get lost out here and never be
found again. What am I saying? *I* am lost out here. Damn
you, anyway, Johnnie."

She and her brother, to whom Heloise had delegated the
task of retrieving Sarah's things since Sarah was too ill to
travel, were over halfway to the Adamson house when they
met with a group of Victoria's colonists in high-spirited pur-
suit of a coyote. Already mounted on his hunter, Johnnie
tossed Verity the sack containing Gemma's forgotten doll as
well as the breads Sarah sent her family. Then, shouting as-
surances of a swift return, he rode off into the distance. Verity knew her brother better than to believe he'd remember
her; going anywhere with Johnnie was an exercise in the
impromptu. It was her own fault for trusting him, but, after
a week of terrible crowding in that tiny house, escape was a
necessity.

Bitterness rose in Verity. Mama had won the fight for the
house's sole bedroom. This left Johnnie and Sarah to sleep
in the sitting room, while Verity laid her mattress beneath
the dining room table. For the past seven nights, she had
been forced to listen to her brother and his temporary wife
giggle happily over each other.

Poor Johnnie. Best he wallow in his happiness now. Mama
intended to see it ended as soon as possible, although it had
already taken longer than she thought. The British embassy

and Papa had managed to ignore her ranting telegrams for the past week. Unwilling to wait another moment, Heloise had taken the bull by the horns this morning: She'd set off to Sir George Grant's home in order to arrange the sale of Johnnie's property and their return passage home.

Verity sighed and looked around her once more. All of that was fodder for the future. Right now, Johnnie's abandonment left her in a touchy dilemma. If propriety said she shouldn't call on an unmarried man without a chaperone, Verity wasn't entirely certain she could remember Sarah's landmarks backwards to Victoria.

It was the doll that settled the matter. The thought of Gemma being without her plaything for another day was intolerable. Surely, the child's presence would serve the facade of decency required of the situation. She'd stay a moment, then get a fresh set of directions for her return trip. That was, if she ever found his home.

"Johnnie, you shouldn't have left me," she muttered as Emeer trotted along. But, then again, why should Johnnie be different from all the other men who'd left her?

The image of Mr. Adamson trying to comfort his distraught niece awoke with that thought. He hadn't abandoned or rejected Sarah, despite what she had done. Perhaps men in the United States were a different sort from those in England. Or, maybe, it was only Mr. Adamson.

Verity's lips gentled into a smile in the memory of Mr. Seth Adamson sweeping his battered hat from his head, his bright blue eyes alive with self-mockery. His irreverent play had struck a chord within her own heart. Then, she freed a hopeless sigh. She was a fool to let her heart fix on him. Once he learned of her past, he could have no compassion or forgiveness for her.

"Look Emeer, we've found another landmark," she said, hope rising as they came across the chalky limestone outcrop Sarah had described.

Emeer's reply was to sidle and snort, lifting his hooves in a nervous dance of fear. Earlier, they'd come across a nasty looking serpent; Verity had no desire to encounter another

one. Although she knew full well snakes couldn't climb, she
was grateful Johnnie had no sidesaddle. Riding astride meant
the train of her black habit didn't reach the ground.

She peered around her. There were no serpents to be seen.
A sudden gust of wind tore at the blue veiling wrapped
around the band of her tall hat and she caught the acrid scent
of smoke. Once again, Emeer reacted nervously.

Verity turned him, looking out over the drying autumn
landscape. There was no sign of fire. Not even a wisp of a
cloud marred the sky's endless expanse.

The wind died, taking the smell with it. "There now,
Emeer, settle yourself. If you are a good boy for a change,
I'll see to it Mr. Adamson gives you a bit of something."

She kicked the high-strung horse back into a walk. According to Sarah Jane's directions, she was now to leave Big
Creek and find the track with the deep ruts, the one to the
right. Verity would know the Adamson home because she
would see a thick growth of wild plums near the buildings.

Or, had she said building? No, a farm always had many
buildings, what with barns, byres, sties and cotes. Verity
shook her head, still confused. Although Sarah had spoken
slowly and given very detailed descriptions, the girl used
words whose meanings eluded Verity. For example, she
would know she'd gone too far if she reached some place
called "A Dugout". This was apparently quite an establish-
ment as it included not only a postal station, but an apoth-
ecary, all run by a man named Gunter.

A curious little structure came into view. Surely, no more
than five yards in length and two in width, grass grew on its
walls, even on its roof. Two minuscule windows were cut
from its green face and a wooden door bisected its length.
There was a great tangle of bushes nearby, the leaves gone
ruddy and dry with autumn.

Did plums grow on bushes? Pulling Emeer to a halt, Verity
studied the foliage, then the building. If this was the Adamson farm, where was the house?

The little construct reminded her of the mossy and ancient
byre she'd seen upon her retreat from the church in August.

Verity smiled in relief. She'd simply misheard Sarah Jane. This was one of the Adamson farm outbuildings, meaning the house lay somewhere nearby.

Dismounting, she led Emeer toward the structure, wanting a look at the strange little thing. Again, the wind rose, sending Emeer into another, fretful complaint. Verity caught him by the bridle to hold him still. Throwing open the panel, she peered inside, blinking at the sudden shift from sunny day to dark interior.

Chapter Five

*S*eth tore the cloth off his face at the sound of a horse's frightened cry. It never occurred to him that Sarah Jane would ride the five miles between Victoria and this house; Sarah wasn't much of a rider. Nor had he expected visitors this early. As a rule, the Brits didn't move before noon. Damn, but if Sarah was on horseback, it could only be with the assistance of a Standiford, but which one?

He leapt to his feet in a rush of water, grabbing blindly for and missing his sacking towel. The door flew open. Turning to warn off Sarah, Seth froze in shock.

Miss Verity Standiford, herself, strode into his house. Dressed in a black riding habit, complete with top hat, she had the Arab at her back. The words left him in a surprised rush. "What the hell are you doing, bringing a horse into my house!"

Miss Standiford came to a halt with a jerk, her gaze darting from the table to the stove, then, like iron to a lodestone, her attention caught on him. Her startled gaze flew down his chest and farther. Only then, did Seth think to clap the cloth in his hand to his most private part. "Jesus H. Christ, I'm bathing!"

She gasped, her eyes widening. The Arab's reins slid from her frozen fingers as the horse backed out into the yard. Seth dared a brief exposure of his backside to grab up his makeshift towel. He clutched it to him and waited for her retreat, but she stood as if rooted to the spot.

The urge to laugh rose. It was obvious Miss Standiford was encountering a naked man where she least expected to find one. This was nothing more than fitting punishment for his lusting after her. "Welcome to my home, Miss Standiford," he said.

"I—I," she stuttered. Her blush began at the top of her blue cravat and crept slowly upward until even her brow was bright red.

Seth's twisted amusement grew. If he let her stand there much longer, she'd be nothing but a mortified puddle in the doorway. "Miss Standiford, you must step outside so I can dress."

His soft command broke her spell. "Oh," she breathed and turned so swiftly, she trod on her habit's train. Trapped in her own skirts, she stumbled to the side. Her hat hit the doorjamb and fell off her head, tearing her snood as it dropped. Braided hair tumbled to her waist.

Seth's earlier disappointment deepened. Once Miss Standiford managed to mount, she'd ride hellbent for Victoria. Her embarrassment over this meeting guaranteed he'd never see her again. It was for the best. Seth frowned. If that were true, then why did letting her go feel so damn wrong?

"Aw, hell," he muttered and leapt out of the tub.

His drawers tumbled to the floor as he snatched up his trousers. Dragging them on, he managed the waist button, then shoved his arms into the sleeves of his shirt. Barefooted, his hair still dripping, he threw himself out the door after her, his mind working for some way to soften what had just happened.

Verity's embarrassment was so deep it made her knees weak. With trembling fingers, she snatched at Emeer's reins. Emeer, who never graciously accepted his riders, slyly lifted his head and danced away from her. She followed him, desperate to escape the enormity of the wrong she'd just committed.

"Hold still, you nasty, spiteful creature," she cried, leaping to catch him.

Emeer again sidled out of arm's reach, his reins dragging in the dirt. He tossed his head over his shoulder to see if she meant to persist in this game. Verity stopped. If she followed him any farther, he'd run for certain, leaving her to walk home.

"I'll see Johnnie sells you." Her threat was an aching cry and neither of them believed it.

Another wave of mortification washed over her. How could she have been such a fool? No, she was worse than that. Even fools knew to knock at strange doors before entering.

Verity squeezed her eyes shut in a futile attempt to regain some semblance of control. It was a mistake. Seth Adamson's naked image, all broad chest, lean hips and long legs, was permanently burned on the inside of her eyelids.

"How could I have been so stupid," she scolded herself as the urge to weep grew.

"Sarah Jane shouldn't have let you walk in that way." Mr. Adamson's voice was soft and it came from just behind her.

Verity whirled on him in surprise. His shirt clung to his wet arms and hung open over his chest. Water droplets gleamed along his collarbone. Another startled gasp escaped her as her mind's eye persisted in showing her his unclad form.

Although shock and embarrassment were the greater of her emotions, a new and disturbing sensation joined them. Fourteen years hadn't dimmed the memory of what transpired between a man and a woman within the confines of a bed. Deep in Verity grew the immoral desire to share that sweet transaction with Mr. Adamson. At these lewd thoughts, new heat stained her cheeks. Verity turned her back on him. It was easier to fight her wickedness when she didn't have to look at him.

"I am so sorry. Can you ever forgive me?" she whispered.

"There's no harm done, Miss," he said, an odd tone to his voice, "save to my pride."

"You can laugh?" Verity glanced over her shoulder, surprised that he still retained his good nature. Her gaze darted downward to his exposed chest beneath the open shirt, then away, to the brightly colored foliage cloaking his home's end.

"Pardon," he said. There was a moment's quiet, then he said, "You can turn around now." Verity turned. His attire, if damp, was properly buttoned and arranged, but his blue eyes still gleamed with amusement.

"You've come too early," he said with a smile. "I meant to meet you in my best, such as it is, not my all together." A sudden frown touched his brow as he glanced around the yard. "Where is Sarah Jane?"

"She was far too indisposed this morning to consider a ride," Verity replied, wishing she was anywhere else but here. Even enduring Mama's complaints was preferable to attempting a casual conversation while her dignity was still in Mr. Adamson's house, crawling around the foot of his bathtub.

"You came alone?" His question was more surprised than disapproving at her lack of a chaperone.

"Not by choice." Between his willingness to pretend the last few moments hadn't happened and her irritation over Johnnie's desertion, Verity's seesawing emotions steadied. "Mr. Standiford abandoned me midway here to chase after a coyote. At this particular moment, I'm of the mind to murder him upon my return." She offered Sarah's uncle a faint, but wry grin.

Mr. Adamson's black brows rose over laughing eyes as he smiled. "Justifiable homicide."

Verity nodded in complete agreement. "I should have done it years ago and spared Sarah Jane her fate. By the by, she sends you her love and hopes you are well."

"I doubt that." His refusal of Sarah's greeting was so absolute, the lines of his face fell into harshness and the bright color of his eyes dulled.

"But, she did," Verity insisted, startled and puzzled by his reaction.

She turned to find Emeer. Now that she wasn't chasing him, the stupid beast stood calmly at the edge of the house nibbling its grass exterior. Verity retrieved the sack of baked goods and handed them to Mr. Adamson.

"Sarah made these for you. I assumed she did so for the sake of family. Is it possible she meant them as a peace offering?"

He took the canvas bag and looked inside of it. Putting a hand in, he retrieved Gemma's plaything and stared a moment longer at the contents. When he raised his head, disbelief still clung to the harsh lines of his face. "It appears I owe her an apology," he said. "You, as well, for inferring that you lied on her behalf. In explanation, I can only say that this affection of hers is a recent development. Given what I've done to her, I think it cannot endure."

"And, what is it you've done?" Verity asked, all the more intrigued by Seth Adamson. As her embarrassment waned, the need to ask him rude and intrusive question after question took its place. More than anything, she wanted to understand this contradictory man.

Sarah's uncle sighed and tucked the doll under one arm, then crossed his arms over his chest. "She'll be none too happy with me after your brother makes her a divorcée."

Verity stared at him in surprise. Although he was right to think Johnnie wouldn't keep Sarah, it astonished her that Mr. Adamson expected this legal maneuver. In general, divorce was an avenue of escape offered only to the wealthiest and most well-connected of men. "You went to the trouble of forcing marriage, all the while believing she'd be cast aside? How is it you are certain Johnnie won't keep her?"

A ghost of a smile touched Mr. Adamson's full lips, self-mockery again waking in his blue eyes. " 'Fess up," he said, borrowing her words from last week. "Even if your brother truly loved her, Sarah's no wife for him. She has neither inheritance nor pedigree to recommend her, and even less sophistication. I can imagine the drawing room's reaction were she to mention she met Johnnie while cleaning and cooking for others.''

"There are no colder hearts than those self-righteous few who deem themselves the elite," Verity agreed, having endured years of that coldness. Her fascination with him grew. "Now you must tell me how a man who lives in a grass house knows my world so well, Mr. Adamson."

He shook his head in refusal, his rough-hewn face touched with a studied blankness. "A boring story, better left untold. How long does she have?"

Verity released a breath of a laugh. Within her grew the certainty that he'd once inhabited the American version of her rigid and proper world. "Longer than you think. Had you found yourself a clergyman, they might have been tied together forever."

"Is that a fact?" Mr. Adamson's face took life again in pleased surprise.

"As much as I'd like to do so, I'm not gloating yet," she warned him. "Mama has only begun this battle. The present delay in Johnnie's freedom is caused by your government's ongoing financial chaos. Be warned, as our embassy can do nothing, Mama intends to spirit Johnnie home and pretend the wedding never occurred. Most likely, our clergy will agree with her, the ceremony being civil, not religious. Either way, know that Sarah will not be left destitute. Trust me, Wilson Standiford always pays."

Try as she might, Verity couldn't keep the bitterness out of her voice. When she saw the question forming in Mr. Adamson's eyes, she held up a forestalling hand. "A boring story, better left untold."

"Touché," he laughed.

Verity glanced around the yard. "Where is Gemma?"

"She's staying another day in Hays with her friend," he replied.

She nodded in acknowledgement, then could think of nothing either polite or acceptable to say. A strained quiet woke between them. When it lengthened beyond comfort,

Verity turned and caught Emeer's reins. This time, he came willingly to her side.

"Well then, if you'll give me Sarah's belongings and describe my route home, I'll be on my way."

There was a brief flicker of disappointment in Mr. Adamson's gaze, then all emotion disappeared from his face. "You'll be wanting your hat before you leave. I believe you left it inside, Miss."

Verity nervously pulled her braid over her shoulder as color again crept over her cheekbones. She'd left far more than her hat in his house. "So I did," she said, attempting to mask her discomfort with an air of insouciance.

Not the least bit fooled, Mr. Adamson smiled at her, but his amusement had no sting to it. "Come inside while I fetch Sarah's things. You can put yourself right while you wait on me. I'll tie him for you." He held out his hand for Emeer's reins.

Verity hesitated. If going inside with Mr. Adamson wasn't the proper thing to do, it was sensible. She could hardly ride home bareheaded. Without hat and snood to contain it, the thong at the end of her braid would soon slip, leaving her hair flying in the wind. She released the gray to him and, once more, entered the earthen house.

Without an unclothed man to trap her gaze, Verity looked around her in interest. Although the atmosphere was dim and musty, the walls gleamed a fresh white. A tiny squared stove sat toward the center of the room. At the wall behind it stood several trunks, an assortment of basic tools tucked behind them. To the right there was a table, cloaked in ivory linen, and three chairs. Two books lay at the center of the table. In the corner was a dry sink next to a cherrywood display cabinet filled with precious knicknacks.

On her left, curtains made from the same green sprigged material that made up Gemma and her doll's attire, separated the room's end into what appeared to be sleeping areas. Verity shook her head in amazement. And, she'd thought her brother's house crowded? To live, eat, cook, sleep, even bathe, all in one room set in the middle of nothingness was quite beyond her comprehension.

Her host moved past her to push aside one of the curtains, revealing the hidden bed. The piece was fine far beyond the structure that housed it. Verity's glance flowed from bed to cabinet to linen tablecloth. There was enough quality here to confirm her belief that Seth Adamson hadn't always been a poor man.

Mr. Adamson returned to the table with a paltry pile of clothing. He set down the doll, then emptied the baked goods from the sack. Turning the canvas bag inside out, he began to fill it with Sarah's meager possessions.

Verity reached for one of the two books on the tabletop. Opening it, she found in it a study of land laws. "What are these?"

Mr. Adamson looked up, then his jaw tightened as he saw she meant the books. "I'm studying to become a lawyer."

Verity shook her head, uncomprehending. "Lawyer?"

"Barrister," he translated.

"You can do that without going to university?" The words came out in a thoughtless rush. "But of course you can, or you wouldn't be doing it," she amended, trying to soften the abruptness of her comment.

"The United States is a wondrous land of opportunity," he said with a short, sharp laugh. "Here, even a Republican who lacks any formal education can become president. Your hat, Miss Standiford?" It was a rather blatant hint that he wasn't willing to expound on the subject.

Verity found her hat near the open door. Her snood was trapped inside, shredded beyond use by its combs. And, she without a single hairpin. Perhaps if she replaited her hair as tightly as she could and stuffed it into her hat, it would stay confined for the duration of the ride. An impossibility, but what choice had she?

Pulling the thong from her braid's end and tucking it into her glove, she shook her hair loose in preparation for a new braid. It was as she sectioned thick stuff in preparation for replaiting that the possibility of hairpins in Sarah's belongings occurred to her. She turned on her host.

"I don't suppose," she started. The remainder of her words died unspoken. Mr. Adamson was watching her, his face soft in masculine appreciation of her unbound hair.

Verity's heart lifted to a new beat. It wasn't right that he should look at her that way, especially when they were alone in his house. It wasn't right, but, after more than a decade of invisibility, his interest made her feel alive in a way she'd forgotten existed.

"Suppose what?" he asked, his voice suddenly husky.

The intimacy of his tone filled her, rendering her speechless. She forgot what it was she'd meant to ask. Outside, the wind rose until it soughed and gusted around the house. Emeer cried out in sharp complaint.

Mr. Adamson lifted the filled sack and crossed the room, stopping far closer to her than need be. At his nearness a disturbing warmth flowed through Verity until every muscle softened and all her defenses were laid low. The desire to lean into the shelter of his body grew urgent. She wanted his arms around her more than she wanted to breathe.

Her gaze lifted to his face. His hair was still damp and it lay in dark tendrils around his face. One curling strand clung to the corner of his jaw. The upward lilt of his mouth haunted her, begging for her touch. Verity sighed. His eyes were so very blue.

As her gaze met his, his eyes half closed and he freed a slow, quiet breath. His attention drifted to her mouth. Verity shivered in reaction. Before she realized what she did, her lips parted in the hope that he would kiss her.

"You should go," he whispered.

"I should?" she asked, uncomprehending.

So enmeshed was she in the sensations waking between them, it was another moment before his words registered. He was warning her against him. She must turn and run. Immediately. To stay would be madness, for if she stayed, he would do more than kiss her. Not a muscle responded. With dignity already dead, all that remained in her was the incredible need to feel his mouth against her own.

He raised a hand. Dear Lord, but where was her pride? She must tell him he could not touch her.

Verity sighed as his fingertips came to rest against her cheekbone. She shivered as he traced the curve of her cheek. He extended his fingers into her hair. She leaned her head into the cup of his palm. Seth's skin was rough and calloused, but, in all her life, she'd never felt anything more wonderful.

Her eyes closed, her imagination again supplying the hard curve of his bare shoulder and the way his naked chest had gleamed in the sun. His thumb moved softly along the turn of her lips, a gentle caress. Then, he withdrew his hand.

Even though her skin was still alive with his touch, Verity's relief was sudden and complete. His seduction had been very effective. Had he continued his caresses, she was certain she wouldn't have resisted him, no matter what he asked of her.

Still trapped in the bemusement he'd wakened in her, Verity opened her eyes. Seth's expression was tight, a small crease marking his brow. A muscle quirked angrily on his jaw line.

Horror seared a line through her soul. What had she done? Men knew only two sorts of women: those they slept with and those they married. Her behavior of the last moments branded her as the former.

Until this moment, Verity hadn't realized how much she wanted to be valued and accepted by this man. Her heart ached as he took a step back from her. Why was it the disgust of a man she barely knew would hurt her more deeply than all the scorn she faced at home?

"It would be best if you left now." His voice was quiet, emotionless.

It was done; she'd destroyed herself all over again. Utter despair closed over Verity. The only shred of peace she owned was the knowledge that her lapse of modesty meant never having to bare the tale of her past to him.

Hat in hand, Verity took the sack from him and tucked it

beneath an arm. "Farewell then, Mr. Adamson," she said, damning herself when her voice was thick with tears. She turned toward the door.

"Wait." Seth's hand closed around her elbow to hold her in place.

Verity stopped, but didn't turn to look at him. Her heart pounded, her mouth trembled as he drew her back until she nigh on leaned against his chest. Oh dear God, he was going to ask her into his bed. It wouldn't be the first time such a thing occurred, nor, probably, the last, but it would certainly be the most devastating of the proposals. Outside, Emeer cried again, sounding as desperate to escape as she.

He cleared his throat. "I know I haven't much to recommend myself, Miss Standiford," he said softly, hesitantly, "but that will not always be the case. By winter's end, I will have my law license and a respectable career. Knowing that, would you be willing to let me call on you for the duration of your visit?"

Tears sprang to Verity's eyes as love for him washed over her. Despite all the wrong that had passed between them, he was still willing to pretend she was a chaste woman. Deep in her woke a desperate need to simply tell him yes. He knew nothing of her. If Mama had her way, they'd be gone before another week passed. It would be heaven to immerse herself into the happiness other women knew at being admired and pursued, even for so short a time.

The pain in her heart overflowed, sending a tear burning its way down her cheek. How could she even consider it? Fallen she might be, but she was no liar and deceit was no way to reward his kindness toward her. Besides, there were enough folk in Victoria who knew her tale. It wouldn't take long before someone made it their business to inform Seth. Oh, but telling him would hurt worse than anything she'd ever done.

Verity cursed herself as a coward and drew a fortifying breath. "It would be cruel of me to allow you to continue thinking me a woman worthy of your affections." When she opened her mouth to continue, the words refused to come.

His hand slid up her arm to rest on her shoulder. "I think I am the better judge of who is or is not worthy of my affections." There was a hint of confusion in his voice.

"Not in this case," she breathed, her hand closing so tightly over her hat's brim, it crumpled. "Fourteen years past, when I was Sarah's age, I'm afraid I erred much as she has done. Where you have been kind and understanding toward Sarah, my sin drove my father into a rare rage." To this day, Papa's vengeance stunned her.

"Instead of forcing a wedding, as you did, Papa offered my lover a goodly sum to disappear. The man who'd sworn his undying affection left, caring nothing for what became of me." She paused to draw a shaking breath. "Having heard my tale, you will understand why I must refuse you. You have been kind and deserve better than another man's leavings."

With that, Verity tore free of his grasp and fled into the yard. She could only pray he'd do her the courtesy of letting her leave without further comment. It would destroy her if he pursued her, changing his honest proposal into the one she'd expected.

Stunned, Seth watched Verity rush from his house. Well, here was his explanation for why she was a spinster. No matter how pretty or how rich, her digression from the strict moral code of her society had destroyed her.

Pity flickered through him as he remembered the world of his youth. Women who erred as she had were shunned and isolated. It was vicious punishment. At the thought of her suffering, Seth wanted nothing more than to take her in his arms and shield her from those who hurt her.

Then, his heart lurched in new joy. In refusing his attentions, she revealed her care for him. Where she could have given him a simple no, leaving without any explanation, she'd shared the tale of her downfall, making certain he understood her refusal had nothing to do with him.

Hope roared to life. If there was nothing for her in her own world, what reason had she to refuse him in his? One more time, Seth followed her out of his house, set on preventing her escape.

Chapter Six

A brutal gust of wind caught Verity's loose hair as she rushed from the house, sending it swirling around her face. Emeer was crying and fighting at the end of the house, his reins caught in the plum's scrubby branches; his eyes were wide with fear. She dropped what she held and raced to him. When he tried to lift again, she caught and clung to his bridle. "Emeer, no!"

The wind took the words from her lips at the same time it sent her hat careening across the yard. This time, the acrid smell of burning grass was strong enough to make her cough. Verity whirled and squinted into the reeking, dusty wind.

A coppery-brown cloud rolled toward her, spreading ever wider as it moved. In those places where it found wood, it lingered, spiraling upward to towering orange heights, distant plumes of smoke were faded black against the dusty sky. Where there was only grass, it raced along close to the ground.

Fear spiked in her. No matter how much she hated the emptiness of her life, she had no desire to die, at least not by burning. Her need to escape was as deep and desperate as the fear driving Emeer's panic.

"Seth, come swiftly!" she shouted toward the house, crisis driving all pretense of formality from her. The fire seemed miles off yet; they could still outrun it, but only if Seth came now. Emeer's terror shortened the length of time he would tolerate their combined weights.

Verity reached into the dense bush to release the reins. His efforts to free himself had resulted in a tangle of leather and thick, horny branches. Twigs cut into her gloves and tore at her sleeves, while the wind kept pushing her hair before her eyes. The horse tossed his head and pulled.

"Behave and I'll free you," she said, trying to keep her voice soothing.

She opened the knotted end and pulled one side free as another blast of burning air hit them. Emeer screamed, the whites of his eyes visible. Verity's grip on him slipped. Once more, he tossed his head and, this time, found new freedom of movement.

He reared back, pulling desperately, and branches broke. Verity stumbled aside as Emeer's hooves flashed over her head. The reins fell from the bush, bits of leaves and branches still tangled in them.

"Let him go." Seth's shout was barely audible over the wind.

His words sent fear exploding inside her. "No!"

As she leapt for Emeer's bridle to keep him from escaping, Seth caught his arm around her waist and drag her back from the horse. He drew her close against his chest as Emeer turned. In a beautiful display of expensive horseflesh, his mane and tale streaming in the wind, Emeer fled from the yard.

"No," Verity screamed again, bursting free from Seth's hold.

With terror nipping at her heels, she grabbed up her heavy, trailing skirt and chased after the horse. The unwieldy cut and weight of her garments made her impossibly sluggish; by the time she'd gone ten yards, Emeer had disappeared. Panting against exertion and the heavy air, Verity stopped, all hope of living to tomorrow extinguished. Tears of self-pity woke, but anger followed swiftly on its heels.

She turned to vent her rage on Seth. The yard was empty. He was gone!

Even as logic insisted Seth couldn't have escaped without her, Verity stared at the filthy, roiling smoke in the distance. The wind battered her, tearing at her hair. Sharp grains of dirt stung her face and smoke ate at her lungs just like panic ate at her soul. Not only would she die a fiery death, but she would die abandoned.

The banging of the grass house's door against its inner wall was barely audible over the raging wind. Relief and chagrin filled her. She wasn't abandoned; he'd only gone into the house. Chiding herself for a fool, Verity hurried after him.

The force of the wind held the door pinned to the earthen wall. Turned askew on the table and held in place by the books, the tablecloth fluttered; the bed curtains streamed. The tiny windows were now shuttered with thick wooden panels, making the interior all the more dim. Seth leaned over one open trunk.

Verity wrestled the door away from the wall. It took all her strength to force it shut. The wind wailed in complaint as she turned the latch to keep it out. Relief soared in her, then crashed. What sort of protection was a wooden door against a fire? She turned on Seth. He was still searching through the trunk.

"You've killed us," she cried, her fright stronger than her anger at what he'd done. In the sudden quiet, her voice was much louder than she'd expected. She gentled it before continuing. "Why did you let Emeer go?"

Seth straightened and turned, calmly pulling on a pair of heavy gloves. There was nothing in his face to indicate concern, much less worry over the coming fire.

"Verity, there's no use in trying to outrun one of these fires. They move on winds made in their own heat, skipping over some places and decimating others. Here, we have what we need to fight the fire. If we'd ridden off, we might have found ourselves surrounded by flames with no hope of survival."

"You cannot believe we will survive a fire in a grass house?" It was a startled cry.

His mouth twisted into what was almost a grin. "I'm sure as all get out hoping we do." He took a shovel from the wall behind the trunks, shoved his feet into his boots and started toward the door.

"Where are you going?" Shifting to stand between him and the door, Verity reached out as if to grab him by the arms, then caught herself. Her hands fell back to her sides. "Don't leave me here."

Seth watched her, his expression quizzical before it softened in what might have been understanding. "Verity, I'm not leaving you. I need to dig a firebreak, or rather refresh the one I plowed last spring. If there's time after that, I'll soak down the house."

"Yes, soak down the house," she said, taking courage from the thought that wet grass couldn't burn. "Do that first."

"It's more important to put a ring of barren dirt between us and the flames," he said in refusal.

"The house first," she begged.

At her plea, Seth lifted his hand and brushed his knuckles against the curve of her cheek. Even this brief touch took away her breath. "Trust me, Verity, the firebreak is more important. Now, I'm wagering we have an hour before the fire reaches us. If we're to survive, I have work to do."

Torn between her desire to believe they could live past the flames and her fear they would not, Verity didn't stop him when he moved past her. The moment he turned the latch, the wind tore the door from his hands, once more slamming it against the wall. She turned, strands of hair flying around her, and watched as he walked a bit from the house. "Soak the house, please?" she whispered.

He placed his shovel to the dirt and begin to dig. There was a precise and efficient rhythm to his movements, a competency that eased some of her terror. That was, until she again breathed in the acrid scent of the fire. Panic moved up another notch.

An hour, indeed. He might be competent, but it just wasn't

possible for him to finish this before the flames reached them. If she wanted the house soaked, she'd have to help him.

That thought stopped her cold. What use could she possibly be to him? Her skills were limited to riding a horse, painting a decent landscape, and playing the piano. She could even sing if she had to. But, fight a fire?

Her lips twisted in disdain. How hard could it be to dig? Ignorant farmers seemed to manage the activity well enough. Her heart steadied with the thought. No matter what, it was better to try digging than to sit in here and wait to die.

Well then. Gathering her hair into one hand, she found the thong in her glove. Once it was braided and tied, she turned to the wall. The only tool whose purpose she recognized, beyond the shovel Seth used, was a hoe. She took it and stepped outside into the gritty wind, closing the door behind her.

Shoulders squared, her weapon in her gloved hand, Verity crossed the yard. The roar of the air was deafening, dirt and smoke stung her eyes. Her skirt twisted and tangled around her legs as if it wished her to topple. She picked a spot a few feet behind Seth, meaning to work in the opposite direction around the house. Then, for the first time in her life, Verity lifted a garden tool, hefting it high over her shoulder. It hung in the air for a brief instant, until she brought it singing downward at the grassy earth.

The blade bounced off the hard ground. Not even the tiniest clod of dirt flew into the thick and turbulent air. Dismay shot through her. This digging was harder than it appeared.

Rearranging her grip, she once again raised the tool. This time, she brought it downward with all her might. The blade bit into the ground with such suddenness, Verity flew over the handle. Her impact with the ground brought tears to her eyes. She rolled over, but was too stunned to do more than stare upward into the dusty air.

Seth appeared above her and extended his hand in invitation. The very blankness of his expression said he was laughing at her. Verity glared at him as she struggled back to her feet. "This is not amusing," she yelled at him.

"Did I laugh?" he shouted in return, his brows lifted in innocence even as his eyes sparked in amusement. "I would never do that. Besides, I surely appreciate you wanting to help me. Would you like me to show you how to use it?"

With a nod as her reply, Verity reclaimed the betraying tool. Seth came to stand behind her, bringing his arms around her and laying his hands atop her. When he'd rearranged her grip on the handle to suit him, he rested his lips against her ear so he could speak to her.

Verity drew a sharp breath in reaction. Even in the depths of this crisis, his nearness woke a sudden jumble of sensations. But, of all of them, the comfort she found in his arms was the most precious.

"Lift it slowly."

When she did as he commanded, he stopped the hoe's rise at waist level. With his hands over hers, he guided the tool downward into the earth in a series short, sharp motions. Clod after clod of dirt broke free. "Steady and firm. Now you, while I watch."

With Seth yet standing directly behind her, Verity repeated what he'd done. Success was a heady feeling. She looked at him from over her shoulder, smiling against her achievement.

He leaned toward her to once again aim his mouth at her ear. "Well done," he said, a smile in his voice. "Now, your aim is to turn the earth so nothing burnable is left exposed. You dig right, while I go left. Verity, as the fire nears, you'll swelter dressed in that thing. If you find yourself overheating, don't hesitate to shed your jacket and skirt. This is no time for an overactive sense of propriety."

Verity started in shock. Remove her clothing? She turned, ready to protest that she wasn't that sort of woman, but Seth was already walking back to his discarded shovel. He couldn't possibly believe she'd shed her clothing.

Still shaking her head at the very thought, Verity set to work. This time, ground broke and earth turned. It wasn't long before she found a rhythm in her movements and not much longer after that before she was panting, giddy from the heat.

Her habit was too hot. Made from thick wool, it was meant for cool autumn riding. Worse, the jacket had a mannish cut and fit tightly to her torso and arms. Every time she lifted the hoe, she swore the jacket's tight sleeves cut into her flesh. She supposed it wouldn't be too improper to remove her jacket.

Leaning the hoe's handle against her hip, she tore off her outer garment and examined her arms. No blood marked her fine, white cotton blouse, even though her arms throbbed in relief. The wind tore the garment from her hands. Sleeves flying, the jacket cartwheeled out of the yard.

In that same instant, her tightly buttoned collar began to choke her. She unknotted the blue silk cravat. It slipped from her fingers and fluttered into the distance. She laid her collar wide, then glanced down at her heavy skirt. No, not her skirt, surely never her skirt.

While she did wear trousers beneath her skirt, as did every woman she knew, that garment wasn't meant to be seen. Then, the thought of dying because of her 'overactive sense of propriety' washed over her. How much faster could she work without it?

Verity shot a swift look over her shoulder to Seth. His back was to her, his attention fully focused on the task at hand. Once more, her gaze slipped to the threatening, coppery cloud. The need to continue on past this day became steel in her heart. This was no time for modesty.

Tearing at the skirt's fastenings, she kicked it off and to the side. Dressed now in dark trousers and boots, with her blouse collar open, Verity drew a deep, freeing breath, or rather as deep a breath as her tightly laced corset would allow. No, that was beyond consideration, even if death were imminent.

Once again, she lifted her hoe and began to clear the ground. The heat grew until it was searing and the driving wind worked to permanently embed dirt into her skin. Where there had once been blue sky, there was now a roiling blackness.

By the time she rejoined Seth at the back of the house, he having gone the greater distance, her breath burned in her lungs. Gentleman that he was, Seth didn't let his gaze stray to her trousered legs. His face was spattered with dirt, except where sweat had turned it to mud. Like her, he'd opened his shirt collar and rolled up his sleeves over strong forearms.

"Are we finished?" she yelled to him.

"Your side's not wide enough," he called back. "It must match mine. If you're game to go another round, I'll begin soaking the house."

Verity stifled her moan of despair, finding a new respect for uneducated farmers. If the fire didn't kill her, this digging surely would. Her back muscles strained and her arm muscles burned. The palms of her gloves had given way, being too thin to tolerate the pressure of a wooden handle, and her hands were tender and sore. But, she'd succeeded. As long as she agreed to dig, he would wet down the house.

"Of course," she shouted.

This time, she bent more slowly to her task. It took every ounce of will power to continue lifting and dropping the hoe. New blisters formed atop her first set. She tried pausing, but each time she did her fingers stiffened. When she wanted to begin again, they resisted her efforts to close them around the hoe's handle.

As she once more joined her ring of earth to Seth's, she straightened slowly, her body screaming in protest. Blinking back exhaustion, Verity immediately slid into panic. Great gouts of black smoke billowed around her, the sky as dark as night. Flames danced only a stone's throw from their firebreak, the fire promising death in its hoarse and crackling voice.

Seth appeared out of the darkness, a bucket in each hand. He wore a colorful scarf across the lower half of his face, but the rest of him was covered in sooty mud. Stopping before her, he set his buckets at her feet, then pulled the scarf off his face.

"Here, take these inside and wait there for me." His voice was raspy and hoarse with smoke.

"You have to come in now," she coughed to him, catching him by a sleeve. "You'll die out here."

He shook his head. "I need to finish the roof."

She opened her mouth to protest it was too late, but the smoke seared her lungs. All she could do was cough. By the time she'd caught her breath, he'd disappeared.

Bent close to the ground, a line of flame reached out toward their barren ring of dirt. Tiny fires broke out in a dozen places near the newly turned earth, the doomed grasses releasing a peculiar squealing sound as they took light. Verity stared at her fate. Only a fool would think they had any chance of survival.

Cowardice turned her toward the house. If she was going to die, it would be far better if she didn't have to watch death coming for her. Gingerly lifting the buckets, her arms trembling against their weight, she picked her way to the door.

Squinting against the bitter air, she set down her burdens and used the heels of her hands to turn the door's wooden handle. Water sloshing over their edges, she lifted her buckets over the threshold, then wrestled with the wind until she shut out the reeking air. Panting and coughing, she leaned on the door. The air in here was far cleaner, the atmosphere gone humid with the dousing. Tears born of smoke tangled with those awakened by her fear of dying. She stumbled blindly to the table and fell into a chair.

Her hands throbbed. Carefully, slowly, she peeled back her ruined gloves, biting her lip to keep from screaming as the thin leather seemed to take her skin with it. Huge blisters covered her palms, some of them already seeping. Verity freed a wavering hiccough of a laugh. She'd torn her hands to shreds for nothing; she was still going to die.

On the table top, its green sprigged dress blown over its head, lay Gemma's rag doll. Verity picked up the plaything, touching one stuffed and fingerless hand, remembering how Gemma had touched her cheek. Worse, she was going to die, never having even seen Gemma again. Tears filled her eyes for having missed even one more of the girl's kisses.

Then, the tears spilled over, not for herself, but for the children. What would happen to Gemma and Sarah if their uncle died? Neither Mama nor Papa would offer to take them.

For the first time in her life the normal impatience she felt for her parents blazed into rage and she damned them both for lacking enough depth of character to care for someone besides themselves.

She caught herself in the next moment. Anger such as this was a pointless exercise. Her parents were who they were. Verity set the doll back onto the table, carefully straightening its arms and legs, then finger pleated its tiny dress. There. Now it was all laid out as if for burial.

As she pulled back her hand, she caught sight of her blouse's wristband. It was a horrifying shade of dirt brown. When she opened the button and turned back the cuff, thinking to hide the color, the contrast between her clean arm and filthy blouse was too great to endure. Her skin began to itch beneath its layer of grime.

She stared longingly down at Seth's washcloth, which lay where he'd dropped it, near a pot of what must surely be soap. This time, her laugh had a touch of hysteria to it. Didn't one always wash the body before burial? Well then, in the few moments she had left to life, she'd make herself as clean as she could without actually undressing and bathing.

Chapter Seven

*E*yes streaming, Seth staggered across the yard toward the soddy. Even with the bandana across his mouth, each breath seared his lungs. His back felt like it was on fire and he was certain the faint crackling he could hear over the fire's roar was his hair singeing.

He tore off his gloves and felt his way along the house's warm, damp sod until he found the doorway. As he opened the door, reeking, smoky air streamed past him into the interior. He started inside, then couldn't resist. Like Lot's wife from the Bible stories he'd learned in his youth, he turned to look behind him.

They were engulfed, the fire chewing all around their ring of barren earth. Awakened by the heat, a mist rose from the sodden yard and house to tangle with the smoke. He might as well have been standing on a steamy island in hell. Seth's heart plummeted. Jesus, but what sort of fool was he, believing they had a better chance here rather than riding off on the Arab?

Nearly falling inside, he slammed the door, a paltry defense against certain death. He yanked the scarf from his face, then tore off his shirt, just in case he was right and he was on fire. The tub stood before him, its tepid depths offering to douse flames as well as relieve his overheated skin.

He kicked off his work boots and stepped in, yet trousered. Water spilled over the tub's edge as he dropped into its depths, then sank below the surface. When he rose, sputtering and coughing, he leaned back against its side, savoring the blessed coolness as his vision cleared.

Wavering circles of light appeared in the otherwise gray and smoky atmosphere; Verity had lit the lanterns. They swung slightly, set into motion by the draft as the steady wind penetrated around the door and shutters and down the chimney. One of the soddy's supporting beams creaked against the battering.

Seth's hopes for the future dimmed even further at the sound. If it gave, the roof would drop, crushing them both beneath its weight. Within him grew the certainty that his life wouldn't extend past the next half hour.

As he rubbed the remains of smoke from them, the wish grew that he could do the same with the bitter stinging in his heart. Damn, but if he died now, it would only confirm that his life had been nothing but a series of cheats. Education and his father had been taken by the War, while Matt squandered their inheritance and lost their home. Then, insult to injury, Seth was left with Matt's children to raise. Now, nature seemed set on stealing what little he had left.

"Would you like the cloth?" Verity's voice was barely audible over the noise, but there was no mistaking the sadness in her tone.

Seth turned in the tub to look for her. She was seated on the floor near the back wall, her knees drawn up and her arms wrapped around them. As she raised her head, her clean skin gleamed in the low light, while her open collar revealed the smooth line of her throat. Soft wings of honey-colored hair curved against her cheeks, then swooped on back into a long braid. Her eyes were still slightly red and swollen from the smoke. Or, had she been crying?

He sighed. She didn't want to die any more than he did. The urge to comfort her drove away his self-pity. Placing his hands on the tub's sides, he started to rise, then glanced down. The water's surface was scummy with mud and soot. He could hardly offer her comfort as filthy as he was.

"I think I would," he replied. Dripping water, he rose to his feet and stepped outside the tub. To appear to bathe before her, even if they both knew he still wore his trousers, seemed uncomfortably intimate.

As she came to her feet, Seth meant to glance away and preserve some semblance of modesty for her. Instead, his gaze locked onto her trim hips and legs clad in her trousers. He forced his eyes to focus on her toes. The full length of her slender calves in her tightly fitted boots remained in his field of vision. She offered him the cloth.

To distract himself from his somewhat lewd preoccupation with her legs, Seth turned his back to her and swiftly wiped away the majority of the dirt and soot. He finished the job by scrubbing his exposed skin and hair with the sacking. Throughout his chore, there was no sound from Verity.

His depression deepened. The thought of her death hurt even worse than that of his own. In this last hour, Verity Standiford had made herself beyond precious to him. Not only was she a marvelous woman who had survived shunning while still able to laugh at herself, but she was strong and capable as well. When the crisis arose, she'd joined him, working at his side as his equal and done a damn fine job at it, too.

He turned toward his trunk, meaning to retrieve a pair of his workday trousers, only to find Verity sitting on it. Her arms were crossed and her head, bowed. Once again, he damned God. After all life had cost him, it wasn't fair that he should find the one woman he wanted and now loved with all his heart, only to lose her before he'd even once held her in his arms.

That realization hit him like a punch. It was beyond comprehension that he would die without ever having kissed her. Before he knew what he meant to do, Seth curled his finger beneath her chin and lifted her head.

Verity blinked back her tears and tried to smile, a pretense of courage. It was her brave attempt that set the need to touch her, hold her in his arms, and love her, to exploding beyond his control. If he was going to die, he was damned well going to go with this woman in his arms.

Verity caught her breath in surprise as Seth leaned toward her. It hadn't occurred to her he would kiss her. When his mouth settled softly atop hers, she breathed against the sweetness of his caress. The scent of smoke still clung to him, but his skin was cool from his dunk in the water.

Her eyes closed. His lips moved against hers as his hands closed over her arms, the slight pressure of his fingers urging her to rise. Her lips yet clinging to his, she did as he bid.

Once she was on her feet, he embraced her and drew her close against him. She breathed deeply as she savored the strength of his arms around her. Cautiously, she rested her aching hands against his damp, bare skin. Even as light as her touch was, she felt the beat of his heart, steady and strong.

A shudder shot through her, the pleasure loosening fear's iron grip on her heart. Outside, the fire roared, but here, in Seth's arms, there was nothing but sweet enjoyment. As long as he held her, there would be only heaven for what remained of her life.

She let her mouth soften beneath his, pleading with him to use his passion to carry her beyond her fear. Seth slid one hand up her back until he cupped his palm around her head. Threading his fingers into her hair, his kiss grew in intensity, demanding her own passion in return. Verity answered him with all the desire he woke in her.

The sounds of fire and wind, the creaking of the house, it all disappeared in the heat they made between them. Gasping, Seth tore his mouth from hers, then traced a line of kisses down the curve of her throat. When he reached her collarbone, Verity leaned back her head, her fingers coming to loosen the highest button. She opened her blouse, offering him more of her to kiss. He obliged. With each button she opened, his mouth descended, until his kiss hovered on the swell of her breasts above her corset.

Shivering at the way his mouth moved on her skin, she

combed her fingers through his wet hair. Every inch of her was alive with the feel of him. He reached around her and tugged at her loose blouse. It dropped into a bunch around her elbows. As she shook the garment off her arms, he straightened, his hands traveling up the exposed undergarment, until he traced his fingertips along its upper edge. Then, his hands fell away and he stepped back.

"Verity," he said, his voice soft and harsh, "stop me."

She raised her gaze from the masculine swell and fall of his chest to look at him. His mouth was taut as he battled his need for her, his eyes burned bright blue with desire. Verity sighed, loving him all the more. He wanted her, but he fought himself to protect her from his seduction.

Behind him, the air had grown thick with smoke. It was oozing into the house through the gaps above the door and shutters; she saw it swirl and twist in clouds around the lanterns. They didn't have much longer.

Verity shook her head, then reached down and tore open the corset's front opening. The garment fell to her feet, forgotten. She watched him as she breathed deeply, her breasts expanding into the sheerness of her camisole.

Seth made a sound deep in his throat. Beneath his sunbrowned skin new color awoke. Using his finger's tip, he outlined the fullness now exposed to his view. Verity waited for embarrassment to rise in her. She'd never allowed Richard this sort of freedom; their couplings had been completed in modest darkness. Instead, all that lived in her was the need to feel every inch of this man against her.

Shivering against his play, Verity wrapped her arms around his neck, glorying at the feel of her naked arms against his bare skin. She pulled herself tightly against him and touched her mouth to his ear. "Love me, Seth," she breathed.

He leaned his brow against hers. "I do," he murmured, pressing a kiss against the tip of her nose before he claimed her mouth as his own once more.

His kiss seared her. She gasped as he lifted her into his arms and carried her to the curtained bed opposite them.

Shouldering aside the fabric, he set her gently onto the mattress. As she sank into its feathery depths, he caught her braid's end and loosened her hair before he lay beside her. Her boots fell to the floor.

Here, near the wall, Verity could feel the fire's heat, even through the thick sod. Fear again rose in her, driving away pleasure. "Seth," she cried softly, knowing he couldn't hear her over the noise.

His hands were at the fastenings on her trousers. Verity lifted her hips as he eased the garment down her legs. When he'd bared her knees, he touched his mouth to its inner curve. Her trousers joined her boots. As he pulled off her remaining undergarments, he touched his mouth to the curve of her thigh into her hip. The caress jolted Verity out of her fear. A dark throbbing woke deep inside her, the cry of her body for his, as he kissed his way down her legs to her ankles.

He shifted on the bed until he straddled her, his hands splayed across her midsection. As he inched his hands upward to gather the fullness of her breasts into his palms, Verity ran her knuckles along the waistband of his wet trousers. She smiled as her touch made his skin quiver in reaction. Lifting her head, she touched her mouth to the smooth surface of his belly. Seth freed a sharp sound and leapt from the bed to tear off his only garment.

Once again, all of him was hers to view, but this time she stared at him in open appraisal. Her breath caught in appreciation. Oh, but he was as much man as she could ever want.

Even the smoky light showed her the strong curve of his shoulders and arms. It found the masculine swell of his chest and gleamed on the slim line of his hips. Verity's gaze caught on the part of him most male, the corners of her mouth lifting in new appreciation. Nor was there any doubting his desire for her.

He returned to lay alongside her. Verity studied his face, loving the slight twist of his nose and the full curve of his lips. His wonderful eyes were soft with need, but there was a question lurking in the depths of his gaze. Even now, he was offering her the opportunity to retreat. Her need for him expanded from the momentary distraction of pleasure into forever.

When he touched a finger to her mouth to trace its outline, she turned her head until she could press a kiss into his palm. Seth made a gentle sound and lowered his head to kiss her again. Although it was an almost passionless press of flesh to flesh, he stroked a hand downward past her breast. When he reached her hip, he used his fingers to draw fine lines along the sensitive skin of her abdomen.

As his fingers moved lower and found the core of her femininity, she cried out in surprise and pleasure against his mouth. Sensation flooded her in warm and trembling waves. She arched against it.

Seth shuddered at her reaction, but didn't cease his torment. The power of the sensation grew until she was awash in it, leaving her greedy for more. Groaning softly, he pushed her back onto the mattress, shifting until he lay atop her. Verity cradled his body into hers, her embrace tightening as she opened herself to him.

At her invitation, Seth tore his mouth from hers to kiss her cheek, her jaw, then nuzzle at her ear. With a low moan, Verity arched beneath him and made him one with her. The wall beside her grew warmer still. Time was very short. She moved beneath him, the taunting lift of her body begging him to follow where she led.

When he complied, pleasure tumbled atop pleasure in Verity. She moved with him, delighting in how she could make him gasp. Then, his movements became more insistent and it was her turn to gasp.

He was speaking to her, his voice ragged and hoarse, but Verity was beyond understanding. She cried out as her body found every bit of joy he could give her. As from a distance, she heard him respond in kind, his movements urgent in his own need. When he collapsed atop her, panting, her arms tightened around him, delighting at the way passion ebbed into contentment.

He rolled to the side, taking her with him. Still holding her close, Seth touched his mouth to her cheek, her jaw, her ear, then eased back from her. Verity sighed at the softness in his face. It was love for her he wore in his expression. Sadness touched her heart. How could she die now, when this is what she would lose?

"Marry me, Verity," he said, his voice deep and soft. "Stay with me."

Joy tore through Verity, no less powerful than the fire that worked to destroy them. She would have it all, a husband and even a child. The memory of Gemma's hand in hers shot through her, as sweet in recall as it had been in reality.

Then, happiness died. If by some miracle they survived the fire, nothing would have changed. She was still the fallen Miss Standiford; she could never be his wife. Pain boiled up in her, rendering her speechless. Biting her lip against her tears, Verity shook her head.

Seth's brow creased, some of the happiness dimming in his face. "Why not? You care for me, I see it. I know this sort of life is beneath you, but joining me cannot be any worse than what you are condemned to now."

His words drove away her pain. When she spoke, her voice was still ragged with tears and barely audible over the wind's persistent moan. "How can you think I would refuse you for any reason on your part? Seth, you said you studied to be barrister." She lay a hand on his shoulder, her fingers alive with the feel of him. Suddenly, death was preferable to life without Seth.

"You don't wish to marry me because I will be a lawyer?" There was more of confusion than accusation in his voice.

Verity again shook her head, wiping at a wayward tear. "A barrister needs a wife who is beyond reproach. What sort of position can you secure, what sort of clientele might you serve, that could accept a fallen woman as your wife?" A tiny, painful cry escaped her.

She rolled away, putting her back to him before she had to watch him realize she was right. "If you marry me, you destroy your future. I cannot allow you to do that."

"I see," he said, then pressed a kiss to her shoulder.

Verity loosed another cry as her desire for him reawakened, only to splinter on the wall she had to build between them. "Do not touch me. I cannot bear it. If we live through this, I will have to leave you and I think that will be worse than death." Reaching blindly over her head, she found a pillow. She pulled the thick cushion over her head and sobbed into the blankets, her keening almost as loud as the wind. It wasn't long before exhaustion, brought on by the crisis and her exertions, overtook her. Verity dropped into a deep and uneasy sleep.

Seth waited until he was certain she slept before he curled his body around hers and drew her into his embrace. Although a trifle upset with her well-meant refusal, the power of their lovemaking still awed him. Damn, but he wasn't content with only one joining; he wanted her for the rest of his life. But, how was he going to do that, when her refusal was based on the misguided notion that she protected him?

He let his hand graze along the silken length of a graceful arm, then twined his fingers between hers. She started in her sleep, jerking her hand from his. Catching her wrist, he turned her hand palm up, then frowned at the line of blisters crossing it. His admiration grew. She hadn't uttered a single word of complaint.

Nope. Never, no matter how she protested, he would never let her go. There was a way to wring marriage out of her. He just hadn't found it yet. Seth's eyes narrowed in determination as he pondered the issue.

As the moments passed, something changed in the room. Silence crept over him until his ears almost rang with it. He eased from the bed, then rushed to open the door.

Except for the circle of yet steaming grass that was the soddy's yard, there was nothing but charred ground and smoking desolation for as far as he could see. Seth fought back a triumphant yell. Then, grinning like an idiot, he leaned buck naked in the doorway to confront his future. If they could live through this, there was a way to force marriage down Miss Verity Standiford's throat.

The means to his end came sneaking up from the back of his brain. Seth's mouth once again lifted as euphoria swept over him. And, once the shock had passed, she'd surely see the humor in it. Turning back into the house, he went to his trunk and found his work clothes. He had himself a wife to catch.

Chapter Eight

"Verity, it's time you rose."

Seth's voice startled Verity out of her exhausted sleep. She sat straight up, uncertain if he'd truly spoken or she had only dreamed it. Something was sizzling. She breathed deeply. The sour smell of burnt things was strong, but, along with it came the warm and comfortable scent of frying—ham?

She eased to the bed's side, the sheets warm against her ever so bare skin, and peered around the curtain. Morning light streamed in through the two small windows. The air in here was still thick with dust and where the sun's heat hit it the particles whirled and circled in a joyful dance.

Seth stood at the stove, dressed in a worn pair of trousers and nothing more. A single beam of golden light shot through the nearest window to lay bright shadows across the masculine contours of his chest. For just that instant, Verity let herself believe they were man and wife already and that this was the normal beginning of their day. Then, reality settled heavily on her shoulders.

If this was morning and he was frying ham, then they had survived the fire. Falling back onto the mattress, she blinked at the muslin overhead, the thought of never again seeing Seth aching in her. Then, she grimaced. If she wanted to return to Johnnie's home, she'd have to send word to her brother. There'd be no hiding the fact that she'd spent an unchaperoned night with a man.

She rolled her eyes. Good Lord, but Mama would have a tantrum over this for certain. It wasn't beyond Mama to tell all of Victoria about this in a vindictive snit.

Verity waited for shame to wash over her, instead, there was only irritation at the intolerance of others. In that instant, she knew she couldn't return to either Victoria or England. Yesterday's happiness had changed her forever. She loved Seth and didn't care a pin for what others said about their supposed sin.

The need to hold onto her precious happiness tore through her. The United States was a very large country. Wasn't there some place they could go where no one knew or cared about her past?

Oh, but what if she'd already convinced Seth he shouldn't want her? Verity sat up and leaned out of the curtain, the thin fabric clutched to her chest to hide her nakedness. "Seth?" It was a soft and tremulous cry, filled with the worry that he'd rescinded his offer.

He turned toward her. His face was haggard and there were deep rings beneath his eyes, but his smile was glorious. Verity breathed out a slow sigh. He still wanted her.

"Well now, you're awake at last. There's a nightshirt at the end of the bed for you. It won't cover all of you, but it will have to do. Your clothing is filthy. Everything is buried ankle deep in dust and soot. Thinking you might want to straighten your hair, I put Gemma's hairbrush under the shirt. Hurry, now. We have an urgent appointment." What sounded like a quick laugh escaped him, but it was hard to tell as he turned swiftly back to his frying pan.

Verity frowned at him. An appointment? Whatever was he talking about? Confused, she shut the curtain and reluctantly pulled on the voluminous shirt.

The shirt hit her at the knees, the sleeves dropping over the tips of her fingers. Even trousers were better than this. She rolled back the cuffs until her hands were exposed, swiftly using the brush before she pushed back the curtain.

Seth turned at the sound of the moving curtains. His face almost glowed with happiness. Cocking a hip against the table, he called out in a voice that was far too loud. "Now that's much better. You're dressed, if not fully decent."

Verity stared at him. "Why are you shouting?"

"That's my sister I hear in there, Adamson!"

Verity's eyes widened at the sound of her brother's voice. With a yelp, she leapt from the bed's side to the middle of the room, then glanced around her in the ridiculous urge to hide. Such a thing wasn't possible in a one-roomed house.

Her hand flew to her loose hair, then she tried to drag the nightshirt down over her knees. Another impossibility. Verity turned on Seth. He was still leaning casually against the table, his arms crossed over his bare chest.

"It's my brother," she hissed. "I don't care how filthy they are, give me my clothing. Hurry, put on a shirt."

Seth only smiled at her, nothing but masculine appreciation of her semi-dressed form in his expression. "I think I like you in my clothes, almost as much as I like you in my bed," he said, a tangle of longing and laughter in his voice.

Johnnie pounded angrily on the door. "Open up, you piece of cheap American trash!" This pronouncement was followed by a choked sound, then the door flew wide and Verity's brother stepped inside, rifle in hand. Johnnie's face was streaked black with soot, his fine hair tangled and his shirt, grimy.

Behind him came the same little man who'd wed Johnnie to Sarah. Today, the justice's horrid brown suit was grayed with a fine layer of dust. Gemma stood at his side, her hand in his.

"What are you doing here?" Verity cried, wishing she could sink through the dirt floor and disappear.

While the men smiled at her, Gemma paid her no heed as her gaze swept the sooty house. When she spied her doll on the table top, she released Mr. Jenkins with a happy cry. Dust flew as she raced to the table and grabbed up her precious plaything.

Verity took a step back toward the shelter of the curtained bed, but ran into Seth. The man she'd believed she'd loved until this very moment put his arms around her to hold her where she stood. She turned in his embrace. "Let me go," she begged quietly. "I don't want to be seen this way."

"I don't think I can do that," he replied, his voice equally as low while a smile quirked at his mouth.

There was a tug on the nightshirt's hem. Verity looked down. Now cradling her doll close, Gemma stood beside her. A frown touched the child's brow as her bright blue gaze took in Verity's loosened hair, bare legs and oversized shirt. Verity's heart crashed through her feet and deep into the hard, dirt floor. Oh Lord, but what could Gemma think of her now?

Seth's niece held up her doll. "You brought her home to me?" she asked tentatively. Verity could only nod. If not for Seth's strong arms, she would have followed her heart through the floor.

Gemma sighed in satisfaction and leaned her head against Verity's hip. "I told Mina you would, so I didn't worry," she said. "Uncle Seth says I should ask you to stay with us. Will you? I would like that."

Verity went dizzy with happiness. Gemma wanted her. Reaching down, she claimed one of the girl's hands. Gemma's grip on her fingers had the feel of permanence to it.

"Well, well, well, what have we here?" Johnnie asked, his voice hard as he eyed his sister in her masculine nightwear. His face resolved into a ludicrous expression of harshness as he thrust out his chest. It was the role of an outraged father he was playing this time.

He lowered his rifle toward Seth. "Since you've made yourself free with my sister, you'll do right by her or die." He ruined the performance with a giggle. "Pardon, but I couldn't resist," he said to Seth.

"I had it coming," Seth said, as friendly as could be. "Jenkins, you can commence with the marrying."

"What?" Verity cried, turning in Seth's arms to look at the men behind her, then back to Seth. "What is this?"

"Why, darlin', it's a wedding or don't you recognize it? Your brother has caught us in a compromising situation and he has no choice but to see the honorable thing done." Seth's eyes crinkled at their corners as he finally gave way to his smile. "Your refusal didn't sit well with me and I'm afraid you'll slip away before I can convince you of your error. This is the expedient solution."

"Oh do hurry and agree with him, Ver," Johnnie said, his tone now petulant. "I'm like to drop. Spent the whole of last night fighting the demmed fire, I did."

Verity leaned on Seth in astonishment. "You did this," she cried, trying not to laugh. "You tricked me into this. You are a horrible, conniving, underhanded—"

Seth cut off her protest by pressing his mouth to hers. Verity melted into his embrace. As his kiss deepened, she brought her arms around his neck to hold herself closer. He not only wanted her, he had arranged this wonderful farce to keep her.

"Marry me, Verity," Seth murmured as he straightened to look into her face. There was still a spark of worry in the depths of his eyes.

"What choice have you left me?" she replied, trying to sound harsh and failing at it.

Seth's brows rose as he awaited her true response, not this halfhearted concession. What a fool she'd been to refuse him last night and Verity thanked God he hadn't listened to her.

"Yes," she told him, the word leaving her in a wondrous rush. She laughed to free some of the joy caught in her heart. "Poor man, you don't know the sort of trouble you're buying here. I should warn you, I'm outspoken and bold, sometimes even rude. And, I walk into houses without knocking."

New sparks came to life in Seth's eyes, these having a great deal more to do with lust than worry. "A terrible habit, one that as my wife, you must immediately rectify." He turned her in his arms until they faced Justice Jenkins. "Jenkins, we are at your convenience. Hope you won't be insulted if we do it again before a preacher. I'm not leaving her any possibility of escape."

"None taken." The justice grinned beneath his thick mustache as he fumbled in his pocket for his book. "This here's my favorite part. Dearly beloved—"

Historical Note

*V*ictoria, Kansas truly existed. It was founded by Sir George Grant, who brought with him an intrepid, but entirely unprepared band of Englishmen and women. They came to the frontier with their finest china and silver, while lacking the more basic skills, such as cooking and cleaning. All in all, they suffered the indignities of frontier life with great panache, arranging wonderful dances, coyote hunts and banquets.

The colony survived not only the fire, which happened somewhere between the middle of September and the end of October (I have been unable to pin down the exact date), an invasion of locust the next summer and, in the following year, a terrible winter. It was Sir George's death on April 28, 1878, that signalled the end of the colony. The British began to depart, some returning to England, while others drifted toward Topeka or farther westward.

To the best of my knowledge, there were no Standifords or Adamsons in the area. The spacious house with the stone foundation that Johnnie was building did exist. In reality, it was constructed by two sons of a Scottish nobleman. According to Elizabeth Stramel, it still exists. When the brothers decided to move westward, they gave it and all its furnishings to one of the German locals.

A WISH TO BUILD A
DREAM ON

❧

Vivian Vaughan

To

Bobby and Stephen

For teaching me the measure of a son's love

And the depth of a mother's.

Following an unusually wet winter, spring wildflowers bloomed early in the valley of the Pedernales. Andie Dushane trudged up the hill, carrying an old tomato can filled with a mixed bouquet of bluebonnets and Indian paintbrushes. When she reached a well-tended grave, she knelt on the rocky ground and settled the flowers against the crude wooden cross.

"Oh, Samuel," she whispered near tears, "tell me what to do. I know I promised not to give up, but it's so hard. I don't know much more about ranching now than I did before you died. And with only a child for help . . . Oh, Jordan's a good boy, Samuel. You'd be proud of him. And I'll never let him forget you. But it's been two years; I can't hold on much longer."

Wiping a tear off her cheek with the back of a callused hand, she focused on the flowers instead of on the rock-blanketed grave. The rocks were necessary to keep away varmints, but even after all this time they still brought visions of Samuel's skeletal frame and memories of his last wretched days and pain-filled nights, of his emaciated body and dull, lifeless eyes, of his fevers, which she had been unable to break, and his deliriums, which echoed endlessly through her mind—

"Don't leave me, Andie. Don't leave me alone."

She hadn't. She sat night and day, day and night, holding

him, bathing him, praying for him. In the end, he left her.

Oh, Lord, would she never forget the bad times? Until the end of her days would she hear only his cries and never his laughter? See only his wasted body and never his beautiful strength?

She felt guilty thinking about herself, her husband's dying had been so hard. But living was hard, too. Rays of the setting sun streamed over her shoulder and glinted from the golden centers of the orangy-red Indian paintbrushes. Gold, which in any other form was scarce as hen's teeth on the Dushane ranch. Andie was broke. She had failed to make a living for their son.

"I've been offered a job in town, Samuel. Cooking at Long's Cafe. Uncle Kipp found it for me. He's been lookin' after Jordan and me better'n most blood-relatives would have done. We can sleep in his back room, if I take the job. I know I promised to raise Jordan on the ranch, but . . ." A muted sob drowned her words.

"Ma." Jordan's warm hand touched her arm. "You still miss Pa, don't you?"

She nodded. Jordan knelt by her side.

"I miss him, too, Ma, but he wouldn't want you to sit out here cryin'." The child's maturity added to Andie's misery. At nine, he should be in school, have friends, be a boy, while he was still young. She looked into his small, sad face. A little round face that was even now lengthening to the oval shape of his pa's.

Reaching, she tousled his towhead. Samuel had been fair, too. Even before his illness, Samuel had blistered rather than tanned beneath the strong Texas sun. But that hadn't diminished him; a lifetime of hard work had produced a strong, firm body.

She glanced away from Jordan's hazel eyes, for they, too, were like his pa's. Serious, now, as Samuel's had been at times; but a deep streak of playfulness had run through both father and son. More often than not it showed in their eyes. And in their smiles. Samuel's smile had lit up his eyes and the whole world with them—Andie's world, at least. How she longed to see that smile again, even in her dreams.

Jordan's hand sought hers. "Don't cry, Ma. You never used to. You used to laugh." He brightened. "And dance." Jumping to his feet, he pulled her up beside him. "Remember how you an' Pa used to dance in the moonlight? It was your most favorite thing. Remember?" Speaking, he tugged her away from the grave, to a rock-free clearing. "Come on, Ma. Dance with me."

Without further prompting, he grabbed her around the waist and stepped off, singing, "Lou, lou, skip to my Lou. Lou, lou . . ." What his voice lacked in timbre, it made up for in enthusiasm.

Andie followed her chest-high son, her heart lodged in her throat. Dancing with Jordan didn't ease her loneliness, but it brought her back to the present. The present, where her duty to her son outweighed every other concern.

Stopping abruptly, Jordan pointed to the sky. "Look, Ma. The wishing star."

The wishing star, indeed. Gazing forlornly at the Evening Star, Andie wished for one thing—the healing spirit of youth.

"Star light, star bright," Jordan recited. "First star I've seen tonight. I wish I may, I wish I might, have the wish I wish tonight." His eyes were squinched tight. His sincerity tugged at her heart.

"I wish for a new husband for my ma. For her birthday."

"Samuel Jordan Dushane! I do not need a new husband!"

"Yes, you do, Ma. Ranchin's almighty hard work, an' lonely, too. You need someone . . ."

Dropping to her knees, Andie cradled him against her shoulder. "I have you, Jordan. You're all I need." She held him back, smiled wanly into his serious eyes. "How could I be lonely? You're the spittin' image of your pa, his own flesh and blood. And mine. Don't you see? You're part of us both. Having you is like having him." She pressed the child's face to her shoulder again, lest he see the small but, to her mind, necessary falsehood. "Your pa was a good man, Jordan. The best. And I intend to see that you grow up just like him."

I

"Don' take no sass, lil' gal. Chuck wagon cook runs the show, an' you let 'em know you know it first thing out o' the chute." Uncle Kipp's instructions echoed through Andie's head the whole day long, interspersed with her own admonition that she should have stayed home and taken the job at Long's Cafe instead of heading off to cook for a herd of trail drive cowboys.

But Uncle Kipp and Jordan found her the job and insisted she take it. She hadn't needed much encouragement; Miz Long's dollar a day couldn't compare with cattle drive pay.

"Reese Catlin's got some burr under his saddle blanket," Uncle Kipp explained after Jordan brought her the startling news that she had been hired to cook for a trail herd headed for Kansas. "Wants to drive the first herd into Wichita this spring, an' he's payin' fightin' wages to get the job done— three hundred dollars, double the goin' rate for a chuck wagon cook."

Three hundred dollars! Three hundred dollars would see them through the summer and winter, too. With three hundred dollars, she could hold onto things a while longer.

"What did he say about me bein' a woman?" Andie had quizzed.

"Nary a word," the old mercantile proprietor insisted. "Catlin's a no-nonsense trail boss, Andie. Built up a right proper reputation for hisself in the cattle country. Ain't heard nary an ill word spoken against him, neither. I wouldn't send you off with someone I wouldn't trust alone with my own mama."

Jordan was especially excited. "He ain't married, Ma."

"Isn't, Jordan." She smiled, rueful. She took Jordan's meaning, while realizing the futility of his wish. Even if she were in the market for a husband, Reese Catlin wouldn't be a candidate. From Uncle Kipp's description, he must be in his doddering years. But why spoil Jordan's fantasy?

She'd had a week to tie up things at home and provision

the wagon; a week for Uncle Kipp to tutor her in the ways of a chuck wagon cook. Now that week was up, and she had arrived at the appointed site. She glanced around, pleased.

All was in order. Pot roasts and potatoes steamed in Dutch ovens; sourdough biscuits rose beneath flour sack towels. In the black iron pot, frijoles burbled merrily, while Andie's culinary speciality, six sour cream pound cakes, lovingly baked before she left home, were wrapped in brandy-soaked towels.

"Make the first meal count," Uncle Kipp had cautioned. "Thataway, if there's any dissentin' cowpoke among 'em, he'll be won over 'fore he can spoil the barrel."

The first dissenting cowboy turned out to be the night horse wrangler, Night Hawk, who rode into camp midafternoon to help set up. A tall, rawboned kid, with a head of shaggy brown hair that Andie vowed to tackle first when the drovers lined up for her barbering skills, he had been visibly taken aback at finding a woman in camp.

Andie sliced him a hunk of cake. "I'm told Mister Catlin hired only the best, which must mean you're an expert at working with stock horses."

"For a fact, ma'am. This'll be my third year up the trail."

She ladled a dipper of mustang grape syrup over the cake. "Night Hawk," she mused. "How did you come by such a name?"

The first taste of that buttery, brandy-flavored cake lit up the boy's eyes. He spoke around bites. "My job's to keep track of a hundred and twenty head of horses and two extra wagon mules in the dark o' night, ma'am. That calls for eyes like a hawk."

"No doubt. Well, my job is to keep a dozen hardworking, hungry men fed. I'm an expert at that."

Night Hawk glanced up from his empty tin plate. "You surely are that, ma'am. Might I trouble you for another piece?"

By the time he had eaten half a cake, Night Hawk was eating out of Andie's hand, true to Uncle Kipp's predictions. He inspected the fire trench and allowed how diggin' it was his job, an' he an' Jordan would take care of it in the future. He helped Jordan put up the canvas tepee Uncle Kipp had insisted Andie bring along for privacy. Together the boys snaked in firewood, which they stored in the hide hammock slung beneath the wagon—Night Hawk called it a possum sack. After that, he called it a day.

"Time for me to get some shut-eye, ma'am. I'll crawl on up in the wagon there and get my forty winks 'fore it's time to relieve ol' Hank, the day wrangler."

"Boy, oh boy, Ma!" Jordan danced from foot to foot. "This trip's gonna be better than goin' to a circus!"

Andie hugged him close. Something told her he might not allow much hugging in the months to come, not in front of a dozen cowboys. Tears sprang to her eyes, as a gossamer vision warned of the changes this trip could produce in her precious young son.

"Isn't this a perfect campsite, Ma? That Reese Catlin must be a real smart man."

"It's Mister Catlin, Jordan. Everyone calls the trail boss mister. And yes, he did choose a good campsite. As to how smart he is in other matters, we'll have to wait and see."

"He chose Night Hawk. He's the best wrangler ever."

She grinned. "Unless I miss my bet, you and Night Hawk are going to be great friends."

"Yahoo!" Jordan had been looking out over the prairie. When his eyes widened suddenly, Andie followed his gaze to a rider who approached from the direction of the cattle herd. A fissure of trepidation speared through her confidence.

"That must be Mister Catlin." She whispered a silent prayer that the trail boss would find her work acceptable. She needed this job so badly. "His message said to expect him by sundown."

"Mister Catlin?" Jordan rushed to the chuckbox and picked up a bucket. "I'll fetch some water from the creek."

"We don't need . . ." But he was already out of sight. Andie turned to the approaching rider. The last rays of sunlight splashed over the prairie, burnishing the early spring grass a greenish gold. A muted scent of wildflowers wafted on the evening breeze. Sundown, her favorite time of day.

Or it had been. She suspected that sundown on a trail drive might be more hectic than tranquil, what with twelve hungry men arriving to be fed at one time.

The rider headed straight for the wagon. Uncle Kipp had warned her to keep a gun handy, and indeed her loaded six-shooter was stashed in the chuck box. But this rider would surely be Reese Catlin, who was obviously a punctual man. She liked that.

For the hundredth time she wondered why he was so dead set on getting to Wichita ahead of the other herds. Was it a wager? Pride? Greed? Whatever, she would have to thank him. For his need, or greed, would be her reward. Her salvation.

The rider skirted the camp to the lee side, a practice necessary to keep dust from flying into the food, according to Uncle Kipp. Andie watched him hitch his horse, a big dun with black mane and white stockings. The man was big, too. When he turned toward her, she was startled to see that he was a young man.

Mid-thirties, she judged with quickened heart. His brown handlebar mustache didn't have one gray hair that she could see. Uncle Kipp had spoken so reverently of him, she had assumed Reese Catlin to be in his fifties or better. Maybe this wasn't Mister Catlin. The thought brought a stirring of panic. She glanced to the spring. No sight of Jordan. She moved toward the chuck box, eyeing him warily as he approached.

The Stetsoned man halted in the middle of the clearing. His spurs stopped jingling. Silence pervaded the camp. But although he stood head and shoulders above her, he didn't appear threatening. Her uneasiness waned.

He removed his hat, rubbed his sleeve over a sweaty brow. He glanced around. His eyes lingered on the fire, where supper waited. His gaze moved to the wagon, hesitated on the brand on its side—an entwined RC—moved to her. His brown eyes were the darkest she had ever seen, like a bar of baking chocolate. But they offered no threat. Rather, he looked confused, as though he had lost something.

"Where's Andy Dushane?" His question ended on a high note.

According to Uncle Kipp, the cook was in charge of the campsite, so Andie stepped forward and extended her hand. "I'm Andie Dushane. You must be Mister Catlin. Welcome to camp, sir. Coffee's hot. Let me pour you a cup."

He took her hand, squinting as though bewildered. "You . . . ?"

"I've prepared pot roast and—"

"You're Andy Dushane?" His eyes widened to the size of silver dollars. "But you're a . . . you're . . . a *lady*."

The word lady, though softly spoken, staggered her. "You didn't know?"

"Know? Hell, if I'd known I wouldn't have . . ." Reese dropped her hand like it was a hot pot lid. He looked around the camp, then back to her, one brow quirked, as if he expected her to confess to pulling a prank.

"Uncle Kipp didn't tell you . . ." She glanced down inadvertently. When she looked back, his eyes were taking her in, too, what wasn't hidden beneath the voluminous canvas apron. Her stomach fluttered. "That I'm a woman?"

"A woman!" Reese spun away. He stepped to the fire, where, using a pot hook, he lifted first one lid, then another, releasing mouthwatering aroma each time. He moved to the wagon, looked in, inspected the provisions and the sleeping occupant. Gaining momentum, he strode to the back of the wagon, to the gateleg table, called the lid. After he had examined every cubbyhole in the chuckbox, he lifted the flour sack towels that covered six dozen rising sourdough biscuits. His eyes at last settled on the cakes, five and a half pound cakes.

Andie felt sick. She fought a futile urge to berate the absent Uncle Kipp for his subterfuge. Slipping a tin cup from its corner, she filled it from the pot on the fire and set it on the table before Reese Catlin, even though an unwritten law of the trail permitted no one but the cook to touch the lid.

"Let me cut you a piece of cake, Mister Catlin. I thought this first night—"

"Damn it to hell, woman. The boys won't stand for this. They'll stampede faster than lightnin'-spooked cattle. And I've got to get this herd to market."

And I have to have this job. Desperation clawed its way up her throat. She took a deep breath to steady her voice. "I understand." Picking up the cup, she held it toward him. After a cursory glance, he accepted it. "Uncle Kipp explained your goal to drive the first herd into Wichita."

He gulped a swallow of hot coffee and glared at her.

"To do that," she continued, "you have hired the best men available. No greenhorn, wet-behind-the-ears kids looking to play cowboy. You've hired the best."

"Dang right and they'll . . ."

"That includes me, Mister Catlin. I'm an excellent cook. I can keep your men fed and healthy."

"There's more to bein' a trail cook than lightin' a fire, Andy . . . uh, Miz Dushane." He glared at the wagon as if it, too, offended him. "You expect to drive this rig five hundred miles? Over prairies and mountains, through rivers and rain storms, across mud flats and bogs?"

"Indeed I do." At his skeptical frown, she added, "Six years ago on our move from Virginia to Texas, my husband broke his leg. I not only set the break, but I drove us the rest of the way, without aid of cowhands to ferry the wagon across rivers or fix broken axles or hitch the team or build campfires, all of which I understand are customary on a cattle drive."

"How many men have you cooked for at one time?" Reese challenged. "Not just one meal, but three a day, at three different locations, to which you have to move your kitchen and set up all over again? How many meals have you prepared in pourin' rain or blowin' gales when the Man Upstairs would have trouble keepin' a fire goin'? How many—"

"Mister Catlin, I accepted this job because I'm a widow with a child to raise and because I need the money to hold onto my ranch. Even so, I am beginning to regret my decision.''

"That makes two of us. I've been regrettin' it several minutes now.''

His admission took the life out of her. "I'm not one to stay where I'm unwanted,'' she said at length. "As soon as Hank arrives with the remuda, perhaps you would be kind enough to loan me a horse so I can return to town.''

"Town? Town's half a day's ride away. I can't let a lady ride off into the night by her lonesome.''

"Then forget my gender. Consider me an employee, duly terminated. On second thought, I won't wait for Hank. I'll take one of the mules.''

"Like hell you will.''

"You have two more in the remuda,'' she reminded him. "And I'll send this one back. Don't worry, I'm not about to stand between a man and his greed.'' She strode angrily toward the mule, calling down the hill, "Jordan. Oh, Jordan. Come runnin'.''

Reese caught up with her. "Me and my greed?''

"Uncle Kipp said you had a burr under your saddle blanket. He didn't explain what sort of burr.''

"I'll assure you, ma'am, my reasons for needin' to get into Wichita ahead of the rush account for a lot more than greed.''

When she reached to untie the ground hitch, he stopped her. His callused palm was rough and warm against her hand, and for an instant, pleasing. How long had it been since a man touched her? More than two years. But that had been Samuel, her loving husband. And this was—

"You can't ride a dang mule,'' Reese was saying, "even though I have a hunch you're nigh onto bein' as stubborn as one.''

"Stubborn? Me?'' Andie struggled to free the rope, but he wrested it away. His voice was harsh.

"Climb up on the back of that animal, an' you'll know stubborn. She'll kick you clear to kingdom come.''

"Which at the moment is an infinitely more desirable place than here, where I'm unwanted."

While she was trying to interpret Reese Catlin's strange expression, Jordan dashed into the clearing. "What's wrong, Ma?"

Reese gaped at sight of the boy. "What're you doin'—"

"Howdy, Mister Catlin. Did'ya eat some of Ma's cake? Ain't she the best cook ever?"

Reese swung his gaze from Jordan to Andie, then back to Jordan. "Your ma? Why, boy, I oughta have your hide—"

Andie jumped between them. "Keep away from my son, Reese Catlin." Jordan peeked around her apron.

"Don't be mad, Mister Catlin. We didn't go to pull the wool over your eyes."

"You didn't, did you? You and ol' man Kipp set me up real good. You must've had a barrel of laughs after I left. Hell, he's probably still slappin' his leg and flappin' his lips. Son of a biscuit eater! I've been hoodwinked."

"So have I!" Chagrin roiling in her stomach, Andie shoved Jordan toward the mule. "Climb up on Bessie Mae, Jordan."

"That's not Bessie Mae," Reese corrected. "It's Bertha Jane. If you can't tell your mules apart, how'd you expect to drive 'em?"

"I don't. Supper's on the fire, Mister Catlin. Jordan and I will be on our way."

"On your way? What'll I do for a cook?"

"That appears to be your problem."

"You took the job."

"And you made it clear that I'm undesirable. I don't hold it against you. You hired me sight unseen. Uncle Kipp and Jordan have some explaining to do, though."

"What will I do for a cook?" he demanded again.

"Hire another one. With the wages you're paying, you shouldn't find it hard to come up with someone."

Reese removed his Stetson and kicked a clump of new grass with the toe of his boot. She watched his anger wane. "I don't have time to beat the bushes for a cook, ma'am.

Fact is, just anybody won't do. I have a herd to get to market, and the way I'm fixin' to work these boys, I'll need an expert to keep 'em fed and happy.''

"You just fired your expert, Mister Catlin."

"I did not. You quit."

"I'm no quitter."

"No? What else do you call leavin' a man high and dry? Hell, the biscuits aren't even baked."

"I'm sure you or one of your dough-brained drovers can figure out how to set Dutch ovens in the fire."

"That's not the point." Reese focused on his hat brim, which he twisted in his hands. "I might not like it, ma'am, but you're all I've got. I've tasted your cookin'. If everything you make is as good as those lemon pies Kipp sells, you'll do a better job fattenin' up my cowboys than I will fattenin' the steers."

Andie's heart turned over. A lock of brown hair had fallen over his forehead. She resisted the motherly urge to smooth it back. He might be a respected cattleman and a master trail boss, but at the moment Reese Catlin looked more like an overgrown kid. A kid who had been called to task and had the good sense to know when he was whipped.

"Try her pound cake, Mister Catlin," Jordan urged. "It's yummier'n that ol' lemon pie."

"Jordan," Andie warned.

"Don't go, Ma. Mister Catlin needs us."

Before her Reese continued to twist his Stetson. "That's a fact, ma'am." When he looked up again, the expression in his brown eyes gave her insides a good hard twist.

"What about the men? You said they would stampede."

"With the aroma comin' from those Dutch ovens, I figure your supper'll convince 'em otherwise." He grinned. "And if it doesn't, ma'am, you and I'll find some way to let 'em know who's boss. We run the show around here."

"I know the rules, Mister Catlin. You run the cowboys and cattle; I run the wagon and camp." Uncle Kipp had tutored her in the sharp division of power around a cattle camp, and something warned her that now was the time to stake her ground. "If I stay, I will expect you to do your job and leave mine to me."

Supper was a disaster. Well, all except the food, Reese acknowledged. By the time the boys headed into camp for the evening meal, he still hadn't recovered from learning that Andy Dushane, a renowned trail cook according to ol' man Kipp, was in fact Andie Dushane, a more comely than average widow with curly black hair and eyes the color of the prairie in springtime. The fact that she was an excellent cook, no doubt the expert she claimed, wasn't likely to hold water with the boys.

Reese introduced them one by one, and to a man of them, the cowboys' eyes bugged out, before they turned to him, expecting to hear that their legs were being pulled or their lassos yanked. Every man jack of them let him know by one silent gesture or another that they hadn't signed on to any petticoat operation.

All except Reese's best point man, Tom Lovejoy, who wasn't known as Lover because he was fond of his mama. Which added to Reese's growing list of reasons to send Andie and her fibbin' son back to town at first light.

But if he did that, what would he do for a cook? He hadn't been exaggerating—hell, he wasn't sure the point could be exaggerated—when he told her he intended to work these cowboys so hard only the best of cooks could keep them on the job.

To give her credit, Andie played her role to a T, like she'd been schooled at it, which, no doubt, she had, by that connivin' ol' man Kipp. First, she called the men to supper with vigor.

"Come an' get it, less'n you want me to throw it in the possum an' head the lot o' you out for Wichita with empty bellies!"

The men lined up, all right, even though they balked like a dozen ol' muley cows. But little Miz Dushane didn't blink an eye—or let up issuing orders.

"Wash in the basin, then toss it under the wagon."

"We gener'ly don't toss out water after only one use, ma'am." Grumpy, first in line, was also first to challenge the cook, a dangerous thing under normal circumstances, which these definitely were not. Andie smiled when she replied.

"Generally doesn't count, Grumpy. Toss out the water."

With all the commotion about her being a woman, Reese hadn't figured she'd remember more'n one or two names from his introductions, but dang if she didn't fool him again. She recalled every one and put the right faces with 'em, too.

"Clean water and a clean towel." She added to her list of rules with the regularity of a Texas dust storm, handing each cowboy, as she spoke, a fresh flour sack towel. "Community towels breed germs. I'll doctor your ailments, but I don't intend to cultivate them."

The men fired skeptical glances at Reese, but he nodded in agreement with the cook. What else could he do? If he ended up having to keep her, he couldn't undermine her authority the first night out. Besides, if she wanted to spend her time washing, that was her business, long as she didn't use up all the water with her Miz Clean Crusade. He'd talk to her about that—if he ended up having to keep her.

Grumbling and wary, each man picked up his eatin' irons and tin plate and headed for the fire where Night Hawk was first to lift the lid off a Dutch oven. Before he could spoon out food, however, Andie stopped him.

"Mister Catlin, would you oblige us with grace before these hungry drovers dish up the vittles?"

The ground rocked under Reese's feet at that, but the stampede he felt had nothing to do with four-legged critters. From the hush that followed her request, he figured every man jack of the boys was thinkin' the same thing. It was lookin' more an' more like the decision of whether to keep the cook might not rest entirely on his shoulders. She had stepped on three rattlesnakes already. Before he could come up with something appropriate in the way of grace, she stepped on another.

"Remove your hats, please—while we speak to the Lord, and while you eat."

Every dust-stung cowboy eye in camp swiveled to Reese's. He saw in an instant that their indulgence was wearin' thin. Campfire etiquette did not require a man to remove his hat. Never had, never would. Hell, his neighbor might step on it or spill gravy on it. But the camp was the cook's domain. By unwritten law, Cookie made the rules, and every cowboy was obliged to follow 'em, even the trail boss.

Reese removed his hat and the boys begrudgingly did likewise. "For this food we're about to receive, may we have grateful hearts. Amen." Silently, he added his own prayer for a cook. A male cook of undetermined competence. *Real quick, Lord.*

The food quieted 'em down. Even Reese. By the time he served himself and sat cross-legged on the ground, tin plate balanced cowboy-style on his calves, silence pervaded the camp. Glancing around, he found each man's eyes trained on his own plate. No one spoke. No one rose for coffee. Every drover was pacified by succulent roast beef and garlic-flavored potatoes. Reese's ire began to abate. He couldn't fire her till after breakfast, anyhow. Henry Morgan was the first to speak.

"What'd you do to these taters, ma'am?" Henry questioned of a sudden. Known as Professor for the books he packed in his saddlebags, Henry was one of the two seasoned point men Reese felt fortunate to have hired. "I'll be a monkey's uncle, if my ol' grandmammy didn't cook 'em the same way back in Mississip."

"Thank you, Professor." Andie spoke lightly, with a trace of humility in her voice that Reese instantly admired. "It's an old family recipe from Virginia. If we get our herd in ahead of the competition, I'll be delighted to share it with you."

Our herd? Reese cast a wary glance around the seated cowboys to see how they took that. Most of them were so busy cleaning their plates, they hadn't heard. Or, they chose not to react—for the moment, he cautioned himself.

More praise was quick in coming when Andie passed the biscuits. The kid followed his ma carryin' a tub of butter. Real butter. On a trail drive they settled for sorghum with a little bacon grease stirred in. Hellfire! Had she spent all his money on tender meat and cow's butter?

The wagon had appeared well-stocked. But was it? Did she know how far it was from one supply station to the next? Did she know how to stretch groceries to fit the distance? Did she know anything except how to cook?

And how to set a man's world to spinnin'?

With her dark hair pinned up, he hadn't missed the delicate line of her nape, nor for that matter, the graceful way she gestured with slender fingers. It took a man's full attention to keep from imagining those fingers runnin' across his chest at night, or his own, snakin' up the soft skin on her neck.

Uncomfortably, Reese realized he wasn't the only man among them to have noticed Andie's attributes, even though most of said attributes were hidden beneath billowing apron and swaying skirts. He watched Tom Lovejoy watch her pass the biscuits.

Reese didn't mind that Lover charmed the ladies at every stop from South Texas to Kansas, as long as he did his job. Possessed of boyish good looks and what Reese had heard one girl refer to as eyes that looked like bluebonnets sparklin' with dew, Tom Lovejoy was the best point man in the business. And two good points were essential to the success of this drive. Like Andie said, Reese had hired the best, experts in their fields to a man of them:

Lover and Professor at point; four swing riders—Pop and Monte to the north, and Woody and Dink on the south; bringing up the rear, the three Tahlman brothers—Gimpy, Grumpy, and Goosey—rode drag. These were men who knew how to trail twenty-five hundred cattle ten miles a day, while the herd thought it was out for a morning stroll. With these men, his cattle should gain weight, and, by turn, his pocketbook. Every trail boss to follow would envy him.

Reese had thought of everything. At least, he tried. He hired two skilled young drovers for the lowliest job, horse wrangler: Night Hawk for night duty and Hank Sawyer for day shift; the wrangler off-duty would help Cookie set up and break camp. With them to do most of the dirty work, Cookie could concentrate on preparing meals. And last, but most important of all to the success of a drive, Reese had hired an expert camp cook: the *man* who baked those damned lemon pies at Kipp's.

One by one the men scraped their dishes and tossed them in the wrecking pan beneath the lid, then returned to sit around the fire. As planned, Hank helped Andie wash the dishes. Not as planned, Reese thought. Some *man* she turned out to be.

When the dishes were dried and stored in cubbyholes, Andie enlisted Hank and that kid of hers to help turn the wagon tongue toward the North Star, a necessary duty of the cook, for it provided the trail boss with the next day's heading, come daylight; afterward, she placed a lighted lantern on the tongue to guide the guards back to camp in the black of night. Hell, she knew all the right answers. Made all the right moves.

Before retiring to her tepee, she called to the men in general, " 'Night, everyone. Eat all those cakes. I don't want a crumb left in the morning. They'll draw ants."

Left to sit around the fire with his men, Reese watched her go, but his thoughts were far from the harness he mended. When she lit a lantern inside the tepee, his imagination began to play havoc with his brain, so he turned his attention to the campsite. To a man of them, his cowhands were busy eating the best dang sour cream pound cake a man could ever ask for, prepared by a cook that would be the envy of every trail boss in Texas, if she weren't—

Again Grumpy was first to complain. "Dangit, boss, a woman's about as welcome on a cattle drive as a skunk at a church social."

"I'd say she smells a mite sweeter," Tom Lovejoy observed. "And she looks . . . hmmm, makes a man wonder what's underneath that canvas apron . . . don't it, son!"

Reese shook his head in agony. Goosey tuned up his fiddle.

"She'll sure as shootin' cramp our style," Monte allowed.

"Ain't that true?" Dink added. "I've been savin' up tales all winter. I won't be able to tell a one of 'em with a lady in camp."

"You oughta learn cleaner tales," Weasel, called Pop, contended.

"Says you, Pop. You fixin' to clean up your language?"

"What's wrong with my goddam language?"

Reese joined the cowboys' whoops, if a bit feebly.

"Your language'd light a fire of wet cowchips," Woody allowed.

"Hell, Pop, you're the only man I know's been run outta Rosie's Pleasure Palace for unfit language. How you figure on keepin' your mouth clean around a real lady for two months?"

"Or any of us. Hellfire, boss. 'Fore we reach Wichita we'll be explodin' like a pot of boilin' Pecos strawberries."

Rising to his feet, Reese took the poker and banked coals around the pot of fresh coffee Andie had put on for the night guard. "Which one of you's offerin' to trade in his cow pony for the chuck wagon and mules?"

The grumblers fell silent.

"I take responsibility for her bein' a woman," he told them. "I shouldn't have hired a cook sight unseen. So, I'll let you fellers have your say, an' when we take a vote, I'll abide by your wishes. But let me say somethin' first. You know how important this drive is to me. Hell, I was born and raised on that Matthews spread. It's like home, even if my pa was only the foreman. I'd give my eyeteeth to own that ranch, and now that he's decided to sell, Mister Matthews has given me first chance to buy it. If I don't come up with the money by midsummer, he's puttin' it on the market an' takin' the highest offer." Reese scanned the men.

"So I took a gamble," he continued, "on you boys. Each of you is the best there is, and I'm payin' double wages. Oh, you'll earn 'em, no doubt about it. I intend to work you into a lather an' send you out again 'fore you've dried off good. Workin' that hard, I figured you'd need the best grub this side of your mama's kitchen table. So, we have a decision to make tonight. Way I see it, there're two choices. We keep Miz Dushane. You had a taste of her cookin', should be enough to judge her by. Or we send her back to town in the morning and handle the cookin' chores ourselves.''

A groan passed around camp, ending with a sour note from Goosey's fiddle.

"If you choose to send her back," Reese added, "we can try to pick up a cook at Red River Station."

"Only hands at Red River is them that's so sorry no one can git along with 'em," Woody observed.

"On the other hand," Reese added, "if we keep her, and she doesn't work out, we can always let her off at Red River."

"Hell, that's rough territory for a lady."

Reese shrugged. "It's where you get rid of incompetent help. I'll tell you boys again, I'm gettin' into Wichita ahead of the crowd, whatever it takes. If you can't stand havin' a woman in camp, let me hear it now."

"It'll be a hassle."

"You'll have to keep her from usin' up all the water."

"An' makin' us feel like schoolkids."

Tom Lovejoy glanced up from a cigarette he was rolling. "Way I see things . . ." He paused, swiped a long wet line along one edge of the paper with his tongue, then carefully folded the opposite edge over it and stuck them together.

Reese stroked one side of his mustache, waiting.

"Andie Dushane's not only a good cook, she's a looker," Tom observed at length. "She'll add a touch o' home to the monotony we're fixin' to impose upon ourselves."

"And another notch on your—" Monte's attempt to rib Lover was cut short by Reese's explosive,

"That's reason enough to send her packin', right there! I don't have time to ride herd over a bunch of lustin' drovers. If we take her along, she'll be treated with the same respect we'd show our mamas."

Lover struck a wooden match on the sole of his boot. "She don't look nothin' like *my* mama."

"Not mine, neither," Dink added with a laugh.

"That settles it. First thing tomorrow, she goes—"

"You heathens listen up!" Young Jordan jumped from the wagon where instead of sleeping, he must have been eavesdropping. All eyes followed the frail youngster who ran to stand beside the trail boss. "I'm here to protect my ma."

Grins spread across the men's faces. Undaunted, the kid continued. "Ever one of you better keep your filthy hands and eyes to yourselves—I mean, all except Mister Catlin."

It took a minute for the boy's meaning to register, and when it did, Reese felt like someone had waylaid him with the blister end of a shovel. "You connivin' little . . ." His eyes flew from Jordan's innocent expression to the tepee set in the distance. His mouth fell open. *Sonofabitch! Would this nightmare never end?*

Andie Dushane was preparing for bed; at least he hoped that was her intention, for she stood, bent at the waist, head down, brushing her hair in long, graceful strokes. He knew that's what she was doing, for her movements, along with every gentle curve of her body, were silhouetted by the glow of the lantern that rendered the canvas transparent.

Hoodwinked? Dang if he hadn't been, and not just by the old man and the boy from the looks of things. So they thought to catch him in a matchmakin' scheme, huh? Well, it wouldn't work. It would take more than a connivin' old man, a schemin' widder-woman, an' a fibbin' kid to wrestle him into a double harness.

If he didn't need a cook worse'n a muleskinner needed a bath, he'd send 'em packin' and good riddance.

But he did need a cook. And he could take care of himself; hadn't he evaded double harnesses before? Hell, their little plot didn't stand a snowball's chance in a Texas heatwave.

But halfway to the tepee to upbraid Andie for revealing herself in the lantern light, Reese began to wish for a snowstorm, himself. Halfway there he realized that only part of the heat sizzling inside him came from anger.

II

"Haaaw, Bessie Mae! Heee, Bertha Jane!" Two weeks later Andie had settled into the routine of the trail drive, determined to see the job through, in spite of Jordan's matchmaking and Reese Catlin's belief that she was part of the scheme. Jordan, she had reprimanded, with as much success as one could expect from a nine-year-old who was trying to marry off his ma.

Reese was a different story. She had found neither the opportunity nor the courage to explain to him that she hadn't known about or encouraged or approved of the wretched scheme. In truth, she never wanted to think about it again, but she did want him to know she wasn't out to catch a husband, namely him.

"Haaaw!" She cracked the whip across the rumps of the mules Night Hawk had hitched earlier, before climbing up in the wagon to catch his forty winks. The heavy wheels lumbered out of camp, pulling the cumbersome wagon over the prairie; she steered the team in a wide arc around the grazing herd.

Before her, the rising sun glistened from dew-sprinkled grass. Already a morning's work was behind her, and a full day's worth awaited ahead. Jordan sat on the wagon seat, prattling, the one member of the crew who never seemed to tire.

"Grumpy said I could, Ma."

"It's Mister Tahlman, Jordan. How many times do I have to tell you? You must address your elders with respect, even on a trail drive."

"Then there'd be three Mister Tahlmans and that would be confusing. Can't I call him Uncle Grumpy?"

Andie sighed. She still wasn't certain she had made the best decision. Indeed, more often than not, she questioned her reasons for not returning home and taking the job at Long's Cafe.

Oh, her major reason, the money Reese would pay at the end of the trail, remained the same. She needed the money.

But from that first night when he stormed into her tent and demanded she blow out her lantern, she had sensed that money would not be the only factor in her decision to stay or return home.

Memories of their encounter shimmered in the crisp morning air, taking her back to that night in the tepee. The emotions she felt then assailed her now—embarrassment at Jordan's outburst, fear of losing this job, guilt at her own runaway senses.

She hadn't realized Reese Catlin was so handsome, nor so large. She saw him yet, in her mind's eye, filling her little tepee, lantern light playing on his bronzed skin and glistening from the anger in his brown eyes.

But more than his anger, it was the fascination in his eyes that held her mesmerized. He had stood like a moth drawn to the light, gazing at her as though he had never seen a woman in a dressing gown before. And she let him look, as though she had never been admired before. Later, plagued by guilt, she tried to rationalize. It had been so long, so very long. Later still Samuel's delirious pleas haunted her dreams. *Don't leave me, Andie. Don't leave me alone.*

Now, two miserable weeks later, recalling the indecent way she had stood there, still as a dewdrop on a trembling leaf, the guilt of that encounter remained fresh as an open wound.

It lasted mere moments, before Reese finally found his tongue and ordered her to extinguish her lantern. She had quickly regained control. "I'll thank you to get out of my tent, and stay out, Mister Catlin."

When he neither budged nor spoke, she became wary. Had he come to send her away in the middle of the night? Had Jordan's scheme lost her this job?

"We've decided to try you out," he told her.

Relief, though sweet, was short-lived.

"But I won't have you sashayin' in front of the boys, or showin' yourself—"

"Showing myself?" Embarrassment gave way to anguish. "If you think I—"

"It isn't what I think, ma'am. It's those cowboys sittin' out there watchin' you brush your hair. I'm ready to protect a lady's honor with my life, but I don't hanker to have to shoot my own cowboys, leastways not before we get this herd to Wichita."

"Oh!" She had extinguished the lantern with an angry puff. "Why didn't you tell me?"

"I just did." Apparently believing the matter settled, he backed out of the dark tepee. She charged after him.

"Mister Catlin." She stopped inside the open flap, inadvertently, catching his eye.

"Reese," he corrected.

She shrank at the personal request. *The nerve of him!* "Everyone addresses the trail boss—"

"Everyone except the cook. Trail boss and cook are on equal footin'. Since you've decided to stay, we'd best be showin' the boys who the bosses are." He turned to leave. " 'Night, Andie."

She steamed. Pigheadedness was her least favorite male trait. "What makes you think I've decided to stay?" That stopped him in his tracks. Turning, he quirked an eyebrow.

"We decided to try you out."

"I know what *you* decided. I heard it all, including Grumpy comparing me to a skunk at a church social."

"Don't go gettin' riled; he didn't mean any harm."

"I'm not riled. I told you earlier, I have no desire to stay where I'm unwanted."

Although she stood inside the darkened tepee, Reese was in full view with moonlight playing on the broad planes of his face. Again, his eyes took her in, and the perusal jolted her, for in it she saw want of a far different kind than she had intended.

Oh, he believed Jordan's story, she could tell. Skepticism tightened the fine lines around his eyes. But thinking her a hussy out to catch a husband hadn't checked the physical need she saw reflected in his eyes. Saw and, Lord help her, responded to.

Uncle Kipp had called Reese Catlin respectable. In that intense, sensual moment she sensed something in him that was wild. Still, for the life of her, she could only stand there and savor the pleasure of being admired by this determined, pigheaded, and yes, too-handsome, man.

Against her better judgement, she acquiesced. She needed the money. But even then, she retained enough sense to realize that if she were to remain with this drive, it must be on her own terms.

"All right, Reese Catlin, I'll try *you* out. I won't sashay or otherwise flaunt myself in front of the cowboys; to be truthful, I consider it an insult that anyone would accuse me of such behavior. And you will not put me out at Red River."

"Now, Andie—"

"Jordan has relations in Fort Worth. If things aren't working out, we will leave the drive there. You can prorate my pay."

His grin befitted a man who had just won at faro. "If you last to Fort Worth, I reckon you'll have earned it all."

Jordan's voice penetrated Andie's reverie, calling her back to the wagon. "Uncle Grumpy says a boy my age should be ridin' herd. He says when he was nine he was already fendin' for hisself."

"Himself, Jordan."

"Anyhow, he said he'd teach me how to ride drag."

"No."

"Please, Ma."

"No."

"Here comes Mister Catlin. I'll ask him."

A rider galloped toward them from the north. Even from the distance, she recognized Reese. *How quickly one learned*! Aggravated with herself, she cracked the whip, startling the mules. "You will not ask him to let you ride drag, Jordan. Don't make me regret coming on this drive."

"You won't regret it, Ma. Uncle Pop says Mister Catlin's

gonna be howlin' 'round your tepee any night now.''

Andie turned stricken eyes to her son. "What?"

"Uncle Pop says—''

"Oh, Jordan. What did I get us into? More specifically, what did you and Uncle Kipp get me into?"

"Nothin' you won't like better'n a hog likes slop.''

"Jordan!"

"That's what Uncle Gimpy said.''

"The cowboys . . .'' She cast an eye back to the sleeping figure of Night Hawk, then lowered her voice. "They're talking about Mister Catlin and me?" She watched Reese approach the wagon, wishing she could crawl under the seat and disappear.

"Don't let it ruffle your feathers, Ma. That's what Uncle—''

"Ruffle my feathers, my eye!" Embarrassed to her toes, Andie pulled the team to a halt and awaited Reese's directions to the noon camp. *Did he know what the cowboys were saying?*

These meetings had become a daily ritual. Reese left camp immediately after breakfast, while the cowboys caught up their morning mounts and moved the herd out slowly, allowing the cattle to graze if the buffalo grass was dry enough. With the dishes finished, she drove the wagon alongside the herd, until Reese returned with directions to the noon site. Afterward, he rejoined the herd, and Andie, Jordan, and Night Hawk proceeded to the new camp, where they set up and she prepared a hot meal.

Amazingly, given the misunderstanding that brought them together, she was comfortable with Reese. Or had been. She had looked on these meetings as a respite from the grueling work that took up most of her waking hours. In large part, she knew, Reese himself made this possible. Since that first night, he had kept their relationship strictly professional.

Now, with the cowboys' talk, all that was ruined. She couldn't even meet his eye this morning.

"Hidee, Mister Catlin."

"Howdy, Jordan. Andie."

From the corner of her eye Andie watched him remove his Stetson and wipe his brow with his sleeve, motions she could see with her eyes closed, they had become so familiar.

"Camp's six or seven miles ahead," he told her. "Along the Concho River." After she repeated the directions, another part of their daily ritual, he turned to the boy who eagerly hung on his every word. "Jordan, I want you to help Night Hawk fill the water barrel from the river before we pull out."

"Yahoo! Thanks, Mister Catlin. Wait'll you see what my ma's fixin' for dinner. It's a real tummy-tickler."

Aghast, Andie glanced at Reese. His jaws were clenched; those fine lines around his eyes had tightened.

He knew what the cowboys were saying!

When he continued, his tone was brusque. "Once you get past the herd, Andie, wake up Night Hawk."

"He needs his sleep," she argued, determined, in spite of the situation, to defend her right to control the wagon and its occupants.

"Do as I say," Reese shot back. "When you move out ahead of the herd, I want him sittin' on that bench with his eyes peeled."

Trepidation shot through her. "Is there trouble?"

"I cut the trail of a couple of fellers headed west on shod horses. Followed 'em a piece. They appeared to be leavin' the country, but it won't do to take chances."

She relented. "You win."

He shrugged in a pigheaded way that called for a retort, but before she could think of one, he continued pleasantly, "It's a fine campsite with good grazing. Since we're ahead of schedule, an' the boys need a rest, we'll stay there till tomorrow morning."

Overjoyed, self-consciousness fled. "Three meals in one place?"

"Thought you might take a likin' to that."

She sat motionless, soaking in the warmth of his smile, while a rare giddiness gripped her. "I have so many things to do around camp," she babbled. "There's never enough time—"

"Likewise." His gaze focused on her lips. He touched his hat brim and sunk spurs. "Ma'am."

"What'd he mean by that?" Jordan wanted to know.

"By what?" Still in a dither, she stared after Reese.

"What he said, Ma? Likewise. What's that mean?"

"It means . . ." She cracked the whip and headed the team north. "That he has unfinished business around camp, too."

"What kind of business?"

"Oh, you know. Mending harnesses, oiling saddles, washing clothes." But somewhere deep inside her unwanted expectations began to build. Angrily she reminded herself that she was not a giddy schoolgirl looking for a beau, but a widow with the memory of a beloved husband to honor and a strong-willed son to raise in his pa's image. She had no time for dalliances. And nothing awaited her at the next camp but another day of backbreaking work.

As it turned out, she was right, with one exception. After dinner Reese had a surprise. On his way back to the herd, he stopped at the lid where she washed dishes. The biggest part of the surprise was that he stopped at all, for he had avoided her throughout the meal. A couple of times she had caught him studying her, but it was with a distracted look that told her little.

Except that he surely knew what the cowboys were saying.

Now he kept the width of the lid between them and his eyes on his Stetson. "A stray calf took up with us a few days back. What say I get Monte to butcher it for you?"

She watched him study his hat. "Fine."

"How'd you want the meat cut?"

Surprised he would consider her opinion, she gathered her wits. "We can have steaks tonight; I'll use some for breakfast; and the rest . . . save the entrails for, uh, son of . . . uh . . . stew."

Son-of-a-bitch stew was a staple around a cow camp. Uncle Kipp claimed it contained nutrients not readily available on a trail drive in any other form.

That got Reese's attention. Caught off guard, he grinned and slapped his hat against his thigh. "The boys're gonna have a hard time callin' it by name in front of a lady."

The word lady rolled off his tongue like a caress. When Andie caught herself focusing on his mustache, she glanced down at the dish in her hand. Then it came to her. She could kill two birds with one stone. As cook, again according to Uncle Kipp, she could change the name of that stew. "I understand it's the cook's prerogative to call it after anyone she wants."

"You bet. Long as it's after an enemy." He challenged her with quirked eyebrow. "Don't tell me you're claimin' to have an enemy." At ease like that, he was disarmingly handsome.

"I certainly do." She was more than ready to set the record straight. "I'll call it Uncle Kipp Stew." She watched him consider her meaning.

"Remind me not to get on your bad side," he said at length. But instead of the understanding she had hoped for, skepticism tightened the lines around his brown eyes and wariness filmed the gaze he drilled into her before she looked away.

Reese Catlin was one pigheaded man! If he wanted to believe she was so desperate for a husband she would put herself through the rigors of a trail drive to catch one, that was his problem. She didn't need his approval, only the three hundred dollars he would owe her in Wichita—or Fort Worth.

Andie had two objectives for the afternoon, which she intended to tackle with heart and soul—and mind. If she concentrated on her work, surely she could keep Reese Catlin off her mind. Away from him, her brain cleared and she recognized the perfidious nature of her problem—physical attraction, which she had no intention of allowing to get out of hand. She was, after all, a widow and a mother with an obligation to honor her dead husband and to rear her son accordingly.

But let Reese come within shouting distance and reason deserted her, leaving her with a tingling in her stomach and breathless anticipation in her chest. Neither were appropriate;

both she vowed to conquer with an afternoon of hard work.

Her first objective, to fix bear sign, the cowboy's term for doughnuts, required that she set the dough to rise early. That done, she undertook her second mission—freshening the chuck wagon. The cowboys' wagon sheets and blankets, which they wrapped around their extra—make that dirty— clothes smelled to high heaven.

Everything wouldn't get dry by nightfall, so she decided to tackle the clothing first. Climbing into the wagon, she began tossing bedrolls down to the boys.

"You can't do that, ma'am," Night Hawk objected.

"You didn't learn as much as I would have thought in three years up the trail," she observed with a smile.

"What'd you mean?"

She pitched him another bedroll. "The cook can do whatever she deems necessary for the welfare of her charges."

Night Hawk eyed the bedrolls. "Charges or not, them boys ain't gonna take kindly to you messin' with their clothes."

She pitched a bedroll down to Jordan. "They have mothers, don't they?"

"Far's I know, ma'am."

She tossed him another set of bedding. "Their mothers must have washed their clothing."

"I reckon." By this time Night Hawk staggered beneath the weight. Andie jumped to the ground, picked up a wooden box filled with bar soap, and headed for the river, beckoning the two wide-eyed boys to follow.

Jordan struggled along on one side, Night Hawk on the other, the latter muttering, "Do what you like, ma'am, but I'm tellin' you, they ain't gonna like it."

She did what she liked, rather, what she thought best. In order not to mix up the clothes, she spread each bedroll beneath a tree or bush where she could hang that man's clothing.

"The boys like to choose their own sleepin' spots," Night Hawk fretted.

"They can move their bedrolls later. I'm more concerned about not mixing up their clothes."

Night Hawk shook his head. "A passle of things're fixin'
to get mixed up, ma'am, but it's your funeral."

An hour later, she stood with hands to aching back, sur-
veying her handiwork—holey socks and long johns, most of
which cried for a mender's needle, flapped in the breeze beside shirts and britches. Another day perhaps she would find
time to mend.

"Jordan, you and Night Hawk take the wagon down to
the river and fill the water barrel, like Mister Catlin said."

"Sure thing, Ma."

"Sure thing," Night Hawk muttered. "I don't hanker to
be around when the boys ride in an' see their unmentionables
bared to the world."

Andie laughed. "Everything will be dry and rolled in the
bedrolls before they return."

Reese spurred his horse, propelled toward camp by an eagerness he didn't quite understand. He told himself he was
concerned about those fellers whose trail he had cut earlier,
but that wasn't necessarily the case, and he knew it. Those
tracks had beat a steady path west. If it hadn't been for Andie
and the kid, he wouldn't have given them another thought.

If it hadn't been for Andie . . . Everything he did these
days revolved around that woman. He argued that he would
be as preoccupied with any cook, since grub was important
to his success. But that wasn't entirely true. Ordinarily he
would have left Cookie to fend for himself against travelers
or out of work drovers who might or might not be ridin' the
grub line.

He tried to ignore the fact that she was out to catch a
husband, and in that he had been partially successful. To his
good fortune she had turned out to be one heck of a trail
cook. She kept things running at a clipped pace, the way he
liked. No lollygaggin' around. She was up at three in the
morning without so much as a yawn that he'd seen; she had
breakfast ready in a little over an hour, called the boys, and
had them in the saddle by sunup. She prepared dinner with

the same dispatch, with never a grumble. And at supper she was a delight to behold.

Who would have suspected havin' a woman around camp could make such a difference? Oh, the boys groused some at having to clean up their language and curtail their tall tales, but each and every one of 'em was more relaxed and easier going than Reese had ever seen a bunch of cowboys.

She had even made a difference in him. At the start of this drive, red-hot determination stewed in his gut; now, he worked day by day as hard as he ever had, but dang if he didn't accomplish more. And at the end of the day, he returned to camp, not filled with anxiety to be on the trail, but with anticipation of what he would find—a delicious meal hot and ready, served by a woman who was every bit as tempting. Not that he was about to get himself caught in her noose.

Reese was mildly surprised that he found her company so enjoyable, knowing she was planning the demise of his bachelorhood. He put that down to his ability to make the best of any situation. He needed Andie on this drive. So why not grin and bear it?

Of course, he didn't intend to grin where anyone could see him. Cowboys were relentless to a fault at bedevilin' a feller. He may be attracted to her, but he dang sure didn't have to let on in front of the boys.

He had tried to get her off his mind, but so far he hadn't been successful at that, either. Images of that night in the tepee taunted him—her curly black hair brushed to a glow, her two mounded breasts jutting from a white muslin nightshirt. The rest was pure imagination, but Reese was good at that.

Actually, he figured he might be a better hand at imagining than at performing. He hadn't been seriously involved with a woman since Cynthia Roland, a little affair that ended abruptly when her pa discovered Reese to be the son of the Double M Ranch foreman, rather than of the rancher who owned the spread. Reese figured he stepped over a snake with that one.

Afterward he heeded Mister Matthews's advice not to let
a female distract him from his primary goal in life—to become a rancher in his own right. Henceforth, he had limited
his romances to dancing with local girls at barn dances and
infrequent visits to trail-town bordellos, none of which had
entered his mind since two weeks ago, when he rode into
camp and discovered that he had hired Andie Dushane to do
his cooking.

She was preoccupied with supper when he arrived, bend-
ing over the fire, a lid in one hand, a long-handled spoon in
the other. Her skirts bustled up behind her, her waist curved
in, and her breasts pressed down against the taut apron bib.
Loose black curls had escaped her bun and wisped enticingly
against her nape. It hit him then that she was as dedicated
to her work as he was to his.

They were alike in that. Was that what drew him to her?
Of course, they were poles apart in a major way: She was
out to catch a husband, and he intended to sidestep every
loop cast his way.

She turned when he stepped down from the saddle, and
the unguarded welcome in her prairie green eyes set his spurs
to jangling. Try as he did to see a scheming woman in their
depths, he had yet to get past their startling beauty.

He faked composure. "See any sign of those two fellers
I told you about?"

She shook her head. "Did Monte butcher the calf?"

"He'll be along directly." Crossing to the fire, Reese took
a pot hook, lifted a lid, and dipped a spoonful of frijole juice.
His taste buds thought sure they'd died and gone to heaven.
"Mighty fine." Awkward as a spring colt and determined to
conceal it, he glanced around camp. "Did the boys take the
wagon down to the river?"

"Yes, they—"

Then he saw them. "Son of biscuit eater!" For a moment,
he was certain his mind was playing tricks on him. What the
devil was that flappin'—"What in tarnation are the boys'
long johns doin' . . ." His words trailed off. "What're
my . . ." His gaze flew to Andie's innocent expression.

"I was glad to have time to wash, Reese; those clothes had begun to smell up the wagon. Next time I'll do the bedding."

Exasperation flashed through him with the heat of a July Sunday. "Next time, hell! How'd you figure the boys are gonna feel, you handlin' their . . . their . . ." When he met her luminous green eyes, the heat inside him leaped into flame.

Confounded woman! Handling his long johns . . . His loins throbbed at the thought; he glanced back at the bush, as for confirmation. She had done it, all right. There they hung for all the world to see, holey knee and all. Flappin' in the breeze.

"Dangit, Andie, you shouldn't've . . ." Her green eyes held him, beckoned him, promised him . . . The earth rocked beneath his feet. His heart felt like it might beat itself out.

By the time he regained his senses, his hands were two inches from her shoulders. He froze. He had reached for her. His lips trembled. He had almost kissed her. He staggered backwards. Lordy! He almost played right into her scheming hands.

"I'll find the boys," he mumbled, turning toward the river even as he spoke. "Help them with the . . ." On trembling legs he headed for the river. For safety. Freedom.

Andie watched him go, mortified to her toes by her reaction to this man. And by his to her. He had almost kissed her! She had seen it in his eyes, the want, the intent. Mesmerized, she had watched him consider holding her, kissing her. A familiar, but long-forgotten yearning glowed shamefully in her stomach. She pressed both hands against her fluttering heart. He had almost kissed her and she hadn't made one move to stop him. Would she have? Could she have?

Monte arrived then with the slaughtered beef, and she set to work, grateful to have steaks to fry and meat to hang out to cool in the night air.

Come morning, she would wrap the fresh meat in cheesecloth and pack it on the wagon bed beneath a tarp. That should keep it a couple of days. Gradually her emotional equilibrium returned. Andie was good at that, stuffing her emotions back in a corner of her mind, putting on a tranquil face. But not any better than the cowboys, she discovered.

Monte was the first, after Reese, to see the clothes flapping from bushes around camp. After a couple of frowns and a shrug, he thanked her for doing his laundry and rolled his clothes and put them away wet. If she hadn't been busy chastising herself for having almost kissed Reese Catlin, she might have been more concerned about the cowboys' exposed unmentionables. As it was, she had enough on her mind without succumbing to guilt over something that had needed doing in the first place.

While she fried the steaks, Reese and the boys returned with the wagon. Reese put his clothes away, too, avoiding the campfire and lid as though they were located on the outer rim of Hades.

Pop arrived next, snaking in a load of firewood. At sight of the longjohns, his face flushed hot as the fire for which he was so ready to provide fuel.

The others drifted in then—Goosey, who was always quick to help turn the wagon after supper; Woody and Dink, who fought nightly over who would grind coffee for her.

Watching them flush and fidget, the guilt she felt over *almost* kissing Reese took its rightful place behind her regret for embarrassing these men. In two weeks, they had accepted her with a grace she would never have dreamed possible, given their shaky beginning. She had known they were hesitant to wash their own clothes, but she put it down to the chore itself, woman's work, rather than a desire for privacy.

The steaks, biscuits, and mustang grape jelly went a long way toward relaxing them, all except Grumpy.

"Beats me how womenfolk get to be so nosy," he grumbled. "Never knowd a one who'd leave a man to rest in peace." He stuffed his clean clothes down in his bedroll, and after supper, he poured a second cup of coffee at the fire and told Andie, "Next time I'll do my own washin', thank you, ma'am."

Reese sat back against a tree, stroking his mustache and watching Andie fend for herself. Even though she avoided him with obvious ease, he couldn't help looking at her. And liking what he saw. And wishing he had gone ahead and kissed her and gotten it over with. Hell, he'd been wanting to for two weeks now, ever since he burst into her tepee and looked into those innocent green eyes, and . . .

But that was the problem. She wasn't innocent; she was scheming, casting with a narrow loop, her sights set on him. And, by damn, he wasn't gettin' himself lassoed. Not by her, not by any woman. He learned early and well that an isolated ranch was no place for a woman.

His own ma died young, overworked by a well-meaning, but ignorant husband, and Reese's pa had grieved until the day they carried him to his own grave.

Mister Matthews's wife hadn't died, she picked up stakes and ran off. Matthews's reaction was opposite of Reese's pa's.

"Good riddance!" he'd told his foreman. Matthews maintained that for a man to be a rancher of any note, he had to shy away from a double harness, and Reese intended to be the best dang rancher in Texas. But one kiss? What harm could one little kiss do?

As though she heard his thoughts, Andie glanced his way. Their gazes held; Reese began to feel like a too-tight saddle cinch had a stranglehold on his chest. She turned away first, but not before telltale blotches sprouted on her cheeks.

When their gazes collided, Andie's heart raced out of control. She had felt him watching her all evening, but until she met his eyes, she hadn't known what he was thinking. Now she knew. His heated expression was hot enough to sizzle the grease in which she fried bear sign.

No man had ever looked at her that way—except Samuel. No man had ever set her head to reeling and her heart to racing this way—except Samuel.

Samuel, her husband. Samuel, who had loved her long and well. Samuel, to whom she owed loyalty and honor and respect. She couldn't let him lie in that cold grave while she carried on with another man. She wouldn't.

Finished with the bear sign, she emptied them in a crock and tossed them with sugar and cinnamon. "Wait until they cool," she called to the group, "then help yourselves."

"Told you they wouldn't like it none," Night Hawk observed, heading for the horse herd. "Save some bear sign for me."

She worked quickly, anxious to finish her chores and retire before her distress over offending these men turned to guilt, before she inadvertently met Reese's gaze again.

Hank and Jordan helped her wash dishes, like other nights, and Goosey helped turn the wagon tongue toward the North Star, but the silence around camp was anything but ordinary. Although Dink ground coffee, it was without arguing with Woody. Andie wondered whether the men had flipped for the chore, and Dink lost. The peppermint stick wrapped inside each Arbuckles package likely wasn't enough pay for the embarrassment she had caused. Somehow, Andie vowed, she would make it up to them. Somehow—in addition to never touching their clothes again.

She was so engrossed in finishing her chores without drawing attention to herself, that when Tom Lovejoy stepped around the back of the wagon, he startled her.

"Tom! What—?"

His blue eyes danced with mischief. "Any lady who'd wash the smelly ol' clothes of a dozen smelly men deserves something sweet." With a flourish, he produced a bouquet of wildflowers.

"Why, Tom . . ." She buried her nose in the flowers, then cast about to find a jug to put them in. That's when she saw Reese.

He jumped to his feet and headed for the chuckbox with long strides. "What in tarnation're you doin', Lovejoy, traipsin' around out there in the dark? You want t' frighten the dang herd?"

Tom grinned. "Figured someone oughta thank Cookie for her trouble. Why, she washed our clothes, an' cooked us big steaks, an' fried up a batch of bear sign.'' He dipped into the crock of hot doughnuts, pulled one out, and took a bite. ''Man alive!'' His face beamed with delight. ''If these things won't satisfy a sweet tooth, son . . .'' Draping his free arm around Andie's shoulders, he grinned at Reese. ''I figure I know somethin' that will.''

Reese's eyes spit fire. ''Tom Lovejoy, if you don't want to lose your job in the next two minutes, unhand our cook.''

His anger took Andie by surprise. ''Tom didn't mean—'' Reese ignored her.

''I've been waitin' for you to make some damn fool move like this. For the last time, unhand our cook.''

Andie ducked out of Tom's embrace. ''Time for me to turn in.''

But Tom wasn't through. Adding insult to injury he winked at her. ''Don't let an ornery ol' trail boss scare you, Cookie. You've got as much say so around here as him.''

Andie cast a wary eye to Reese, who glared at Tom; she looked to Tom, who exuded mischief. Eager to escape this standoff, she called to the group in general, ''The bear sign are cool now. Come an' get 'em.''

Finally, in a gesture she later recognized as one of defiance, she picked up the wildflowers. Ignoring Reese, she smiled at Tom. ''Thanks for the flowers, Tom. They're beautiful.'' When she headed for her tepee, inspiration struck.

''They're just a bunch of flowers,'' Lovejoy objected to the disgruntled trail boss. ''There's plenty more where they came from. If it riles you for me to give 'em to her, go out an' pick 'er a bunch, yourself.''

''Mind your own damned business.'' Reese knew he was acting the fool. He had known it all the way across camp, known it when he confronted Lovejoy, and he knew it now. But he couldn't help himself. And when he got in a mood like this, it was time to make himself scarce.

Tossing the dregs of his coffee in the fire, he swished his cup in the wrecking pan and dried it off. Behind him the men were beginning to return to normal, what with Andie out of sight.

Goosey tuned up his fiddle with a melody that was a favorite of many a cowboy, "Green Grow the Lilacs." Which was all right, until Gimpy and Grumpy broke out in song.

> Green grow the lilacs, all sparkling with dew,
> I'm lonely my darling, since parting with you.

Reese ignored them, or tried to; Dink and Monte joined to finish the verse:

> I used to have a sweetheart, but now I have none,
> For she loves another one better than me.

Reese headed for his bedroll. But he hadn't taken two steps when Jordan approached him from the wagon tongue, where he had been watching Pop braid a rawhide reata by the lantern light.

"Say, Mister Catlin . . ." The kid's innocent voice gave no hint of bedevilment. "I've been wonderin' 'bout something."

"What's that?" Reese noticed how Jordan glanced back to Pop, but still he didn't suspect a trap.

"That harness you've been mending, sir? I wonder now, is it a double?"

Reese blanched. Behind him, Tom Lovejoy whooped. The rest of the cowboys chimed in. All except the musicians, whose rendition of "Green Grow the Lilacs," gained momentum.

> I passed my love's window both early and late,
> The look that she gave me, it made my heart ache.

Reese grew hot under the collar. Time he put a stop to this nonsense. "Come on, Jordan. Let's you an' me go for a little walk down by the river."

When they were out of earshot, he began by asking,

"What happened to your pa, Jordan?" In typical fashion, the boy was ready with a mature account.

"Doc Wilson never did know exactly what it was. Ma called it the fever. Pa just got weaker an' weaker, till he couldn't even climb up in his saddle. Finally he couldn't get out of bed. Then, after quite a spell, he died."

"An' your ma's looking for a new husband?"

"Oh, no sir. Truth is, she don't want anyone new. She jumped all over me for what me an' Uncle Kipp did. Why, I doubt she'll ever speak to Uncle Kipp again. Me bein' her son an' all, I got off a tad lighter."

Reese considered the boy's claim. Could it be true? Was Andie innocent of the scheme? Or was Jordan a first-rate con artist?

"So, what is it, then? You lookin' for a new pa?"

"No, sir. Well, not really. I mean, I'd be happy to have a man around the place, but I'm the one looking for a husband for my ma. Me an' Uncle Kipp."

Reese hadn't expected such an honest reply. He squinted through the darkness to read Jordan's expression. The kid was dead-serious, or appeared to be. Off to the side, the river lapped gently against the bank. In the distance, a bullfrog karoomped. Deep inside Reese, warning bells sounded. Jordan continued.

"Ranchin's almighty hard work for a woman, sir. I reckon it's lonely for anybody, bein' so far from neighbors an' all. Ma needs someone, Mister Catlin. Other'n me. I hate seein' her lonely."

Reese cleared his throat of a sudden obstruction. "So you picked me?"

"Me an' Uncle Kipp, yes sir, we did."

"I see. Well, Jordan, I'll have to admit I'm flattered. Your ma's as handsome a woman as I've seen, and you're a fine boy. Any man I know would be honored to have you for a son. But these things are generally left to a man and a woman. To be honest, I'm not in the market for a wife. I've got a ranch to put together. Leastways, I hope I will have, once we get back from Wichita."

"You figuring on buying that ranch?" Jordan asked.

Deciding his little sermon had produced the desired effect, Reese turned them toward the campfire. His mouth fairly watered for some of Andie's bear sign.

Jordan grabbed at a firefly and missed. "You think you're gonna like livin' out there all by yourself?"

"I'll like it. I've lived on that ranch most of my life, Jordan. I know what I'm getting into."

"Maybe so, sir. Then, again, maybe you're gonna be as lonesome and miserable as Ma. A big ranch like that, with no woman to cook you sweet things or make your house smell fresh or dance around under the stars with you or give you the sweetest goodnight kisses this side of heaven."

Reese stumbled, caught his balance, and realized without being told that the boy's sights were still set dead ahead— on him. On his freedom, anyhow. But what about Andie's sights? Reese wasn't so sure anymore. He cursed himself for a fool.

Dance under the stars, huh?

"Look, Mister Catlin! Ma's flowers."

Reese glanced down to see that he had stumbled over a bedroll. Hell, Andie had scattered the dang things several rods across the prairie. Well, maybe not that far, but . . .

Then he saw the flower. One long-stemmed daisy, lying at the head of the bedroll. He glanced right and left, and sure enough. She had distributed Lovejoy's flowers among the cowboys. A flower on each bedroll. A hell of a way to apologize.

Reaching his own bedding, he knelt on the ground and picked up the daisy, smelled it. Was Jordan right? Was he destined for a life of loneliness and misery?

And was Jordan further right? Could a warm and sweet thing like Andie Dushane cure those ills?

If he could have one wish tonight, it would be that Andie Dushane was not involved in her son's matchmaking scheme. But who was he to believe? How would he ever know for sure? And dang him! Why did he care? He wasn't in the market for a wife.

* * *

In the days that followed, Reese tried to ignore the suggestion Jordan had planted in his brain, but he wasn't very successful. Every time he looked at Andie he thought about the ranch he had coveted since childhood and dang if he didn't feel a twinge of loneliness.

Loneliness. That's what women were supposed to feel. Men were loners, according to Mister Matthews.

In the following weeks Reese spent less time in camp and more time wishing he were there. Andie filled his thoughts and his dreams and had become his biggest concern. He should have kissed her when he had the chance, he argued. Then it would be over and done with, and he could get back to worrying about making it to Wichita ahead of the crowd.

"Make a list of supplies you need," he advised her a couple of weeks later. He had ridden into camp early, after he finally came up with a real reason for talking to her, rather than the excuses that grew like weeds in his fertile imagination.

At least he thought he had a reason until he lost his train of thought somewhere in the depths of her green eyes. "We'll reach Fort Worth in a few days," he finally managed to explain.

He had caught her kneading dough, which she continued to do, as though unaffected by his presence. "Then it's time for our discussion, Reese."

That knocked him for a loop. "Discussion? About what?" *Had he been that easy to read*?

"Whether you intend to keep me on as cook all the way to Wichita. If not, Jordan and I might as well leave the herd at Fort Worth. It'd be a lot safer than Red River Station."

"Leave you?" Reese's mind spun. He remembered the conversation, but it had taken place so long ago. A lifetime ago.

Trail drives had a way of doing that to a feller. After a few weeks, the drive took on a life of its own. The outside world ceased to exist. Every drive was different; every drive had an atmosphere of its own.

He studied the black-haired woman who was on his mind day and night these days. She was the atmosphere of this drive. Sweet, yet firm. Gentle, but in control. Undemanding, yet commanding the respect of every drover in camp. And that was before you even got to the myriad ways she fascinated and distracted him.

"Dangit, Andie, we couldn't make it to Wichita without you."

Her green eyes fired a slow burn inside him. "I hoped you would feel that way. This has been a rare experience. I feel, well, sort of responsible for the men."

He stroked one side of his mustache, watched her pinch off biscuits and put them in Dutch ovens. For the life of him he couldn't think of anything to reply that wouldn't get him in a peck of trouble. Was she in on that damned scheme or not?

He made a point of studying the campfire coals, hoping to conceal his rattled senses. "Closer to town, I want you to keep an eye out for some fellers who'll likely come out to camp."

She mistook his meaning by a country mile. "You worry too much, Reese. We won't fall prey to unsavory characters, especially not with Night Hawk along."

"Hell, Andie! If I didn't think that, I'd be drivin' this rig myself." She went about covering up the biscuits as though she hadn't turned his world upside down. He tried to concentrate on business. "I'm talking about a man by the name of Edwin Howell. Matthews was supposed to write and ask him to meet with me, somethin' about investin' in the ranch."

"That's wonderful!" The smile she turned on him was genuine and earth-shattering. "Then it wouldn't matter whether we got to Wichita first."

He was standing way too close to her, but when he tried to move away, his feet refused to oblige. "It'll matter. First herd in brings the best prices. I want to use as much of my own money as I can to buy that ranch. I don't like bein' beholden."

A wistful look touched her eyes, making her, if that were possible, even more tempting. "Samuel felt that way, too."

"Samuel?"

"My husband."

"Oh." Reese didn't know what to say. For some fool reason, he felt uncomfortable, hearing her talk about a husband, dead or otherwise. "Jordan said he took his own time dyin'," he offered, "that it was hard on you."

"It was harder on him. But then death is always hard."

"How long's it been?"

"Two years."

Two years. Reese turned away, lest she see the relief—stupid though it was—that flooded him. Two years was time enough to grieve and get on with one's life.

Wiping her hands on a damp towel, Andie studied him covertly. His jaw bulged with the grim set of his teeth. Uneasiness splotched his sun-bronzed cheeks. He had been away from camp more often than not lately, and she realized quite suddenly that she had missed him.

Missed the way he looked at her when he thought she wasn't aware of it; missed her heart quickening when he quirked his eyebrow in response to something she did that surprised him.

She had missed him, and she felt guilty for every minute of it, for she should have been missing Samuel. *Two years.*

"You must have loved him." He spoke with his back to her.

"I still do."

He glanced over his shoulder, capturing her gaze. She wanted to look away, but unspoken questions held her.

"He was a lucky man," he said at length, striking the very heart of her guilt.

"Lucky? He died! A cruel and horrible death."

"But he still has your love."

Her breath caught. She tore her gaze away, confused. She picked up a cuptowel, folded it, pressed the creases against the top of the lid with her fingers. Of course Samuel still had her love. He was her husband.

But he had died. He left her. Alone.

And lonely.

And it had been two years. *Two years.* She glanced up. Reese had turned and was watching her. Her pulse throbbed in her throat. Moments passed.

He recovered first. "So, is this the first time Jordan's tried to pair you up?"

"Pair me . . ." Abashed, she caught her cheeks in her hands.

"Don't let it bother you." Fighting the compulsion to take her in his arms, he strove to sound flippant. "I'm not."

"You're not the merchandise being offered, either."

Without a thought, he pulled her hands away from her face and held them. "Dangit, Andie, you're not merchandise."

Their gazes held. Spread by the warmth of their clasped hands, the yearning became physical. Reason fled; his body trembled with anticipation, too long held in check. He dipped his head.

His lips barely grazed hers, before Andie came to her senses. She ducked, swirled away, but when she would have fled across the campsite, her feet failed her.

Reese caught her arm.

"I'm not out to catch a husband, Reese Catlin," she whispered in a tight voice.

Long moments passed in silence, while he retained a death-grip on her arm and her heart raced out of control.

When finally he spoke, his voice was low and equally strained. "I don't care if you are."

He might as well have dunked her in an icy cold spring. Any heat she felt now was fury. Jerking free, she spun to face him. At the last minute she restrained herself from slapping his bewildered face. "Get out of my sight, Reese Catlin. Just get out of my sight."

They arrived outside Fort Worth three days later. Reese had made himself scarce after their altercation at the chuck wagon, and Andie thought, good riddance! Or she tried to think it. How could she lose her heart to a pigheaded man who thought she was stupid enough to want to drag him to the altar?

The wretched incident had served one purpose, bittersweet, though it was. Andie came to a realization about her own life. Two years was enough time to grieve. For Jordan's sake, she must try to put the past behind her. Day by day now, seeing him with the cowboys, she was aware how much he needed a man in his life. Not to take the place of his pa, but as a companion and role model. And Reese was so good with him. But there she always stopped in panic—pigheaded Reese Catlin, a role model for her son?

By midday the cattle were settled down, leaving the cowboys freer than usual for much of the afternoon. Monte was the first to come into camp to seek her medical attention.

"Caught my thumb in a rope, Cookie. Figured you could dab it with some of that liniment you keep up yonder." He nodded toward the chuck box, where a bottle of whiskey intended for medicinal use had remained unopened since the drive began.

She struggled to keep a straight face. "Whiskey won't do much for a rope burn, Monte. How 'bout a little bacon grease, instead?"

Woody was the next to arrive; he hedged until Monte was out of earshot, then admitted, "Figured we might have a chance to mail letters, bein' so close to Fort Worth."

Andie guessed the source of his uneasiness. "I used to write letters for my husband. Could I help?"

"Why, ma'am, that'd be mighty handy. My penmanship, well, it ain't . . . what I mean is, I'd like to impress the lady with my intelligence an' not the lack of it."

Those chores taken care of, Monte and Woody rode off together, only to return a short time later in the company of a couple of men wearing store suits.

"Run into these drummers, Cookie." Woody winked. "Give 'em that supply list I asked you to draw up."

By now Andie was well acquainted with pranks pulled on a trail drive. Lordy, was she ever! From shortening someone's rope to putting sand or even snake skins in a bedroll, nothing was off limits when it came to joshing a fellow drover. Each man competed to see who could outwit, outfox, or generally get the best of his compadres.

So she wasn't surprised when Woody pretended to be the trail boss. And since Reese had ridden back down the trail with Night Hawk to check on the location of the Sutton herd, she didn't see any harm in going along with the prank.

She handed over the list, then promptly forgot it. Not long after that two other gentlemen, emissaries of Edwin Howell, arrived with a dinner invitation for Reese.

Andie went about preparing supper, paying little attention. The drummers left for town, followed shortly by Mister Howell's men. By the time Reese rode into camp later that afternoon, however, the drummers were back. Andie invited them to supper and went on with her chores. Then just before she called the crew to eat, Reese approached her with a package wrapped in brown paper. His open grin was unexpected and did things to her insides that she strove to conceal.

"From the boys," he explained.

Her hands trembled when she dried them on her apron. What mischief were the cowboys up to this time? Taking the package, she tore back one edge. *Yellow muslin. And lace.*

"Seems they put their money where their mouths have been all this time. They've joined Jordan's campaign."

As though it were a poker straight from the fire, she shoved the package back to Reese.

"Open it, Andie. The boys expect you to."

She scanned the cowboys who watched her with expectant expressions and faces as flushed as the sky at sunset—exactly the way she felt inside. Her hands were still trembling when she tore open the package and pulled out a yellow frock. "What—?" Her eyes found Reese's.

"You're to wear it to Howell's dinner."

"Howell's dinner?" she echoed.

"You're to come with me. Whether Woody ferreted the invitation, or whether, as he says, Howell's men took one look at you and invited you on their own, doesn't really matter."

"It certainly does." Indignation vied with confusion. She scanned the cowboys, whose eyes were riveted on her and Reese. "Where did . . . ? How did they—?"

"Charged it to my account and told me to deduct it from their wages in Wichita. That's why the drummers came back."

"Their wages?" Stunned, she didn't know what to say. She fingered the soft fabric. She couldn't go, but oh my . . .

"It's not unusual." Reese quirked that distracting eyebrow and her pulse rate doubled. "I mean chargin' expenses to the drive and deducting 'em from wages at the end. Buyin' a dress, now, that's a horse of a different color."

"I can't go, Reese. It's a business dinner. It's too important to you."

"You think I could concentrate on business, knowin' I'd left the prettiest gal in Texas home with those cowpokes?"

She clung to control by a gossamer thread. "I can't—"

"You'll be makin' a lot of cowboys mighty unhappy."

Tempted, oh so tempted, still, she resisted. "No—"

"Startin' with me." His eyes held her mesmerized, like that first night in her tepee.

That gossamer thread bound her to him. *Do it, Andie. Do it.*

"Run get dressed," Reese was saying. "We'll have to pull out within the hour to make it."

"But, what . . ." *Do it, Andie. It's a dinner invitation, not a marriage proposal, for heaven's sake.*

Oh, Samuel . . .

Do it!

She dropped her gaze to the dress. "If we're riding horseback, I'd better carry the dress and change there."

"We aren't. Edwin Howell's sendin' his carriage."

An hour later Andie emerged from her tepee light-headed and faint of heart. She had rushed through a bath taken behind a wagon sheet Night Hawk and Jordan hung on limbs that shielded a quiet pool of water. She scrubbed her fingernails and tried to wash camp smoke out of her hair and guilt out of her heart.

Oh, Samuel! What am I doing? What am I doing?

Towel-drying her hair never worked; it left it full and curly. But she had no choice. They couldn't be late. This dinner was too important to Reese. Too important. She shouldn't be going.

Still resisting the idea, she finished dressing and stepped into the camp circle, only to have the drovers jump to their feet like they were in church. Embarrassed to her toes, she obligingly lifted her skirts and twirled once. She felt like a schoolgirl just out of pigtails with a dozen papas to worry over her.

"Thank you. It's lovely, and so are you. Everyone of you."

It was their turn to blush, and they did so in unison. She scanned the group, thanking each man individually, until her wandering eyes alighted on Reese. The sight of him in black broadcloth suit, white shirt, and string tie, took her breath away. He wore polished boots and carried a black Stetson, obviously brought along for a special occasion; his heated perusal left no doubt that he considered this the special occasion.

What was she getting herself into?

When Pop produced a bouquet of yellow daisies, she squeezed back tears. Then Tom Lovejoy, ever one to throw a wrench in things, stepped close.

"Ain't it just my luck? The prettiest gal in Texas, an' she's goin' out with another feller." Plucking a daisy from the bouquet, he stuck it into curls she had pinned on top of her head.

Standing back, his blue eyes twinkled. "Don't mess with it, Mister Catlin. Leastways not till after that fancy dinner you're takin' her to."

Andie ducked her head. Jordan was there, at her side, his eyes round as saucers. "You look awful pretty, Ma." His attention went to Reese. "Don't she, Mister Catlin?"

"You got that right, son." Reese's voice was strained, but

it echoed the awe in Jordan's. Andie didn't dare look at him.

"'Before you come back, Ma, maybe Mister Catlin will dance with you under the stars.''

"Jordan!'' Suddenly she knew she had to get away from these well-meaning, but joke-loving men and a child who thought he had found himself a pa. "Shouldn't we be on our way?'' Her question was more like a plea, one Reese readily accepted.

Injunctions followed them out of camp.

"Behave yourself, Mister Catlin.''

"Don't keep 'er out past dawn!''

Grumpy followed them to the carriage. "A word o' warning,'' he told Reese. "Since you claim not be the marryin' kind, just, well, you know what I mean. Treat her right.''

The sun had set by the time they pulled up to the carved stone portico of Howell's mansion in Fort Worth, but dwindling light did nothing to diminish the grandeur of the place, nor Andie's jitters. "I shouldn't have let you talk me into this.''

"I need you along, Andie.'' Reese squeezed her hand when he helped her down from the carriage. "Lookin' at you takes my mind off bein' nervous.''

They had barely exchanged glances on the ride to town, and she couldn't meet his eyes now, with guilt worrying her mind and anticipation burning in her stomach.

But as things turned out, she enjoyed herself. The meal was delicious—breast of veal glacé, creamy potatoes, and garden vegetables. A butler served glasses of sherry before dinner. After pecan cake and coffee, Verna Howell excused the men for brandy and cigars, and, Andie hoped, a discussion of business.

Verna was a lovely, congenial woman, of an age Andie's mother would be were she still alive. She talked freely of her children, her grandchildren, her friends, and Fort Worth society. By the time Reese and Edwin Howell rejoined them, Andie was fit to be tied. Fortunately, Reese made excuses and they left soon after.

"Well?'' she questioned before the carriage cleared the

drive. Her tensions of earlier had given way to concern for Reese's business. "Don't keep me in suspense. How did it go?"

Reese applied the quirt, setting the matched team on the road back to camp. "I'd give my eyeteeth to know what Matthews wrote Howell about me. If I hadn't known better, I might've thought he was tryin' to sell me on takin' him on as a partner, rather than the other way around."

Relieved, Andie clapped her hands. "That's wonderful!"

They left the dusty cowtown behind. The moon was full and the air soft and fresh. She had become so accustomed to dust and the smell of cattle, she rarely thought about fresh air. Tonight the air seemed perfumed by comparison.

"Another funny thing," Reese mused after a while. "I got the impression Howell thinks you're part of the deal."

Her breath caught. "Me?" *What had the cowboys done now?*

"He kept sayin' how important it is to have a good woman to help build an empire. Said he couldn't have accomplished near what he has without his Verna's being willing to work like a slave—those were his very words—until they got things goin'. Said he owed all he is and all he has to her."

"What a lovely tribute." But it wasn't so much Mister Howell's words as it was Reese's interpretation that set Andie's head to spinning. She tried to scoff it off. "I'm sure most men would say the same thing."

When she felt his eyes on her, her jitters returned. Already her arms burned with his nearness, and the back of her neck tingled. She felt like a schoolgirl riding beside her beau. She immediately chastised herself.

"You didn't know Mister Matthews," Reese was saying.

Grateful for the impersonal topic, she plunged in. "He didn't like his wife?"

"Until she ran off, I reckon. He claims a wife is the sorriest thing a man can have on a ranch."

"The nerve of him! No wonder she left."

Reese chuckled and the sound tripped down her spine. When he spoke again, however, he was serious. "I always thought the moon and stars hung on Matthews's words.''

"No man is right all the time. Or woman, either."

"I'm beginning to see that."

"Then Mister Howell accomplished something far more valuable tonight than financial assistance."

"Actually, a much younger man set me to wonderin'," he replied, ignoring her sarcasm. "Jordan Dushane."

"Jordan?" Caught off guard, she dropped her gaze and nervously reached to tuck a curl behind her ear. Of a sudden Reese captured her hand. She tugged; he tugged.

"I'm just trying to hold your hand, Andie."

"Why?" Already his hand had warmed places inside her that hadn't been touched in years.

"Because you're a beautiful woman and I'm ..." He squeezed her hand and she sat helpless, enjoying it, hating it, confused.

"I'm attracted to you." His voice was tight, as though his chest were as constricted as her own.

"To me?" She jerked free. "A husband-hunting hussy."

"Hussy? I never said—"

"You thought it."

"I did not."

"Don't deny it, Reese. You thought I wrangled this job to snare a husband, namely you."

"Maybe so, but I never thought you were a hussy."

"There, you said it. You think I'm out to—"

"Not any more."

His voice had lowered; he sounded sincere and all the more threatening for it. "What changed your mind?" she asked at length.

"You."

"Don't expect me to believe that." But her heart wanted to.

"I've seen your problem before."

"My problem?" she asked, wary.

"Lived with the same thing most of my life. My ma died when I was young, and Pa never stopped loving her."

"That's wrong?"

"It's wrong to grieve your life away. Pa did that, an' everyone around him suffered. Way I see it, the Man Upstairs gives us one chance at life, and He doesn't promise it'll be a bed of roses."

"I know that."

"He expects us to make the best of things. When difficulties come along, we can't get bogged down in 'em. We have to use them for steppin' stones to something good."

"You're quite the philosopher."

"Nope. Just a man who was a kid one time. The Lord took my ma an' Pa spent the rest of his life wishin' he'd gone with her."

She didn't know how to respond. Without warning, he had opened his heart and let her see the boy inside and she wondered why. What was he asking of her? Before she could question his motives further, he startled her with an abrupt demand.

"Tell me about Samuel."

"Samuel?" She recoiled at bringing ugly memories into this starlit night. But Reese persisted until she relented. "He was sick a long time. He suffered. A lot."

"I didn't ask about his illness. What was he like before? What did he look like?"

"Jordan," she answered simply, because it was true, not because she remembered. "Jordan's a lot like his pa."

"Fair?"

She nodded.

"How big a man was he?"

"Big? I . . . uh . . . He wasted away."

"From what?" The question was simple—and devastating.

She turned to Reese, stricken. "I don't know. I can't remember. I mean . . . I know he laughed a lot, but I can't hear the sound. I know he was tall, but I can't picture him as a well man." She lifted her face to the star-studded sky. "All I remember is the end. He suffered so long."

Silence stretched between them. She regretted her outburst. She had never talked about these things before. That she had now confused her. Then Reese took her by surprise again.

"If you can't remember him, how can you still love him?"

Anger sped to her rescue. "Because he's my husband!"

"He's dead."

Moonlight glinted off the cold surface of Reese's brown eyes, and in that instant she hated him. She swung away, sat stiffly, stared over the horse's rumps. *The nerve of him! The absolute nerve of him!*

He didn't pursue the topic, and they continued down the road in silence. Starlight glinted off the harness leathers and off the polished surface of the carriage. The country was hilly, the road bouncy, and her senses began to cool. Reese's shoulder bumped hers from time to time. Lifted by the gentle breeze, the soft yellow muslin of her skirt billowed over his leg. His masculinity weighed heavily on her mind—his heady, musky scent, his warm chocolate eyes, his robust, healthy body.

Why, oh why couldn't she picture Samuel tall and masculine and healthy? When finally Reese spoke again, his tone was contrite.

"Mad at me?"

"No."

"You can tell me to mind my own business if you want."

She squeezed back tears. "I've never talked about it before."

"Maybe it wasn't time . . . before."

She pondered his meaning. After a while, she admitted, "It's bothered me for a long time. I can't picture him like he was. It's as if he never existed, except as a dying man."

"Maybe you have to find something to live for, before you can let go of those bad times."

"I have something to live for—Jordan."

"For yourself, Andie."

He fell silent after that, and she thought about all he'd said. She was seeing a different side of Reese Catlin tonight. His toughness and compassion made a powerful combination. "You surprise me," she said.

"How's that?"

"Your insight."

He chuckled. "Cowboys have an advantage in that department. With only our horses for company, we tend to think more than most folks." He glanced her way. "Comes in handy, time to time. No offense?"

"No."

Suddenly she realized he had guided the carriage off the road. She watched him set the brake. "What are you doing?"

He chuckled and the sound tripped down her spine. "You think I'd head back to camp without dancin' with you under the stars?"

"Oh, no. I can't." When he rounded the carriage and offered his hand, she refused it. "Please, Reese. No."

"Jordan won't like it if I don't dance with you under the stars."

"That boy." Her voice caught in her throat.

"Come on." His tone was light; he sounded harmless. When she still hesitated, he tugged on her elbow until it was either climb down or be pulled off the seat, or so she told herself.

Even after her feet touched the ground, he held her, still as a heart beat. Moonlight glinted from his eyes; she ducked her head, too conscious of his hands on her waist.

"Please." She stood frozen in place by a mushrooming sense of alarm. "No, Reese. Please."

"Just one dance," he urged. Moving into dance position, he pressed the flat of his palm against her back. She tried not to think about it, but couldn't stop.

His nearness overwhelmed her. It thrilled down her spine like hot fingers. She trembled and her legs grew weak. She felt his gaze on her face but dared not look up. Instead she focused on a shadow that wisped across his neck. *Get it over with*, she thought. *Just get it over with.*

"What do you do for music?" he asked, ignoring her resistance.

"Jordan hums," she mumbled.

"That figures. What tune?"

She swallowed her trepidation. *Get it over with.* " 'Skip
to My Lou.' "

Reese chuckled and again the motion buffeted her senses
like a gusting summer breeze. "How 'bout 'Green Grow the
Lilacs?' " he suggested and immediately started humming.
His enthusiasm undiminished by her objections, he swept her
around the prairie, skirting prickly pear and rocks, she with
stiff spine and locked knees, until finally the song ended.

Relief surged through her. But when she tried to pull
away, he held her fast, changed tunes, and danced her in a
wider circle, ever faster and faster.

She had no choice but to match his long stride. He sang
this time, full-throated, and she felt as if she were drowning
in agony.

> Did you ever hear tell of sweet Betsy from Pike,
> Who crossed the wide prairies with her lover Ike,

"Come on, Andie, sing."

> With two yoke of cattle and one spotted hog,
> A tall Shanghai rooster, an old yaller dog?

Suddenly, without design, she glanced up, looking him full
in the face for the first time. What prompted her to do it, she
couldn't say, curiosity, perhaps, or desperation. He was grinning broadly. And he was so handsome, he took her breath
away. Strangely, she felt herself relax. He was a good dancer,
smooth even on the rough ground. She felt light of foot, as
if they danced on moonbeams.

Or among the stars, she thought, for the sky was clear and
the stars looked close enough for them to reach up and grab
a handful. There must have been a million stars. They glittered from the pupils of his hazel eyes and glanced off the
planes of his high cheekbones, burnishing his familiar sun-
burned skin to a pink glow.

"Having fun now?" He laughed, and the sound settled

over her, soothing her ragged emotions, filling her with joy. *Joy.* She laughed in return.

As she gazed upon his handsome face, a shooting star fell behind him. It seemed to lodge on the blond lock that always hung over his forehead. She reached to brush it away. Instead of hair, she grabbed a handful of stardust. Then she saw him. *Samuel.*

Do it, Andie. Laugh. Dance.

But you need me.

No. I'm no longer sick. Can't you see?

Yes, but . . .

As if it were a mask being lifted by the star, the image of Samuel's healthy face drifted heavenward. He smiled down at her.

Good-bye, Andie. Be happy.

"Andie! What is it?"

She shook her head and focused on Reese Catlin's face.

"What's wrong?"

Reaching, she touched his dark mustache, stroked it. No stardust there. Only soft, silky hair.

"What's wrong?" he asked again.

Dazed, she tried to shake off the feelings that gripped her, then wondered why. They were wonderful feelings. "I remembered something," she said by way of explanation.

"Must have been good." His eyes caressed her face. They were filled with concern and more—a yearning so intense, so raw, it sent a shiver down her back.

"Yes," she said, because something sweet and begging had lodged in her throat and prevented her saying more.

Still his eyes held hers. "I'd never heard you laugh before. I thought you were laughing at my singing." His husky voice echoed the yearning that spread like wildfire inside her. When he pulled her forward, she gave no thought to resisting.

Mesmerized, she watched his lips descend. "I love your singing."

If she had thought the magic of the evening was over, she would have been wrong, for when Reese's lips touched hers, she felt like the shooting star had landed in her head. He must have felt it, too, for he drew back mere inches. Wonder filled his eyes.

He threaded his fingers through her hair and traced the rough pads of his thumbs across her lips.

"Dangit, Andie. I've wanted to kiss you for so long."

Through the fog in her brain she realized that he was waiting for her consent. Her hands slid up his chest and around his neck and then she was in his arms.

His lips opened over hers in a kiss so wet and sensual she felt lost in it. She had heard about stars colliding in outer space, about great rivers plummeting over mountains in powerful rushes of water, but until Reese Catlin pressed her body to his and released her passion with the force of his own, she had not known such power truly existed.

It was as if the heavens had fallen on their shoulders and sprinkled them with glowing promises, promises as old as the stars, yet as new as an early spring morning. She knew without thinking that this was what she had longed for and craved and despaired of ever feeling again; at the same time, it was something totally new, never before imagined or experienced.

When they stopped for air, they were both breathing heavily.

"Dangit, Andie. What'd you do to me?"

"It wasn't me."

"You bet it was." He looked dazed. "I feel like you clobbered me with a dang star."

Weaving her fingers through his hair, she drew his face down for another heart-rending, soul-healing kiss.

This time when Reese drew back to study her face, she could see his yearning, still raw and unrequited. His voice was low and husky.

"I won't ask what you remembered tonight, but I'm a lucky man for it."

Too soon it was time to return to camp. Back in the carriage Reese held her close. Neither spoke until camp was in sight.

"We need to talk about what happened tonight," he said. She snuggled closer. "It was magic."

"Like hell, it was. I don't want you wakin' up tomorrow and pretendin' it never happened."

She watched him long seconds, while the passion of the evening turned to something else. Something she couldn't name—or wasn't ready to confront.

"I know it happened," she told him quietly.

Then they arrived. Reese drew rein in the darkness of a thicket beyond the camp circle. The strains of Goosey's fiddle let them know the men were awake. Alarmed, she envisioned facing the cowboys. "They'll know."

Reese set the brake and turned to her with a chuckle. "They'd figure it out quick enough, anyhow."

"How?" She worked to repin her hair.

"By the smitten look on my face." He tugged her arms around his neck. "Since that son of yours has been right about everything else, let me put one more thing to the test."

"Oh, dear. What now?"

"That you give the sweetest goodnight kisses this side of heaven."

She was still trembling when he handed her down from the carriage and escorted her toward the tepee. They didn't make it all the way, however, for the drovers suddenly burst into song.

> Frog-y went a-courtin', he did ride, Ah-ha, Ah-ha,
> A sword and pistol by his side, Ah-ha, Ah-ha.

Reese squeezed her shoulders. "I think I liked 'Green Grow the Lilacs' better." But the concert wasn't over.

> Where will the weddin' supper be? Ah-ha, Ah-ha,
> Where will the weddin' supper be? Ah-ha, Ah-ha.

Andie laughed to cover her embarrassment. "If I didn't know better, I'd think someone had gotten into my medicine box."

"Us?" the cowboys quizzed in unison.

Racing to her side, Jordan wedged himself between her and Reese. "Did he dance with you in the moonlight, Ma? I told him it was your most favorite thing."

Would she die of embarrassment? She knelt quickly and hugged Jordan to her chest. "What am I going to do with you?"

Reese hunkered down beside them. "I think what your ma means is what would we ever have done without you?"

"You did dance with her! Boy, oh boy! Did you hum 'Skip to My Lou?' It's her favorite."

Reese chuckled, while Andie flushed, and the drovers hung on every word.

"You'll have to leave some things to me, son." Reese found Andie's eyes. "Your ma and I danced to our own kind of music."

In that moment, Andie knew she had come full circle, from happiness, through grief, to indescribable joy. If the drovers hadn't been hovering over them, she would have thrown her arms around this man. But the drovers were there, so she kissed Jordan on the forehead and discreetly bid Reese and the others goodnight.

When she crawled in bed, her body still glowed with the discoveries of this night—and with anticipation of all the discoveries yet to come. She drifted off to sleep with a smile on her lips and a grateful heart. *Thank you, Samuel.*

But in the days to come, she began to fear that night had been magical for her alone. Beginning the following morning, Reese made himself scarce around camp. Although he still watched over her with an eagle eye, except for a few stolen kisses, he acted like that night had never happened.

Andie had not forgotten it. Magical or not, it freed her of her guilt over abandoning Samuel. Whether she had truly seen his healthy face and heard his laughter didn't matter; she now remembered them. Remembering set her free; and freed, her feelings for Reese Catlin ran rampant. Regardless that he didn't appear to feel the same for her.

Worn down by Jordan's persistence and Reese's claim that

it was as safe as riding on the wagon seat, Andie capitulated, and Jordan began riding drag the day after they crossed the Red River. She didn't like it, but Reese was right. She couldn't keep him a child forever.

The wind picked up daily, blowing so hard on occasion that she had trouble keeping the wagon on course. She didn't fear getting lost, however, for Reese insisted she drive closer to the herd now that they were in Indian Territory.

One morning she had passed the point men headed for the nooning place, when Tom Lovejoy caught up with her.

"Hey, Cookie, pull up quick!"

When Tom came close enough for her to see his pained expression, her heart leapt to her throat. "What's the matter?"

Reaching the wagon, he scrambled from his saddle onto the bench seat and stuck his free hand under her nose.

She moved back to bring it in focus. A trail of deep red spots ran down the center; a fiery glow radiated outward.

"Scorpion," he explained. "Burns like a—"

"Scorpion?" Andie drew the team to a halt. "How'd you get stung by a scorpion riding point?"

Tom glanced over at his saddle. "I ran across a bunch of buffalo chips. Thought you might need some fuel."

Andie set the brake. "Fuel? With twelve men bringing me every cow chip in Indian Territory?"

"Well, I just . . ."

"You just thought to get out of the blowing dust for a while."

"Aw, Cookie, don't give me a hard time. I'm painin' something awful."

"I don't doubt it." She jumped to the ground. "Come around to the chuck box and let's see what kind of medicine I have."

She let down the lid, secured the gate leg, and rummaged through the medicine box: Calomel would stop the sting, but she wanted something more. Her eyes fell on the sourdough jug.

After washing Tom's palm, she dipped starter from the

jug and spread it over the injury. "This should draw out the poison." She ripped a strip off a clean flour sack, bound his hand, and tied the ends. "Keep it tied up till supper time."

Hoofbeats drew their attention. Reese reigned to a halt in a swirl of dust and slid from the saddle. "What's wrong? Why'd you stop—" His eyes focused on Andie's hands . . . and Tom's. "What the hell're you up to, Lovejoy?"

"He got stung by a scorpion," Andie explained.

"Ridin' point?"

"He was gathering fuel, Reese. Scorpions nest—"

"Serves you right," Reese barked. "Get back on the job."

"Aw, Mister Catlin, don't go gettin' sore." He winked at Andie. "Thanks, Cookie. Feels better already." Clamping his hat on his head with one hand, he started off, then paused. "If you want dibs on her, Mister Catlin, you'd better speak up. Maybe so she prefers a feller who don't dillydally."

"Tom!" Mortified to her toes, Andie stood still, gripping the lid. She heard Tom ride off. Her skin fairly prickled with Reese's nearness. He cleared his throat.

"Don't let Tom bother you." His tone was gruff. Without further ado, he pecked her on the cheek, climbed in the saddle, and rode off.

Shading her eyes with her hands, she watched him disappear in a cloud of dust. Dillydally? Is that what he was doing? He had warned her not to forget what happened between them that night, but apparently he had done just that. He started this drive a confirmed bachelor, and she had to accept the possibility—probability—that he remained the same.

She was the one who had changed. Thanks to him.

She was the one who had fallen in love. No thanks to him.

Dillydally? Is that what he was doing? The question worried Reese for days. Nights he spent sitting in camp staring at her tepee, pondering the situation.

He slacked off on the men; at least, he didn't feel like he drove them as hard. Daily reports put the closest herd two days back, but that wasn't much leeway in case of trouble.

What worried him more, was that his inner drive to beat the competition was gone. Well, not gone, but the fire in his belly when he thought about the Matthews spread had cooled to a smoldering glow, banked by the kid's threat of loneliness. And he hadn't the foggiest notion what to do about it.

Other than talk to her. They still hadn't had that talk he suggested after the evening she termed magical. He felt it, too, the magic. Sometimes the feeling fit like a solid gold wedding band. Other times it felt like a noose around his neck. Should he give into his emotions? Or trust the lessons learned from his pa and Mister Matthews?

They needed to talk. But dangit, every time he rode into camp early, something always interfered. The cowboys had taken his warning to keep an eye on her to heart. One or another of them was always in camp these days.

Like most things in his life, the opportunity to talk to Andie was provided by an act of nature, in the form of a rip-roarin' dust storm. He had ridden back to check on the drag riders. Their kerchiefs were caked with thick dust; Jordan's blond eyebrows looked like drifts of dirty snow piled against a yard fence. Andie would be fit to be tied if she knew Jordan was back here eatin' all this blowing dust.

"Ride on back to camp, son."

"Uncle Gimpy needs my help, sir."

"Maybe your ma does, too."

Jordan, as was becoming habit, got the last word. "Would you check on her for me, Mister Catlin? Tell her I'm with Uncle Gimp."

Reese grinned at the dismissal. Then he realized he had been handed the perfect opportunity to catch Andie alone. With the wind blowing a gale, every drover in the crew would be on duty. No one would have time to feign an injury or gather fuel or haul water, the excuses used most frequently these days.

He heard the noise before he arrived at camp; it sounded like thunder, but wasn't loud enough. Damnation! Was the wagon canvas being ripped to shreds? Sinking spurs, he arrived at camp only to be astounded by Andie's latest attempt at domesticity.

He slid from his saddle and stood, mouth ajar. Every dang wagon sheet and blanket in the whole camp was flappin' in the wind. She'd tied 'em to every limb and bush in sight.

"I thought this would be good day to air the bedding." At his grim appraisal, she added, "I didn't touch anybody's clothes."

Lifting the flap, he stuck his head inside the wagon, where Night Hawk slept on the men's spare clothes.

"You should have smelled that bedding, Reese. Why, it's a wonder Night Hawk could stand to sleep back there."

He chuckled. "It's a wonder those blankets haven't blown to kingdom come in this gale."

"They're tied down, but maybe I should—"

Suddenly Reese knew it was time to talk. "Wait." He caught her arm and drew her around. He studied her face with its delicate features and enchanting green eyes, the black ringlets that straggled from the bun she pinned at her nape. Words caught in his throat. He pulled her down to the creek, beyond a thicket of cottonwoods and scrub oak. Out of sight of camp, he leaned against a tree trunk and drew her to him.

Their lips met in an earth-jarring coming together that left his senses reeling and his body begging for more. Lolling his head back against the tree, he gazed into her eyes.

She wanted him, too. He could see it plain as day. "We haven't had that talk."

"I know."

"Have you been thinkin'?"

She nodded. "You?"

He nodded. Then he kissed her again, this time an all-consuming kiss that she returned in kind. Her dress buttoned down the front, and suddenly it was undone. His hands found her skin; his lips followed.

"Reese," she murmured, "this isn't talking."

"It's better."

"It's confusing."

He lifted his face, kissed her lips, then settled back. "You don't like it?"

"Yes, I like it. Too much. It confuses me."

"How?"

"That's all I know about you. How you make me feel."

"That's bad?"

"It's wonderful, but . . ."

"I like how you make me feel, too," he whispered against her neck. "I want more, Andie. I want all of you."

She trembled in his arms. "I know. I feel that way, too."

At her admission he splayed a hand over her skirts and pressed her to him. His body reacted immediately and the ache became torturous. Suddenly she began to struggle.

"What is?"

"This isn't talking," she said again.

Reese pursed his lips. He knew what she wanted to talk about. Sliding his fingers into her hair, he pulled her face to his chest. Her warm breath seeped through his shirt and spread hot desire all the way to his loins. "You ready to talk marriage?"

Startled, she faced him. "Are you?"

"To be honest, I don't know." He watched her eyes dim. "How 'bout you?"

She focused on his face, while her fingers played absently, but seductively, through his hair. At length, she said, "If I were to marry again, it would have to be love. A great, desperate love on both sides."

"A great desperate love?" *What the hell was that?* "Like this?"

Again, she took long seconds to respond. "If you have to ask, probably not."

That surprised him. "You givin' up on us?"

"Me? You're the one who said we should talk, then never found time. You're the one who told me not to forget what happened between us that night, then promptly forgot yourself."

She was mad as a spitting adder and lovely as the first rose of summer. He felt like she had grabbed hold of his heart and squeezed real hard. "I'll never forget that night, Andie. It lit a fire in my gut that will never go out. But . . ."

"But you're scared."

"Dang right. It's an awesome task, making another man's wife happy. Raising another man's son."

She kissed his lips softly, taking him by surprise again. *Confounded woman*!

"And what about the ranches?" he argued. "You have yours and with luck I'll have mine, a hundred miles away. You can't sell yours; it's Jordan's inheritance. Where would we live—"

"Reese, Reese. Don't worry about it. Things will work out. One way or another."

"Easy for you to say."

A fleeting sadness, haunting as any melody, flickered, then died in her eyes. She ducked her head. "It isn't easy for me to say."

It hit him then, like a bucket full of lead. The truth. It raced down his spine with the speed of lightning and seared him with both warning and hope. He tipped her chin, forced her to look in his eyes, and saw it there. She was in love with him! Andie Dushane was in love with him. Pleasure raced through his veins, chased by caution, chased by pure, undiluted terror.

His emotions raged. Did he love her? Yes. How much? Hell, how did a man ever know how much he loved a woman? Whether he wanted to live with her all his life?

"Tell you what . . ." He lowered his lips. "While we ponder the situation, how 'bout we keep on practicin' the part that comes natural?"

His kiss muffled an answer he took to be affirmative from her eager response. His hands played inside the opening of her dress, and he had just settled back to enjoy a lengthy, if tormenting, spree of courting when their reverie was shattered by a gunshot.

Andie drew back as if she had been the target.

Reese listened for an answering shot.

"Dang fool cattle!" came a cry from the campsite.

"Night Hawk!" Andie started for the thicket.

Reese held her back. "Stay here. I'll check things out." He kissed her quickly. "Button up, love."

By the time he reached the campsite, all was a confusion of thundering hooves and firing six-shooters.

"Reckon it was them blankets." Night Hawk waved a six-shooter in the air. "All that racket spooked the herd."

Reese watched a blur of patterned hides and clashing horns trample past, not fifty yards distant. "The herd shouldn't have been anywhere near this camp."

Andie came up the hill. When Reese saw her, he went limp. The camp could have been demolished and her with it. To Night Hawk, he asked, "You turned 'em with that six-shooter?"

"Yes, sir. Their rumblin' done woke me up. They was headed straight for camp."

"Jordan!" Andie shrieked.

"I'll see to him." Then to Night Hawk, "Find Hank. We'll need all mounts gathered and ready."

Before he reached his horse, Andie stopped him. "I'm coming."

"Stay here. Put on the coffee. Hell, fill every pot we have with coffee. This may be a long night."

"But Jordan is out there."

"I'll see to him, Andie. Put on the coffee."

III

Supper was forgotten. Forgotten, too, every petty concern that had ever crossed Andie's mind—forgotten, trampled beneath the thundering of reality, the way the red earth was trampled, that night, beneath the frightened hooves of twenty-five hundred cattle. It was a night of loneliness and fear, and Andie Dushane experienced both on the most intimate terms.

The cattle started running near dusk, not an hour before their usual bedding time, and for a while, she was sure they wouldn't stop until they reached China, or wherever in their terror they sought escape.

Fear, fanned by remorse, consumed her. She followed Reese's orders to the letter. She made coffee. Gallons and gallons of coffee. When she used up that already ground by the men whose lives she had placed in jeopardy, she opened another package of Arbuckles roasted coffee beans and ground them herself. Then she ground another package, and another. Soon she had a mound of peppermint sticks, which in the long run she hid, for they reminded her of Woody and Dink. And of Jordan.

She had never been involved in a stampede, but in cattle country, even the word was spoken in hushed tones. Stampedes cost money: Cattle were lost or killed or maimed, many cattle, all at one time. And those that survived lost so much weight by the time they stopped running, their value dropped significantly. Such a loss could cost Reese his dream.

But of much more serious concern, stampedes cost lives. And the men whose lives were at risk this night had become her family.

Then there was Jordan. Her precious son. Frantic with fear for him, Andie searched the camp for ways to keep busy. When she ran out of pots in which to boil coffee, she transferred the frijoles to a Dutch oven and set about scouring the blackened frijole pot with sand and wood ashes.

Jordan, her precocious son, who loved her so much he had inveigled her into the most embarrassing and potentially the most wonderful experience of her life. Seeing her despair, he had set out to change her life; he loved her enough to try to find her a husband, this boy who had adored his own pa.

And he might have succeeded. She and Reese might have gotten together. But now she had ruined everything; her idiotic penchant for cleanliness had placed every drover on the drive in grave danger. Including Jordan, her precious son. Including Reese.

With the coffee boiled, Andie put away the bedding, then set about finishing supper, while night closed around her.

Darkness amplified the sounds—hooves thundering against the hard-packed earth; horn clashing against horn; six-shooters barking in an effort to turn the driving mass of silent, frightened steers. Underscoring it all, the earth rumbled and shook without cease. She felt the reverberations through the soles of her shoes; heard it as utensil clanged against utensil on the side of the wagon; as water sloshed in the water barrel. Finally, she closed the lid to keep things from falling out of the chuckbox.

Gimpy was the first to return. "Boss sent me in," he explained. "Didn't want you here by yourself."

"What about Jordan?" The words clawed their way through a panic-constricted throat.

"Don't worry, none, Cookie. The kid's with Grump."

"Why didn't Reese send him with you?"

"They're on the other side," Gimpy explained, or tried to.

Andie struggled to understand. "The other side of what?"

"Way things are out there, when the boys started turnin' the herd toward that big prairie off to the west, well, it sorta left me odd man out."

"I don't understand. Where is Jordan? Is he safe?"

"Fit as a fiddle. They're on the far side of the herd and at the back of it. Grump'll take care of the lad."

"But they're turning the cattle. What if . . . ?"

The seasoned drover took a seat near the campfire. "Could I trouble you for some coffee, Cookie?"

"Of course."

"An' some vittles? If it's not too much trouble."

No one asked the cook to serve him, but Andie knew what Gimpy was up to. He wanted to take her mind off Jordan. She poured coffee and handed it to him. "Reese sent you?"

"Yes'm. Said you'd likely be scared plump outta your wits."

"I am, that," she admitted, and felt a little better for it. "Where is he?"

"Mister Catlin? Last I saw, he was racin' for the lead. He's the one knows how to stop a stampede; he's the best."

Andie dished a plate of stew, added three freshly baked biscuits, and handed that to Gimpy, too.

"Much obliged, ma'am. Why don't you fix yourself a plate?"

"Me? Oh, no, I couldn't eat." She stirred the stew. "If I had something to put this stew in, I could wash the pot and use it for coffee."

"Coffee?"

At his astonished tone, she glanced around. "Reese said to make lots of coffee."

Gimpy's eyes strayed to the fire, where boiled coffee settled in six Dutch ovens and the freshly scrubbed frijoles pot.

"I imagine that'll be coffee aplenty," he said. "Come on over here an' try to relax some. I've been party to many a stampede an' they ain't near as bad as folks let on. Why I've only knowd of three men kilt—"

"Gimpy," Andie interrupted. "If you don't mind, I'll pass on stampede tales tonight. Maybe later."

"Oh, well, if you feel thataway, all right."

To assuage his wounded pride, Andie took him a couple more biscuits and offered him the pot of fresh honey Night Hawk had collected a few days earlier. She had been saving the honey for a special occasion, but after the stunt she pulled tonight, there probably wouldn't be a special occasion.

Around midnight the drovers began to drift in, singly or in pairs. They came for fresh mounts and coffee, but had no time to eat.

"We'll eat when things quiet down," Monte told her.

"Seen anything of Grump?" Gimpy wanted to know. "Or Goose?"

"They're ridin' with the boss," Dink said. He and Monte had come in together, and together they climbed aboard fresh mounts and headed back into the night, leaving Andie even more frightened.

If Grumpy was with Reese, where was Jordan? The question was so terrifying, she couldn't speak it aloud.

Professor was the next to arrive. Then Goosey. But still no sign of Reese or Jordan.

When Gimpy asked the question he had posed to each drover by turn, Goosey further unsettled Andie.

"Hell, Gimp, it's pitch dark out there. How'd you expect me to know where anybody is?"

Andie was on the verge of sending Gimpy and his worries out to help the others, when Grumpy showed up. *Alone.*

His face, like the others, looked like a racoon's mask, with dust ringing his eyes above relatively clean skin where his bandanna had protected his nose and mouth. Grumpy fit his name in every respect, but he was the most observant of the brothers. He recognized Andie's concern right off.

"Don't worry none about the kid, Cookie. He's with Tom."

"Tom? I thought . . . where's Reese? What happened to—"

"Take it easy, Cookie. They're seasoned men out there."

"I want to know the truth, Grumpy. I'll have to deal with it sooner or later, whatever happens. I caused it."

"You didn't cause anything, Andie."

Reese! His clothing was so sweaty and dust-covered he was almost unrecognizable. Except to her. She was half way across the clearing when she realized what she was doing. She couldn't throw herself in his arms in front of the drovers. She stopped, watching him scan the group with bloodshot eyes.

"Where's Tom?" His tone was sharp.

"Tom?" Terror sped through her with the force of a cold north wind. It blew away her senses, leaving her light-headed. "Jordan's with . . ."

Reese caught her before she crumpled to the ground. She was subliminally aware of his arms around her, of being held close to his chest, of being carried. When he left the camp-site, headed for her tepee, she began to struggle.

"No. Put me down." He neither stopped nor changed directions. "Jordan. I have to find Jordan."

"I'll find him, Andie."

"No. This time I'm going."

In the end she stayed behind again. Reese took Night

Hawk and an extra horse and rode off into the faint light of a dawning day, leaving Andie on Grumpy's bedroll, hovered over by the three Tahlman brothers.

Before leaving he knelt beside her, kissed her forehead, and with a grim set to his mouth that even his mustache couldn't hide, told her not to worry.

It was the longest wait of her life, longer even than Samuel's illness, or so it seemed. She tried to prepare for the worst, but when they returned and she rose on wobbly legs to confront the little group who stood at the edge of camp, she knew that although the worst had not come to pass something dreadful had happened.

Reese supported Tom with one of the drover's arms around his neck. Tom's other arm hung limp. Even from the distance, Andie realized it was probably broken. One side of his face was bloody. His shirt and britches were torn.

Jordan stood beside them, still as death, dazed, she judged, from the vacant set of his eyes and the ashen cast to his skin. She dropped to her knees, extended her arms, but he didn't move.

"Go ahead, son," Reese urged. "I think your ma needs a hug."

Jordan moved then, ran to her, clung to her, and buried his face in her shoulder. She squinched her eyes against the sting of tears. Too soon she had to release him to tend to Tom's wounds.

Tom was more fortunate than she had first thought. The break in his left arm was simple and would heal with time. She set it with trembling hands. The lacerations and bruises on his head and back would heal, too. But until they did, they would be a reminder to all of the courage of this handsome, fun-loving drover.

While Andie rubbed liniment on his battered back, he continued to needle Reese. "Hell, Cookie. If I'd known this was the way to get your attention, I'd have thrown myself in front of a herd of stampedin' cattle sooner."

"Make light of it if you want," Reese retorted, "but you're damned lucky to be alive. You and Jordan both."

Tom's horse had stumbled, as Reese explained, landing Tom and Jordan in a ravine ahead of one branch of the stampeding herd. Tom covered Jordan with his own body, and Jordan came away with no more than a good fright.

"You'll have to stay off a horse for a few days," Andie advised. "Let that break get a good start at mending."

"Ride in the wagon," Reese ordered, his tone curt. Lingering fright, Andie decided.

"Good thing you aired the beddin', Cookie," Tom quipped. "Else I'd be asphyxiated."

"If I hadn't aired the bedding none of this would have happened." Behind her she heard Reese send the drovers back out.

"We'll keep 'em on the move till midday or so. Maybe thataway, they'll settle down enough to graze awhile and hit the bed grounds early."

When he headed for the far side of the wagon, she followed. She watched him dip water into the wash basin and splash his face several times. Finished, he poured the basin of water over his head and swept his hands through his hair, shaking at length like a dog coming out of a creek.

She handed him a clean towel. Their gazes met, then darted apart. "Did we lose any cattle?" she asked quietly. It had been a hard night for everyone, Reese most of all.

"Won't know till it gets good an' light." He spoke in a hushed monotone, and she ached to be in his arms. To comfort and be comforted.

"I'm so sorry."

"For the last time, Andie, you didn't cause that stampede."

"But I . . ."

"Those flappin' blankets weren't the cause. If the cattle had stayed on course they'd never have gotten close enough to camp to hear the dang things."

"Then what—?"

"It was my fault?" he barked.

"You weren't even there. You were—"

"With you." He glanced at her suddenly; his weary eyes

were filled with sadness. He looked defeated. "I was with you and my duty was with the herd. Hell, I almost got your son killed. Don't you know that?"

"Not on purpose, Reese."

"I sure as hell talked you into lettin' him ride drag."

"You were right. I have to learn to turn loose. You'll teach me—" He shook his head, as though pondering a heavy question.

"I'm not cut out for a family man. Tonight proved that."

His claim would have distressed her, had she not known how tired he was. Without a word, she moved into his arms, pressed her face against his heart, and held him.

He embraced her, too, tightly, as though he might never let her go. She felt his lips nuzzle into the top of her head.

"God, Andie, how did this happen?"

Unsure of his meaning, she moved to kiss him, but he stopped her with his lips to her forehead. They stood still as a spring morning, while he gripped her shoulders. Agonizing seconds passed. Then he stepped back, clamped his Stetson on his head, and turned to business. "Pack up and follow the herd."

She walked with him to his horse. He stepped in the saddle. "Soon as it gets good an' light, I'll find a noonin' camp."

A week later they crossed into Kansas, but leaving Indian Territory with its potential dangers did not change Reese's mind. He went out of his way to avoid being alone with her. She dared not press the matter, since she wasn't certain what was wrong.

She suspected, of course. Even before the stampede Reese had shied away from marriage like it was the plague. The stampede, which he considered his fault for being with her, had probably reinforced the opinion that Mister Matthews had planted in his head about a wife being the sorriest thing a man could have on a ranch. The near catastrophes and loss of a quarter of the herd likely added fuel to the fire.

With the romance cooled, camp became a solemn place.

No one joked. Goosey stopped playing "Green Grow the Lilacs" and went back to "Little Joe the Wrangler" and "The Old Chisolm Trail."

Composed as lullabies for spooky cattle, neither did much to lighten the mood; their messages hit too close to home. One told the story of a young wrangler killed in a stampede, the other described the miserable conditions on a trail drive.

Finally she realized that if they were to get back together, she would have to make the first move. Fleetingly, she wondered why she cared. Living with such a pigheaded man would likely be more trouble than it was worth.

She was unable to make herself believe that, however. So, one morning while the cowboys were choosing day-mounts from the remuda, she followed him to his horse.

"Reese, we need to talk."

He focused on his cinch. "Runnin' low on supplies?"

Pigheaded, indeed! "No. We're running out of time."

"Time?"

"For us." Even with her heart breaking, she wanted to stomp her foot at his pigheadedness. "To straighten things out between us."

She watched his shoulders heave, then bunch forward.

"Reese!" she demanded. "Talk to me."

He glanced around. Pain etched the corners of his eyes. Longing filled their chocolate depths. "I almost killed your son."

"We've been over that. I don't hold you responsible. Neither does Jordan. So, stop torturing yourself. It's over."

"It isn't over. It's my way of life."

"It's my way of life, too. And Jordan's."

He dropped his gaze to the cinch. She watched his fingers tremble before he jerked it tight enough to strangle the poor horse. "I don't want to hurt you, Andie."

What was he saying? She felt like he had squeezed her lungs with that cinch. "Whatever's on your mind, say it to my face."

His eyes sought hers. She watched him fight for control. "Grumpy was right. I'm not the marryin' kind."

"Marriage! Who's talking about marriage?"

"It would come to that." Their gazes held. Messages passed between them. Messages of turmoil and anguish, of longing and . . .

Without thinking, she threw herself on him, clung to him, fighting tears. "Damn Mister Matthews!"

He held her gingerly, as if he were as afraid of holding her as he was of loving her. "It isn't just him," he admitted. "I finally understand my pa."

Pulling back mere inches, she gazed up at him. His face was grim; she watched him struggle and knew it was against the very thing she fought so hard to recapture. "What about your pa?"

"The night of the stampede when I finally found Tom and Jordan, when I saw Jordan's little body crumpled beneath Tom's and knew I had put him there, that's when I felt it."

"What?"

"The measure of my pa's grief when he lost my ma."

"Oh, Reese." She reached up, cradled her hand around his jaw. For a second he relaxed against her palm. Then his jaw clenched.

"I can't do it to you, Andie."

"What?"

"You've already been hurt once. I'm not going to be the next man to hurt you."

"You won't be."

"Not if we put a stop to this while we still can."

Her heart stood still. *While who still could?* "What happened to your highfalutin ideas about using troubles as stepping stones?"

"They were hogwash." He stepped in the saddle. "Trust me, Andie. It's best this way." She watched, helpless, as he gathered his reins and turned away.

"Don't tell me what's best, Reese Catlin!" she shouted after him. "I'll love you till my dying day if I want to, and you can't stop me. You love me, too. You're just too pigheaded to admit it. And too, too cowardly to take a chance."

* * *

Andie didn't try again to persuade Reese to change his mind. She wanted to believe she was better off without such a pigheaded man, but wasn't quite able to convince herself.

Jordan didn't ride drag anymore, on Reese's orders, and once he was back in the saddle, Tom Lovejoy relayed Reese's directions to campsites, along with any other information Reese deemed necessary for Andie to know during the day.

His choice of Tom hurt almost more than him not coming himself. During the entire drive Reese had been jealous any time Tom came around her; since the stampede he seemed determined to throw them together. It was as if he were saying, "I don't want you anymore. Take Tom."

Finally they arrived outside Wichita.

"Boss says to plan on campin' there a couple of days," Tom relayed. "It's our last camp. We'll drive the cattle into Wichita to sell, then come back an' settle up."

"We made it." She struggled to conceal her melancholy. "Ahead of the competition."

"You bet. I never doubted it. Ol' Reese Catlin has a reputation for gettin' what he sets his sights on." His gaze lingered on her face. "He's one hard hombre, Andie. Harder on himself than on anyone else." In a moment of uncertainty contrary to his gregarious nature, Tom squirmed in the saddle.

"I know you've been hit a lick by Catlin's reaction to that stampede," he said at length.

"Don't worry about me."

"Fact is, I was wonderin', after we sell the cattle, how 'bout you, me, and Jordan settin' off for Texas on our own."

"Tom! How could you—?"

"Whoa, now, Andie, don't go takin' it wrong. I'm not suggestin' anything that's not strictly on the up an' up. I'd like a chance to get to know you on my own, that's all."

She relaxed. "Thanks. You knew how much I needed a compliment, didn't you? But to be honest, I think I'm due a rest from members of the opposite sex. Uncle Kipp told me about a reputable freight driver; we'll catch a ride with him back to Fort Worth. Jordan needs to spend time with his pa's relations.''

Tom tipped his hat. "Well, think about it. All right?"

"Sure."

Before Tom was out of sight, emotions welled inside her. *Their last camp.* The poignancy of it, the finality of it, brought tears to her eyes; she fought them all the way to the sandy knoll Reese had scouted. The last camp he would lead her to. Possibly the last meal she would cook for him. The last . . .

By the time she drew rein and set the brake, she was beside herself. The mules and wagon were to be sold in Wichita. This had been her last time to hee and haw to Bessie Mae and Bertha Jane. Desperately, she sought control. In the end, she tackled the problem in her usual way, with work.

As soon as Jordan and Night Hawk dug the firepit and had the fire going, she handed them each a gallon jug. "We passed a berry patch back a few rods. Right beside the trail; you can't miss it."

"Fresh berry cobbler!" Night Hawk whooped.

"Yahoo!" Jordan cried. "Mister Catlin's gonna love that, Ma."

Andie turned aside, gripping her emotions. "Wear gloves so the thorns won't get you. And don't quit too soon. I need two full gallons, in case we have visitors from town."

For their last meal together, Andie decided to go all out and fix the drovers' favorites: Grumpy loved frijole pie; Goosey, Saratogy chips; Gimpy's favorite was fried steak, and Tom could eat an oven full of camp potatoes by himself. With the skill of a sorcerer, she kept her mind off Reese Catlin. She wouldn't allow herself to consider his favorite trail food—Uncle Kipp Stew; had she prepared it, she would have called it, and the obstinate trail boss himself, by the stew's rightful name, for he was in her mind, if not in her heart, a son of a bitch of the first order.

She had just fitted the last of the cobbler dough up the sides of a Dutch oven, when she heard a horse approach camp. Her first impulse was to expect Reese. She squashed it. Any hope she allowed into her heart would be sure to come gushing out at an inappropriate time. She refused to ruin the last night she had with him . . . with any of them . . . by crying.

Cautioning herself not to give in to futile hope, that it was surely Tom or Gimpy—or anyone other than the one person she yearned to see—she didn't realize until he stepped from the saddle that the rider had approached camp from the wrong side. Dust swirled around the site, settling on top of the frijoles and in her unfilled cobbler crusts. She spun around.

"How dare you—!" She came to an abrupt halt at sight of a glassy-eyed, highly agitated stranger.

"You're comin' with me." Even as he spoke, the stranger advanced toward her.

Reese Catlin felt like a first class heel. He hadn't meant to hurt Andie. Hell, he'd rather have chopped off his right arm than hurt her. But better sooner than later. On the other hand, he couldn't just ride off into the sunset and let her ride off, too. For days now he had worried with the idea of talking to her, but he couldn't decide what he would say if he did.

It was downright frightening, the way he missed her. He missed the giddiness he felt when he was anywhere near her, the magic when they kissed, touched, held each other.

He missed wondering whether he was falling in love with her. Now he knew. He missed knowing her smile would be the first thing he saw when he rode into camp at night. If she smiled lately, he hadn't seen it, because he had deliberately not looked. But he had a notion she hadn't been smiling. He oughta say good-bye, make sure she understood that his way was best. She called him a coward, and dang if he wasn't. He was scared to death of hurting her. She had suffered enough in her lifetime.

And so had he. He didn't hanker to end up like his pa, pining his life away, wasting his life, when he had so many hopes and dreams. Dreams that were fixin' to come true.

They'd arrived at the last camp well ahead of the next

herd down the trail, a good day and a half, anyhow. He had beat the competition; tomorrow he would learn whether it had been worth the extra effort and money. He had a hunch it would be. Yet, in one way, it was a hollow victory. For he hadn't realized how much he had looked forward to sharing it with Andie.

He oughta say good-bye, wish her well. Hell, maybe he'd even ride down to the Perdernales country to see her sometime, sayin' she was agreeable to such a suggestion. That's what he could tell her. Then at least he would have said good-bye in a way that wouldn't leave her feeling like he'd run out on her.

He didn't leave the herd too early; and he didn't leave without telling the points he was heading for camp. He had learned that lesson, he hoped, for the last time.

It was a beautiful day, not too hot, with a slowly setting sun and a soft afternoon breeze. Riding up to camp he experienced a surge of giddiness he hadn't felt since . . . hell, since before that damned stampede.

He skirted the camp, stepped down from the saddle, reining in his eagerness. He recalled Andie saying she felt good with him, like a kid. That was the way he felt now, riding in, hitching his mount, coming to see her. Then Night Hawk and Jordan rounded the chuck box. The look on their faces brought him up sharp.

"What's wrong?"

They answered in unison. "She's gone!" "Ma's gone!"

Reese's heart jumped to his throat. He glanced around, looked back at the boys, saw their fright. "What do you mean?"

"She sent us to pick berries," Night Hawk began.

"An' when we came back she was gone," Jordan wailed.

"She probably walked off a ways . . . for personal reasons."

Night Hawk shrugged. "Maybe, but lookee here. There's dirt all over ever'thing."

"Her cobblers are covered with it," Jordan pointed out.

Reese forced himself to remain calm. "Could've been a dust devil. Did you call her?"

"Bunches of times."

"In ever direction."

Reese studied the dirt that had blown over the crusts; he crossed to the fire. A layer of dust crusted the bubbling frijoles. He looked out at the mules.

Without warning he recalled the first time he had seen her. What a shock. *A woman! He'd hired a confounded woman for camp cook*! He smiled recalling how she had threatened to ride one of the mules back to town. Stubborn as a mule, he called her then. She wasn't stubborn, he learned later. Only determined. Like him. They were a lot alike—

Then he saw the hoofprints, close to the fire, where a horse never trod. Terror climbed up from his belly. "Who's been here?"

"No one."

"We've been gone," Jordan reminded him.

Night Hawk hunkered beside Reese to examine the hoofprints. "Ain't Indians. They don't generally ride shod horses."

"Generally could get her—" Terror had reached his throat; the words almost strangled him.

"Ain't no cowboy, neither," Night Hawk commented.

"No cowboy worth his salt would ride up to the wrong side of a camp," Jordan claimed.

Reese eyed the footprints that sank into loose sand stirred up by the horse. They hadn't been made by a Western boot. Night Hawk said as much.

"No cowboy'd wear foot gear like that. Might be the death of him, if he were to."

Reese nodded, thinking how that broad flat heel and thick sole could get wedged inside a stirrup. A cowboy needed a high-heeled, pointed-toe boot that would fit easily into a stirrup and slip easily out of one, in case of trouble.

But the trouble here had happened to Andie. Whether at the hand of a cowboy or a farmer or a damned banker, didn't matter.

Following the tracks to the outer edge of camp, Reese had suddenly seen enough. He stopped briefly to reassure Jordan. "Hold down the fort, son. I'll bring her home."

Racing for his horse, he jerked his Winchester from its saddle scabbard and checked the load.

"Want me to call the hands?" Night Hawk asked. "You might need help."

That was true. There wasn't time. "Not yet."

"Where'll you be, case we need to go alookin'?"

"Wherever the hell she is. Follow the tracks." His eyes found Jordan's. "Keep yourself safe."

The sonofabitch hadn't tried to hide his trail, nor had he wasted time. The horse Reese followed made a beeline east, and Reese spurred his mount after him.

Fear gripped his gut. He wanted to blame Night Hawk for leaving her alone at the camp, but if an armed man came lookin' for trouble, a kid asleep in the wagon wouldn't have stopped him.

He wanted to blame himself, and partially succeeded. But mostly he wanted to find her. To find her alive and unharmed.

The tracks led east across the prairie, headed for the distant foothills. Walnut River ran on the other side of those hills, Reese recalled from earlier trips up the trail, with farms scattered along the river bank.

The boot tracks made by Andie's abductor could belong to a farmer. But farmers didn't go around abducting women.

Just this side of the foothills, the tracks veered north. Reese topped a rise and saw a wagon. He forced himself to draw rein and investigate the situation. He wouldn't do Andie any good, if he charged in and got himself shot.

The wagon had a busted wheel. Beside it a man, nondescript from the distance, paced, head bowed. He pivoted at the tongue, reversed direction, then stopped at the back of the wagon. He seemed interested in whatever was inside the wagon for he cocked his head in that direction, waited a minute, then reversed his tracks and paced to the tongue again.

·Reese was still trying to reason through the situation when a woman's scream rent the air. It froze his heart, raised hairs on the back of his neck, and mobilized his brain. Spurring his mount, he galloped down the hill, headed straight for the man, who was so intent on looking at the wagon, he didn't hear the commotion until Reese had drawn rein, slid from the saddle, and raced toward him.

The man turned, wide-eyed. His clothes were rumpled, his hair shaggy, his bleary-eyed expression, anxious.

Reese drew back a fist. "What're you doin' with my woman?" He followed his question with a punch that landed the farmer flat on his back. He bent over the man, heaving, waiting, but his blow knocked the man cold. He turned instantly to the wagon, from where the scream had come.

At that moment Andie climbed over the tail gate and stepped around the side as serenely as if she were in church. Reese's heart lurched.

"Mister Wisdom . . ." Her eyes widened at sight of the farmer, sprawled on his back in the dirt. She looked up. "Reese?"

Their gazes locked. For the longest time he could do nothing more than stare at her. She was safe. At least, she looked that way. His eyes strayed to the bundle in her arms.

"What did you do to Mister Wisdom?" Her voice sounded soft and strange . . . and wonderful.

Reese looked down at the man, who sat up, rubbing his jaw.

"Mister Wisdom?" Reese turned back to Andie. "What the—"

"It's a girl, Mister Wisdom," Andie told the farmer. "A beautiful baby girl. And your wife is fine."

Reese reached her before he knew he had moved. He caught her face in his hands. He kissed her lips. "I love you, Andie." He kissed her again. "I thought I'd lost you." He kissed her again. "I love you."

She started laughing. "Before I would ever agree to marry you, Reese Catlin, you'd have to promise not to hover over me like an ol' mother hen."

"Marry . . . ?" He gazed into the depths of her prairie green eyes, lost in the love he saw there, in the love he felt for her.

Between them the baby started crying. He glanced down, actually saw it for the first time. His eyes found Andie's.

"Marry me, Andie. Now. In Wichita. Today, tonight, tomorrow at the latest." He looked at the baby again. A little pink fist waved spasmodically, gripping Reese's heart with a strange new tender-sweet longing. "And have lots of my babies."

* * *

Roses love sunshine, violets love dew,
Angels in heaven, know I love you.

"Don't you think they're about finished?"

Andie snuggled into Reese's arm. What a day! The cattle brought top dollar and Reese Catlin admitted he loved her, all in the last twenty-four hours.

Below them now, in the dusty cowtown street, the RC cowboys gathered to serenade the newlyweds. Already they had gone through "Green Grow the Lilacs," "Careless Love," and "Drink to Me Only with Thine Eyes." They were on the sixth repetition of the third stanza of "Down in the Valley."

Know I love you, dear . . .

Reese kissed the top of her head.

"It was a perfect wedding, Reese. I loved everything about it. Even the berry cobbler, sandy crust and all."

He eased a hand down her side, feeling her curves beneath the yellow muslin dress. "I'm not sure how most women would take gettin' married in front of a campfire, but I suppose it was proper enough for an ol' trail cook like yourself."

"I wanted it that way for Jordan and the drovers. They're the ones who brought us together." She plucked at the yellow skirt. "This dress, bought with their hard-earned money."

Know I love you . . .

Reese squeezed her closer. "I didn't deduct. Figured a bridegroom oughta spring for his bride a dress."

"Oh, Reese."

Angels in heaven, know I love you.

" 'Night, boys," Reese called over the song's final notes. "See you in camp tomorrow."

"Take good care of Jordan," Andie called down.

"Hey, Ma," he called up. "We wired Uncle Kipp 'bout your birthday present."

"Thank you, honey. It's the best present I ever got."

"Yahoo! You be . . ."

But Reese was already pulling her back inside, where he closed the French doors, drew the drapes, and took her in his arms. "When's your birthday?"

"Jordan thinks it's today."

"Today? What's this present you're so proud of?"

She laughed and hugged him with both arms. "You."

At his quirked eyebrow, she explained. "Not long before he met you at Uncle Kipp's, Jordan made a wish on the Evening Star."

"Oh?"

"He wished for me a new husband—for my birthday."

For the longest time, Reese held her, quiet and still. At length, he said, "Lucky I came along when I did."

"When wishes come true, Reese, there's usually more love than luck."

"It was love that brought me back to that camp," he admitted. "You're more important to me than that ol' Matthews spread or even the fear of ending up like my pa. When I rode into camp and found out some fool had carried you off, I knew the only thing that mattered was being with you, loving you, forever.''

He kissed her then, cupping her face in his hands, bringing her lips to his. He moved gently, worshiping, adoring, loving, while he released her with all but his lips and in no time had her disrobed.

Then he bent his head and nipped kisses along her neck, across her chest, found her breast. When she trembled against him, he lifted her in his arms and carried her to bed.

''Ah, a real feather mattress.''

''The finest hotel in Wichita, ma'am. Nothin's too good . . .'' His words caught. The sight of her lying unclothed in the middle of the bed stoked a flame that had been kindled long ago, that first day when he tried to fire her and she tried to quit.

She lifted her arms. ''Come here, Reese.''

The sound of her voice calling him to their bed trilled along his senses, softer than a spring breeze, enchanting him.

The heat of her skin when he lay beside her melded them together. He inhaled her sweet rose-scented skin, with its lingering of wood smoke and cinnamon, and he knew his heart had found its rightful home—in hers.

''Wanta know what I've been dreamin' about?'' Whispering into her lips, he moved over her. Her hands trailed up and down his spine, shooting spears of pure desire to the source of all life.

''What?'' she whispered back.

''This.'' With a strong thrust he entered and filled her. The impact was startling, for both of them. He could see it in her eyes, the need, the want, the joy.

He paused, absorbing the moment, its magnitude, its magic, and the unbelievable fact that she was his and he was hers . . . forever.

He began to move, watching her all the time, unable to take his eyes from hers. They smoldered, her green eyes, while she moved with him, steadily climbing higher and higher, until in one brilliant fiery instant they leaped together toward the exploding sun. A few moments later, he collapsed beside her, drawing her close, but not close enough. She could never be close enough.

"Some say dreams are wishes," she whispered seductively.

He kissed her tenderly. "Today you've made all mine come true. And to think, it started with a boy settin' out to find his ma a husband."

"And himself a pa."

"I'll do my dangedest with him, love. But we'll never let him forget his real pa." He kissed her then until the only thought in either of their heads was of each other. Mindlessly he wanted her again. "I can't get the image of you holdin' that baby out of my head," he mumbled against her skin. "What say we try again for one of our own?"

Turn the page for an excerpt from an
exciting new romance
by Antoinette Stockenberg.

Enjoy this preview of
DREAM A LITTLE DREAM.
At bookstores everywhere
in June.

Prologue

It loomed on the hill like a Disneyland dream: Fair Castle.

He felt a dull ache of pleasure at the thought that it was still intact, still standing—despite the fact that it was standing a few thousand miles too far to the west. Grateful that its American owners hadn't broken it up for salvage or turned it into condos, he lifted his binoculars for a better look.

It seemed bigger than in the photographs, smaller than in the paintings. The word that sprang to mind was *pleasing*. It had good bones. From its soaring facade to its small domed turrets, Fair Castle was a satisfying mix of harmony and oddity.

He swept his glasses in a broad arc to the south and then to the north. He had to admit that the Americans had chosen their site well: a high knoll with sweeping views of the mid-Hudson valley, itself on fire with early autumn color. He could easily have been standing at the edge of a wood in England.

He focused his glasses on the main entrance, marked by a massive arched door. Centuries of ancestors—*his* ancestors—had passed through those doors. As always, the thought was bitter. He put it aside. He was about to get into his car and drive around to some other vantage point when the door of the castle swung open and a young girl burst through it, her laugh carried high on the wind.

She was ten or eleven years old, with auburn hair and a

gait like an ostrich. Clutching something red—a plume?—
she ran down a path that led to a side promenade, then hid
behind a huge stone urn, waiting.

He swung his glasses back to the entrance. Out strolled a
taller, older, calmer version of the girl. Mother? Sister? From
that distance, it was hard to tell. One thing was certain: The
two were related. He watched as the older one cupped her
hands to her mouth and, in a voice that echoed through the
valley, called out to the younger.

"Izzzz-a-belle . . . Isabelle!"

She yelled something else, but he couldn't make it out.

It drew the girl out from the long shadow of the urn. After
waving the red plume through the air like a victory banner,
she handed it over to the woman, who smacked her on the
head in return. Then the two went inside, clearly still friends.

A grim smile played on his lips, then died. *The heirs*, he
thought. *Pity*.

Wrapping the strap of the binoculars around the hinge, he
slipped the glasses back into their case and laid them on the
rear seat of his car. He was about to drop behind the wheel
when he drew out the glasses again for one last look. *Fair
Castle*. There it was. Dramatic. Potent. Irresistible.

His. Whatever it took.

*From the battlement they watched together as he threw the
binocular telescope onto the front seat of his vehicle and then
made away.*

*"Will he be up to the quest, my love?" she asked in a
pale echo of her former voice.*

"He is determined to have it. I see it in his face."

*"Aye," she agreed. "There is a ruthlessness there that he
would do well to disguise, or it will defeat his purpose, and
ours."*

"He will not be defeated."

*"I believe you. He has come at last, the issue of our de-
sire. Flesh of our flesh, blood of our blood, he has walked
till now in darkness. We will make that darkness flare."*

"It galls me that it must come to this. I should not have failed you the first time, my sweet."

"Shhh. Too late for that; too late. You loved me with all your heart. Eventually you gave up your soul. A woman cannot ask more than that."

"You deserved more than that. Much more."

"Shhh."

The cloud of dust raised by the wheels of the vehicle began to thin. Eventually it settled back into the dirt from which it rose.

"We have waited a small eternity," she mused, "for him to claim his birthright."

"And now," her mate said, "his time—our time—is come."

Chapter One

"Hand me the vambrace."

"You bet." Elinor lifted the small piece of armor and looked it over carefully. "Huh. No dents on this one either, Chester," she said. "There goes my theory about our man being left-handed."

Her stepfather hardly heard her. Chester Roberts was focused completely on the task at hand: assembling a complete suit of armor—the first in his collection of knightly odds and ends—for display in the great hall of Fair Castle.

Chester had gone more insane than usual at an auction on the day before, plunking down a huge sum for half a dozen boxes filled with what he hoped were carefully wrapped pieces of a suit of armor. For all of last night and most of the morning, he and Elinor had been working feverishly to get the steel contraption up and standing before the arrival of their first tour group. But it wasn't as though a sixteenth-century suit of armor came with a set of directions. Did the fan plate go on before or after the knee cop? Did the tasset hook directly to the tace? And why didn't the chain mail fit?

"The suit's a composite, no doubt about that," Chester had told his two stepdaughters as the three of them unpacked the boxes on the night before. "But the auctioneer absolutely, positively guaranteed that all the pieces will fit."

Too bad it wasn't in writing. Nearly done now, they seemed to have several pieces left over—which was fine with hem—but it was obvious that part of the chin piece was missing. Without the chin piece, the thin rod of the mannequin's neck showed through, completely ruining the illusion of strength.

Chester sighed as he fit the vambrace over the wooden forearm that should have been a knight's warm flesh. "I suppose I shouldn't carp. A little tweaking, and that German chin piece of mine should work just fine."

"Besides, they did give you the extra pair of gauntlets," said Elinor, nudging her stepfather's mood back up. Big, balding, and bearded, Chester Roberts was still a kid when it came to emotions.

She watched him slip first the left, then the right gauntlet over the mannequin's wrist-stumps. Almost done.

"Too bad Izzy's in school today," she added. Her ten-year-old sister had been nearly as excited as their stepfather on the night before. "She's missing the best part."

"Mmm," Chester answered, hardly hearing her. He went back to the box, reached down to the bottom, and came up grinning. "And now, the crowning touch!" he said, holding the visored helm in both hands for Elinor to see.

With utmost care, he climbed to the second rung of the stepladder with it. Carefully, slowly—ecstatically—he began to lower the gleaming orb of steel over the featureless head of the mannequin.

"Oh, wait!" Elinor suddenly cried. "We forgot the plume!"

"You're right! We forgot the plume!"

Chester set the helm on top of the ladder and Elinor handed him a magnificent red ostrich plume, all too new, which he tried with fumbling hands to fit into the slot designed to hold it.

No luck. The quill was too large. Frustrated, Chester jabbed at the helm so awkwardly that the thing jumped from the ladder and hit the floor with a horrendous clang, skidding to a stop at the feet of Elinor's mother and the small group of tourists she'd just led into the hall.

"Chester!" her mother snapped, jumping back. "You've scared us half to death!"

Oblivious to his wife's annoyance, Chester ran to the helm and picked it up as if it were a puppy run down by a truck. "Oh, *no*," he said, shocked by his clumsiness. "If I've damaged it . . ."

"Chester. It's armor," his wife said with a quick lift of one eyebrow. "Do think about it."

"Still and all . . ." He ran his hand over the gleaming skull, feeling for dings. "It'd be tragic."

"Not as tragic as spending every last cent—" She bit off the rest of the sentence and swallowed hard. Susan Roberts would much rather die than argue in public.

But Susan Roberts, stunned by her husband's latest extravagance, was clearly still fuming over the suit of armor.

"Elinor—dear," she commanded her daughter, "would you mind escorting our visitors from this point? I've just remembered I have a desperately urgent call to make." She swept past the group with a graceful shrug, headed, no doubt, for the aspirin. "I shan't be long."

Shan't. Someone in the tour must be European, Elinor decided. Her mother never dragged out her *shan'ts* for Americans anymore.

"Sure. I'll be glad to," Elinor said cheerfully, dismayed by her mother's mood. With every return visit to the castle that she made, she found that her mother seemed more bored, more weary. Was it with Chester? After only five years? Could it be with Fair Castle itself?

I'm beginning to lose touch with them all, Elinor realized. She was becoming caught up in her blossoming career as author and illustrator of children's picture books. And with the big-city distractions of New York. And, of course, with Tom. But Tom was over now. It was time to come home; time to reenergize. Without Fair Castle, without her family, there would *be* no children's books. All of the inspiration for her medieval stories was right here, smack dab in the castle.

Putting her fears and worries aside, Elinor turned to the five women and three men who were waiting patiently to hear how the hell an English castle ended up on the banks of the Hudson River.

"Well! Hello, everyone!" she said, making herself sound chirpy. "As I'm sure you've learned," she began, "we're a family-run castle. As a matter of fact, there are three generations living under this roof: my grandparents, my mother and her husband, and my sister. I was raised here, too, and still come up from New York City to visit whenever I can."

She swept them all with a good-natured grin and added, "Yes, it's a little eccentric—but not by sixteenth-century standards. Besides, we're all in the arts. People expect us to act this way."

Most of them chuckled, instantly put at ease by her friendly, confidential manner. Elinor said, "We're very good at pinch-hitting, so let me pick up where my mother left off. You know that Fair Castle was one of the last ones built in England, right? Good.

"Though the castle is English," she said, slipping into a tour guide's voice, "it resembles the tower houses being built in Scotland during what's now regarded as the golden age of castles over there.

"The walls aren't as thick as Scottish tower houses, and obviously there are too many entrances for Fair Castle to be impenetrable. But the original owner was still a conservative man by English standards. After all, by the 1550s no one in England was building strongholds anymore."

She went on with her spiel, sizing up the group while she talked: three ladies with gray hair and sensible shoes who looked like seasoned travelers, a young couple holding hands who were clearly there for the romance of it, and a ponytailed college kid in hiking books and backpack who'd no doubt stumbled onto the castle by chance.

And, of course, the European. He wasn't German; not Italian. Not Dutch, Slavic, or French. British? Could be. He wore a tweedy jacket and an air of reserve. Or maybe he was a Scot; there was something stern and unforgiving in his blue eyes as he swept the vaulted hall that loomed around and above the group.

Elinor had been giving tours of the castle for fourteen years—ever since she was sixteen—and was very, very good at reading people.

"Ta-dah!"

Everyone turned toward Chester, who'd finally got the plume in the helm and the helm on the mannequin. Fair Castle's knight in shining armor was ready for battle—or as ready as he was going to be, until he got his German chin piece and a mace or a halberd in his grip.

Chester had his ham-sized fists planted firmly on his hips and was beaming like mid-May sunshine.

"As you can see," said Elinor, flashing her stepfather a victory sign, "we've just acquired a wonderful new addition to our collection of armor and weapons. The suit dates from the sixteenth century, although some of the components are not original to it. The armor is in very fine condition—the guy who owned it must've been in the reserves," she quipped.

Apparently her flippancy annoyed the fellow in tweed. He decided to set the record straight. "Actually," he said, "by the end of the century the use of armor in warfare had declined."

All heads swung toward him. Elinor said, "I'm sorry?"

The man's smile was thin, aloof, superior. "The reason the armor is in such fine condition," he said in a clipped accent softened by a burr, "is that by the mid-sixteenth century, military strategy had changed from the medieval period. Armies had to be capable of long marches and quick maneuvers."

"Oh!" she said, taking it in. "In other words, by then armor was becoming—"

"Obsolete," he said as he glanced around the cavernous hall.

Uppity son of a gun, Elinor decided. She pursed her lips while she searched her brain for a snappy comeback. Not a one came to mind.

"I haven't had time to research that particular subject," she answered, feeling the color rise in her cheeks.

"Of course," he said absently. "Please continue."

"Thank you."

Just what she needed: a know-it-all. Every once in a while someone like him came bopping along, an expert on some tiny little niche of history who just had to let everyone in on it.

Smiling gamely, Elinor resumed the tour. "We tend to think of the great hall as the place where the lord ate with his knights and their ladies," she said as their heels echoed on the slate floored hall. "But by the 1550s, that practice had all but ended. A nobleman ate apart in other rooms from his entourage and appeared in the great hall only on ceremonial occasions."

One of the gray-haired women said, "Why even have a great hall, in that case?"

"Status," Elinor said. "Consider this the forerunner of the modern two-story foyer. Great halls did have other uses, of course. Servants were sometimes fed there, and once in a while the host would put on a play or celebrate a feast in one."

She glanced at the blue-eyed expert, expecting him to put in his two cents. But the man was listening quietly. Apparently she'd misjudged him.

"It's so old, so big, so . . . old," said the young woman, snuggling into her boyfriend's side. "Is it haunted?"

It was the number one question that tourists asked.

Elinor gave her the usual answer. "All castles are haunted," she said with a mischievous smile. It was what visitors wanted to hear, but her sense of honesty made her add, "If you're asking if any of us has ever seen a ghost, the answer—darn it—is no."

A sympathetic chuckle rippled through the group. Elinor had no intention of confessing that she absolutely, positively, did not believe in ghosts. It would be bad for business.

"Hey! Those are pretty cool," said the boyfriend, pointing to Chester's antique sword collection mounted high on the wall above the vast stone fireplace.

The weapons were mounted high for one reason: safety.

Two years earlier the castle had been broken into and three of the swords stolen. Nothing else had been taken. Elinor's mother was certain that the swords were now being used in black masses and other unspeakable rites.

Elinor's grandmother, who *did* believe in ghosts, had another theory altogether. She was convinced that the original owners had simply come to claim their stuff.

Elinor was tempted to toss in those tidbits—just to get a rise out of the surly guy in tweed—but she kept to the standard story line. "The sabres and backswords and rapiers are from the period," she said, then added lightly, "but the dress swords and the boarding cutlass are just impulse buys."

A few more impulse buys like the swords and the suit of armor, and Chester will be the rest of the way into the poorhouse. The thought came and went like a shooting star, but it fed Elinor's growing sense of unease that all was not well financially at Fair Castle.

"What's that weird one on the end?" the young man asked.

Elinor said thoughtfully, "It's Asian, I think. Some sort of ceremonial sword."

"African," the man in tweed said. "An executioner's sword."

Elinor blinked. How would he know *that*, for Pete's sake?

"Our visitor from—Scotland? England?—sounds pretty sure of himself, so it must be true," Elinor said with a cutting glance in his direction. Just where was her mother, anyway?

"England," he said. "Near Berwick-on-Tweed."

"What? Oh. Well, that's a border town," she said flippantly. "It's practically in Scotland."

"Don't tell that to my ancestors. They fought hard to keep it in England." By now there was a militant glint in his eye.

Elinor suspected that he used both his good looks and his cultivated accent to intimidate poor, ordinary Americans. Well, tough. He could be English, he could be Scottish, he could be the devil himself, for all she cared. His highhandedness annoyed her intensely. Intensely.

Turning deliberately away from him, she began pointing

out the simple detailing in the rough-hewn, drafty, but still imposing hall. Fair Castle was no sissy country house, she explained, back on automatic now. Though fairly comfortable, the castle was the last of a breed: a four-story tower that was immune to fire, anarchy, raiders, and neighbors with grudges.

Better. She felt in control of the tour again. It was much easier when her back was to the man; she was almost unaware that he was there.

Almost.

"On this floor," she said, "we'll tour the chapel, the buttery, and the kitchen. On the next level we'll view the great parlor, the dining chamber, and the library. And we'll peek in the archives room, which houses a growing collection of works on English history—in fact, an eighteenth-century scholar will begin a stay at the castle tomorrow to do some research," she said, unable to resist a smug glance at the Englishman.

"After that we'll stroll down one of the unusual features of Fair Castle, an outdoor gallery. And finally, we'll go up to the roof and enjoy the wonderful view from a delightful turret where you'll all be served tea."

It was that cup of tea in the turret that made Fair Castle such an unusual tourist attraction. Elinor had come up with the idea herself and had designed their brochure around it; she was very proud of the whole thing.

Ah—but today they had an Englishman in their midst. Nuts! He'd have his own ideas about a proper tea. Nuts! They didn't even serve clotted cream. And that high-school kid they stole from McDonald's to serve the tea—oh boy. If the Brit was expecting a sweet little lass from the Cotswolds, he was in for some first-rate culture shock.

Elinor looked around without much hope for her mother, then began taking the group along the ceremonial route to the great chamber.

She paused before a wall hung high with half a dozen portraits, four of them acquired by Chester at auctions. "Portraits came into fashion in the sixteenth century," Elinor explained. "Generally they were displayed in an indoor gallery, but since we don't have one, we've hung them here."

She pointed to the fourth portrait of the group. "See the woman with blond ringlets wearing the dark panniered gown and rakish feathered hat? That's Lady Norwood, wife of one of the owners of Fair Castle. Her first name was Elinor; she died in 1780. The portrait of her was one of the possessions that got thrown in with the sale of the castle; so was the one of Lord Norwood—her husband, Charles—to her left. The baron died much earlier than she—but then, life spans were short back then. The paintings aren't by Gainsborough or Reynolds, obviously, but we think they're wonderful."

One of the women in sensible shoes said, "Didn't you say your own name was Elinor, dear?"

Elinor grinned. "My grandfather liked the name so much that he got my mother to name me after her. Except for the hair and the eyes and the nose and the body, I think we look identical, don't you?" she quipped.

"Elinor! Hateful woman! I am jealous of her still."

"She meant nothing to me."

"I know; I know. And yet I cannot rid myself of the notion that somewhere, somehow, she is smug in her triumph."

"It is because of the family who flaunt their possession of the castle. They are the ones who keep alive the vile myth."

"Fie upon them, then! They shall feel my wrath."

"No. Not yet. We must wait. And watch."

"But we have waited generations! How much longer—?"

"You have little patience. In that, you are not changed."

"And you, my love, are too at ease with eternity."

ANITA MILLS
ARNETTE LAMB
ROSANNE BITTNER

*Join three of your favorite storytellers
on a tender journey of the heart...*

Cherished Moments is an extraordinary collection of
breathtaking novellas woven around the theme of mother-
hood. Before you turn the last page you will have been swept
from the storm-tossed coast of a Scottish isle to the fury of
the American frontier, and you will have lived the lives and
loves of three indomitable women, as they experience their
most passionate moments.

THE NATIONAL BESTSELLER

CHERISHED
MOMENTS

No one believes in ghosts anymore, not even in Salem, Massachusetts. And especially not sensible Helen Evett, a widow who lives for her two teenaged kids and who runs the best preschool in town. But when little Katie Byrne enters her school, strange things begin to happen. Katie's widowed father, Nat, begins to awaken feelings in Helen that she had counted as dead. But why does Helen get the feeling that Linda, Katie's mother, is reaching beyond the grave to tell her something?

As Helen and Nat each explore the pain of their losses and the joy of their newfound love, Linda Byrne's ghost plays a bold hand, beseeching Helen to uncover the mystery of her death. But what Helen finds could make her the target of a jealous killer and a modern Salem witch-hunt that threatens her, her family...and the magical second-time-around love that's taking her and Nat by storm.

BESTSELLING, AWARD-WINNING AUTHOR

ANTOINETTE STOCKENBERG

Beyond Midnight